CRITICS ARE CHARMED BY JANA DeLEON!

UNLUCKY

"The quirky characters keep the action moving and I'm sure Mallory has been sitting next to me every time I go to the casino."

—Barbara Vey, *Publishers Weekly* Beyond Her Book Blog

"With original, smart and comedic writing, DeLeon delivers a three-dimensional hero and heroine, a community of offbeat secondary characters, a complex and intriguing plot with a hint of paranormal and a fascinating peek into the world of casino poker."

—*Romantic Times BOOKreviews*

"Ms. DeLeon has an excellent knack at weaving the total story together. She gives the right amount of mystery and suspense with plenty of romance and lots of laughter thrown in. I enjoyed every page and found it hard to put down. I think many people will be putting *Unlucky* on their keeper shelves."

—Once Upon A Romance

"Ms. DeLeon provides a great plot and a lot of mystery. The heat that sizzles off of Mallory and Jake keeps you turning the pages to see what will happen next. And right when you think you have it all figured out, you realize you don't. Things are never as they seem on the bayou!"

—The Romance Reader's Connection

THE NEW BODYGUARD

Maryse stared at Luc in disbelief. "You actually want me to spend every waking hour of my day with you? Take you everywhere I go? We don't get along all that great in the few minutes a day we're in contact at the office. How the heck do you think we can manage an entire day?"

Luc shrugged. "I get along just fine. You're the one with the problem."

Maryse felt her pulse quicken. Luc was right. She was the one with the problem. The main problem being that even a minute around Luc LeJeune led to thoughts that she had no business thinking. How in the world was she supposed to manage an entire day? "I have to go shopping today. And I am *not* selecting undergarments with a man."

Sabine laughed. "You don't even wear underwear, Maryse."

"I do on Sundays," Maryse grumbled, feeling her independence slipping away.

"It's only Friday," Luc said, and grinned. "You've still got time to change your mind."

Other books by Jana DeLeon:

UNLUCKY
RUMBLE ON THE BAYOU

JANA DELEON

Trouble in Mudbug

LOVE SPELL

NEW YORK CITY

*This book is dedicated to Cari Manderscheid, Cindy Taylor,
Angela Garzetta, and Sarah Saunders,
strong women and great friends...you know why.*

LOVE SPELL®

February 2009

Published by

Dorchester Publishing Co., Inc.
200 Madison Avenue
New York, NY 10016

ISBN 10: 0-505-25784-7
ISBN 13: 978-0-505-52784-4
E-ISBN: 1-4285-0605-5

The name "Love Spell" and its logo are trademarks of Dorchester
Publishing Co., Inc.

Printed in the United States of America.

10 9 8 7 6 5 4 3 2

Visit us on the web at www.dorchesterpub.com.

ACKNOWLEDGMENTS

To Colleen Gleason, friend and critique partner extraordinaire, for keeping me honest and always making me work harder. My parents Jimmie and Bobbie, brother Dwain, sis-in-law Donna, and beautiful niece KatiAnne, for all your continued support. To the fabulous staff at the Jefferson Hotel, in Jefferson Texas. Maybe I'll get to see a ghost next time! To my editor, Leah Hultenschmidt for agonizing over the cover (it's fabulous!) and every word in between. And to my wonderful agent, Kristin Nelson, for understanding why this was the series I absolutely had to write and working with me and the publisher until I had the opportunity to.

Trouble in Mudbug

Chapter One

"I still can't believe she's gone," Maryse Robicheaux murmured as she stared down at the woman in the coffin.

Of course, the pink suit was a dead giveaway—so to speak—that the wearer was no longer with them. For the miserable two years and thirty-two days she'd had to deal with her mother-in-law, Maryse had never once seen her wear a color other than black. Now she sorta resembled the Stay-Puft Marshmallow Man dressed in Pepto-Bismol.

"I can't believe it either," Sabine whispered back. "I didn't know evil incarnate could die."

Maryse jabbed her best friend with her elbow. "For Pete's sake, we're at the woman's funeral. Show some respect."

Sabine let out a sigh. "Maryse, that woman gave you holy hell. And her son was worse. I don't even understand why you wanted to come."

Maryse stared at the casket again and shook her head. "I don't know. I just felt compelled to. I can't really explain it."

And that was the God's honest truth. She'd had no intention of attending Helena Henry's funeral. Yet after her morning shower, she'd stood in front of her closet and pulled out her dark navy "interview" suit and matching pumps instead of her usual work clothes of jeans, T-shirt, and rubber boots.

Looking down at Helena, Maryse still didn't know why

she was there. If she'd come for some sort of closure, it hadn't happened. But then, what had she expected—the dead woman to pop up out of the coffin and apologize for bringing the most useless man in the world into existence, then making Maryse's life even more miserable by being the biggest bitch on the face of the Earth?

It wasn't likely when you considered that Helena Henry had never apologized for anything in her entire life. It wasn't necessary. When you had a pocketbook the size of the Atchafalaya Basin in Mudbug, Louisiana, population 502, people tended to purposely overlook things.

"I think they're ready to start," Sabine whispered, gesturing to the minister who had entered the chapel through a side door. "We need to take a seat."

Maryse nodded but remained glued to her place in front of the coffin, not yet able to tear herself away from the uncustomary pink dress and the awful-but-now dead woman who wore it. "Just a minute more."

There had to be some reason she'd come. Some reason other than just to ensure that Helena's reign of terror was over, but nothing came to her except the lingering scent of Helena's gardenia perfume.

"Where's Hank?" Sabine asked. "Surely he wouldn't miss his own mother's funeral. That would be major bad karma, even for Hank. I know he's a lousy human being and all, but really."

Maryse sighed as Sabine's words chased away her wistful vision of her wayward husband in a coffin right alongside his mother. If her best friend had even an inkling of her thoughts, she'd besiege her with a regime of crystal cleansing and incense until Maryse went insane, and she was sort of saving the insanity plea to use later on in life and on a much bigger problem than a worthless man.

"Hank is a lot of things," Maryse said, "but he's not a complete fool. He's wanted on at least twenty different charges in Mudbug. This is the first place the cops would look for him. There's probably one behind the skirt under the coffin."

Sabine stared at the blue velvet curtain for a moment, then pulled a piece of it to the side and leaned down a bit. Sarcasm was completely lost on Sabine.

"Cut it out," Maryse said and jabbed her again. "I was joking. Hank wouldn't risk an arrest to come to the funeral, karma or no. The only thing Hank liked about Helena was her money, and once the estate is settled, Hank's bad karma can be paid in full."

Sabine pursed her lips and gave the blue velvet curtain one last suspicious look. "Well, it's going to be hard to collect the money if he's playing the Invisible Man."

Maryse rolled her eyes, turned away from the Pink Polyester Antichrist, and pointed to a pew in the back. "Oh, he'll be lurking around somewhere waiting to inherit," she whispered as the music began to play and they took a seat in the back of the chapel. "Even I would bet on that one. With any luck, someone will grab him while he's in close range."

Sabine smirked. "Then he'll collect momma's money and work a deal with the local cops through Helena's friend Judge Warner, and everything will be swept under the rug as usual."

"Yeah, probably. But maybe I'll finally get my divorce."

Sabine's eyes widened. "I hadn't even thought of that, but you're right. If someone grabs Hank, you can have him served." She reached over and squeezed Maryse's hand. "Oh, thank God, Maryse. You can finally be free."

Maryse nodded as the song leader's voice filtered

through her head. What a mess she'd made of her life. She hadn't even been married to Hank thirty days before he disappeared, leaving her holding the bag while numerous bookies and loan sharks came calling. If they'd lived in any other state but Louisiana, she would have already been divorced, but Louisiana, with its screwed-up throwback to Napoleonic law, had only two outs for a marriage—either you served papers or you produced a body. No exceptions.

She'd had no choice but to ask Helena for help. Hank hadn't exactly borrowed money from the nicest of people, and if Maryse wanted to continue to live in Mudbug, she had to pay them off—pure and simple. That was two years ago, and despite the efforts of four private investigators and several angry friends, she hadn't seen Hank Henry since. Oh, but she'd seen Helena.

Every other Friday at seven A.M., Helena appeared like clockwork at Lucy's Café to collect on the debt Maryse owed her, along with the 25 percent interest she was charging. Now the old bat had the nerve to die when Maryse was only two payments short of eating breakfast in complete peace and quiet.

She turned her attention to the pastor as he took over at the front of the chapel. He began to read the standard funeral Bible verses, meant to persuade those in attendance that the person they loved had moved on to a better place. Maryse smirked at the irony. *Mudbug* was the better place now that Helena had exited. She cast her gaze once more to Helena, lying peacefully in her coffin . . .

That's when Helena moved.

Maryse straightened in her pew, blinked once to clear her vision, and stared hard at Helena Henry. Surely it was a trick of the lights. Dead people didn't move. Embalming and all that other icky stuff that happened at funeral homes took care of that, right?

Maryse had just about convinced herself that it was just a lights and shadows trick when Helena opened her eyes and raised her head. Maryse sucked in a breath and clenched her eyes shut, certain she was having a nervous breakdown that had been two years in the making. She waited several seconds, then slowly opened her eyes, silently praying that her mind was done playing tricks on her.

Apparently, it wasn't.

Helena sat bolt upright in the coffin, looking around the chapel, a confused expression on her boldly painted face. Panicked, Maryse scanned the other attendees. Why wasn't anyone screaming or pointing or running for the door? God knows, she hadn't been to many funerals, but she didn't remember the dead person ever sitting up to take part.

She felt a squeeze on her hand, and Sabine whispered, "Are you all right? You got really pale all of a sudden."

Maryse started to answer, but then sucked in a breath as Helena pulled herself out of the coffin.

"Don't you see that?" Maryse pointed to the front of the chapel. "Don't you see what's happening?"

Sabine cast a quick glance to the front of the chapel, then looked back at Maryse with concern—no fear, no terror . . . nothing to indicate that she saw anything amiss.

"See what?" Sabine asked. "Do we need to leave? You don't look well."

Maryse closed her eyes, took a deep breath, and dug her fingernails into her palms, steeling herself. Even though it was the last thing in the world she wanted to do, she forced her gaze to the front of the chapel.

Yup, her nightmare was still there. And, just as in real life, she didn't want to stay silent for long.

"What the hell is going on here, Pastor Bob? For Christ's sake, I'm Catholic," Helena ranted. "If this is some sort of weird Baptist ceremony, I don't want any part of it." Helena paused for a moment, but the pastor continued as if she'd never said a word.

Maryse stared, not blinking, not breathing, her eyes growing wider and wider until she felt as if they would pop out of her head.

Helena turned from the pastor and surveyed the attendees, narrowing her eyes. "Who dressed me like a hooker and shoved me in a coffin? I'll have you all arrested is what I'll do. Damn it, someone drugged me! What are you—some kind of weird cult?" She paced wildly in front of the coffin. "I'll see every one of you assholes in jail, especially you, Harold." Helena stepped over to the nearest pew and reached for her husband, Harold, but her hands passed completely through him.

Helena stopped for a moment, then tried to touch Harold once more, but the result was exactly the same. She frowned and looked down at herself, then back at the coffin. Maryse followed her gaze and realized Helena's body was still lying there—placid as ever.

Helena stared at herself for what seemed like forever, her eyes wide, her expression shocked. The pastor asked everyone to rise for prayer, and Maryse rose in a daze alongside Sabine, but she couldn't bring herself to bow her head. Her eyes were permanently glued on the spectacle at the front of the chapel. The spectacle that apparently no one else could see.

Helena began to walk slowly down the aisle, yelling as she went and waving her hands in front of people's faces. But no one so much as flinched. As she approached the back, Maryse's heart began to race, and her head pounded with the rush of blood. She knew she should sit down, but she couldn't move, couldn't breathe.

All of a sudden, Helena ceased yelling and stopped in her tracks about ten feet from Maryse's pew. Her expression changed from shocked to worried, then sad. Maryse tried to maintain her composure, but the breath she'd been holding came out with a whoosh. Helena looked toward the source of the noise and locked eyes with Maryse.

Helena stared for a moment, her expression unchanged. As the seconds passed and Maryse didn't drop her gaze, Helena's face changed from sad to puzzled, and she started walking toward the pew. Maryse held in a cry as Helena drew closer. A wave of dizziness washed over her. Her head began to swim. One step, two steps, and then the apparition was right in front of her.

That's when everything went dark.

Maryse came to surrounded by a circle of black. For a moment, she thought she was in a tomb, but then her vision cleared, and she looked upward to the concerned and curious faces of the other funeral-goers. Helena's funeral, she remembered instantly. She was at Helena's funeral.

"Maryse, are you all right?" Sabine leaned over her, worried.

Maryse sat up on the floor and felt a rush of blood to her head. "What happened?"

Sabine shook her head. "I don't know. The pastor was praying, and the next thing I knew, you were on the ground."

An elderly lady standing next to Sabine handed her a Kleenex and chimed in, "It looks like you fainted. It's probably the heat."

Maryse took the tissue, wondering what the hell she was supposed to do with it, and nodded. It was a more diplomatic response than pointing out that the chapel was air-conditioned, so that theory didn't exactly hold water. Maryse rose from the floor, wobbling a bit on the uncomfortable high heels, and perched at the end of the pew. Deciding there was nothing more to see, the other funeral attendees drifted out the door and away to the cemetery for the interment.

Maryse rubbed her temples and looked over at Sabine. "I swear, I don't remember a thing. What happened?"

Sabine frowned and gave her a critical look. "I'm not sure what to tell you. You started looking kinda weird in the middle of the service and asked me if I saw something, but I have no idea what. When we rose to pray, you were white as a sheet, and while the pastor was praying, you must have passed out. By the time I opened my eyes, you were already hitting the ground."

"It must be stress," Maryse said. "That's the only explanation."

"Maybe," Sabine said thoughtfully, then placed one hand on Maryse's arm. "Are you going to be okay to drive?"

Maryse nodded. "Yeah, I'll be fine. I was a little dizzy at first, but now I feel fine."

Sabine narrowed her eyes. "Are you sure? I have an appointment in twenty minutes or I would do it myself, but I can call Mildred if you'd rather someone give you a ride."

Maryse waved her hand, rose from the pew, and gave her friend a smile, hoping to alleviate some of her worry. "No use bothering Mildred while she's working." Maryse glanced down at her watch. "Speaking of which, did you close the shop for the morning?"

Sabine shook her head. "Raissa agreed to cover for me until noon. Mrs. Breaux's coming in for her tarot reading right after lunch. That's the appointment I can't miss.

Mrs. Breaux absolutely hates getting a reading from Raissa."

Maryse stared at her. "But Raissa has real psychic ability. You're just shamming."

Sabine rolled her eyes. "I know that, but do you really think these people want to know the truth? If they did, they'd drive the hour to New Orleans and see Raissa for a dose of reality. The only reason Mrs. Breaux keeps coming back is because I tell her what she wants to hear."

"But how long can that possibly last? I mean, sooner or later, she's going to figure out you're never right."

Sabine shrugged. "Doesn't matter. Raissa says she'll be dead by year-end anyway, so the charade doesn't have to last much longer. Her soul's fine though—very clean, actually—so she should do well in the next round." Sabine took a step closer and gave her a hug. "Give me a call later. And think about taking the afternoon off, please."

Maryse nodded, not even wanting to consider how Raissa knew when Mrs. Breaux would expire, then made a mental note to avoid running into that psychic anytime soon. Death was definitely one of those things where ignorance was bliss. "Thanks, Sabine. I really appreciate you coming with me on such short notice. And don't worry. I'll be fine from here on out."

Sabine didn't look convinced, but there wasn't much she could do. She gave Maryse an encouraging smile and turned to leave.

Maryse gave her retreating figure one final glance and looked back to the front of the chapel. What in the world had happened? There was something in the back of her mind, but it was fleeting, like a movie on fast forward. Something important that she needed to remember, but it was flashing too fast for her to lock in on it.

What could cause a young, healthy woman who spent most of her time outdoors to faint in an air-conditioned building? The answer hit her all at once and she gasped.

Helena!

The image of Helena Henry crawling out of her coffin and yelling at everyone in the chapel made her shudder all over again. And that look in her eyes when she'd seen Maryse watching her . . .

But how was that even possible? Helena Henry was dead. There was no mistaking the bitter-looking woman in that casket for anyone else—despite the hideous pink suit and Vegas-showgirl makeup.

The only explanation Maryse had was that she must have imagined the whole thing. All the strain of trying to find that idiot Hank and paying off his ridiculous debts to that devil-mother of his must have caused her to break. That had to be it. The dead didn't show up to their own funerals and call people assholes.

She paused for a moment. If they could, though, she'd have bet Helena Henry would have been the first to volunteer for the job.

Certain her current line of thought had gone way too far, she left the chapel and made her way to her truck, anxious to get away from the overwhelming feeling of death. It was barely noon, but it was definitely time for a beer. Maybe she'd pick up something from the café on the way home— like a bag of boiled crawfish—then take a shower and a nap. Just a bit of a refresher.

After that, she needed to contact her attorney and make sure he was prepared for a Hank appearance and was ready to serve him the divorce papers. She pulled into Mudbug, all eight buildings of it, and parked in front of the café. Turning off the truck, she stared out the windshield at her

reflection in the café window. She didn't even want to
think about having to face Hank. She wasn't even sure it
was possible without trying to throttle him.

Maybe she'd have fries, too—fries and *two* beers and forget she'd ever known Hank and Helena Henry.

Maryse awakened midafternoon, surprised she'd slept so
long. But napping any longer was a luxury she couldn't afford. She'd already lost almost an entire day of work. If she
hurried out to the bayou, there might be enough daylight to
take some pictures and satisfy the state's latest request for
images of bayou foliage.

Just as she was about to crawl out of bed, she felt the hair
on her arms prickle as if she were being watched. Her cat,
Jasper, stiffened and let out a low growl. Before she could
figure out what had upset him, he leaped from the bed and
shot out the cat door built into the window beside the bed.

Shaking her head in amusement at his antics, Maryse
caught a flash of bright pink out of the corner of her eye
and looked up to find Helena Henry standing in the doorway of her bedroom, studying her like she would the fabric
on designer sheets.

Maryse felt her back tighten from the tip of her neck all
the way to the base of her spine. This couldn't be
happening—not after only two beers.

"Well, hell," Helena said finally. "That solves it." She
took a few steps closer to the bed and looked Maryse
straight in the eyes. "You can see me, can't you?"

Maryse nodded, unable to speak, unable to blink.

"I thought for a moment at the chapel that you'd finally
lost your mind, but I should have known better. You're far
too practical to let something like a funeral take you down.
Especially *my* funeral." She blew out a breath and plopped

down on the end of the bed. "This is certainly unexpected but will probably come in handy."

"Handy?" Maryse managed to croak out, her mind whirling with confusion. There was a dead woman sitting on her bed. Weren't they supposed to float or something? "But you're . . . I mean, you are . . ."

"Dead?" Helena finished. "Of course I'm dead. Do you think I'd wear polyester in the summer if I were alive? And don't get me started about the color, or the low-cut top and the skirt that is way too short." She stared down at the offensive garment. "Makes me want to puke."

"But how . . . why . . ." Maryse trailed off, not sure where to go with the conversation, not entirely convinced she was actually having the conversation. Finally, she pinched herself, just to make absolutely sure she was awake.

Helena gave her a grim smile. "Oh, you're awake, honey. And I'm really dead, and you're really sitting in your bedroom talking to me." She scrunched her brow in concentration. "Although, I suppose it's not really me but the ghost of me. Hmmm."

"But at the funeral, you looked confused, surprised . . ."

Helena nodded. "It was a bit of a shocker, I have to admit. Waking up in a coffin in the middle of my own funeral service. Took me a couple of hours to sort it all out, but once the memories came together, it all made sense."

"But why me? Why in the world would you be visible to me?"

Helena shrugged. "Just lucky, I guess."

Lucky? Lucky! Good God Almighty! Maryse could think of plenty of words to describe being haunted by her dead Antichrist mother-in-law, but lucky sure as hell wasn't one of them. "Please tell me you're going to go away and haunt a house or a cemetery or something."

Helena shook her head. "Can't do that just yet. I have a bit of unfinished business here. And much as you may hate it, it involves you. Plus, there's that nagging problem of letting my killer get away, and as long as I'm hanging around, I figure I might as well do something about that, too."

Maryse jumped up from the bed. "Your killer? The newspaper said it was respiratory failure from your asthma."

"Respiratory failure, my ass. My lungs may have given out, but it was only after I drank whatever the hell was put in my brandy snifter. I collapsed right afterward."

Maryse absorbed this information for a moment. Certainly what Helena implied was possible, but if she was right, that still left a huge question unanswered. "Who did it?"

"I don't know, but they were clever. I haven't had a drink of brandy in a long time. Could have been there for a day or a month for all I know." Helena shrugged. "Guess I'll just have to figure out who wanted me dead."

Maryse stared at her. Was she kidding? A shorter list would be people who *didn't* want her dead.

"I think that might be a bit difficult," Maryse said finally, trying to be diplomatic. After all, she didn't know anything about ghosts. Maybe they could do curses or something. This *was* Louisiana.

"You weren't exactly the most popular person in town," Maryse continued and braced herself for the blow up.

Helena surprised her by pursing her lips and considering her words. "You're right," she said finally. "There are probably plenty of people who weren't sad to see me go. The question is which one was desperate enough to take action?"

Maryse thought about this for a moment and began to see Helena's point. When one really boiled down to the nitty-gritty of the situation, there was an enormous difference between preferring someone was dead, or even wishing them dead, and actually killing them. Still, the word "desperate" brought her missing husband to mind.

"You're thinking of Hank," Helena said, and gave her a shrewd look. "Of course I thought of him, but I don't think that's the answer."

Maryse started to open her mouth in protest, but Helena held up one finger to silence her. "I'm certain he won't be sad to hear I'm dead. But quite frankly, Hank lacks the brains to carry out something like this. If he ever tried to poison someone, he'd never think to use something the coroner wouldn't detect. He'd probably go straight for rat poison or whatever was closest."

Maryse studied Helena's face carefully, trying to discern whether she was being sincere or sarcastic. She couldn't find any evidence of sarcasm. Well, that hung it all. If Helena was talking trash about Hank, the woman was most certainly dead.

Oh, how a little murder changed everything.

"Okay," Maryse said, chasing away the great visual of Hank Henry rotting away in a prison cell. "What about Harold?"

"Hmm." Helena scrunched her brow in concentration. "It usually is the spouse, especially when there's money involved. But as far as Harold's concerned, I was worth more alive than dead. With the bequests I left to various people and organizations, he actually comes out on the short end of the stick, and he's probably known that for a long time."

Maryse threw her hands in the air. "Well, if you've got a logical reason for why Hank or Harold aren't guilty, then I don't know why you bothered to come here. I obviously don't have the mentality to think like a killer." She took a deep breath and rushed on before she could change her mind. "I don't think I can help you, Helena."

There. It was out in the open. She bit her lower lip and looked at Helena, hoping she would politely agree and go away.

Helena gave her a withering look and shook her head. "Sorry. You have something I need."

Maryse felt her breath catch in her throat. Helena already had something in mind, and Maryse knew with complete certainty she didn't want to hear a word of it. "What in the world could I possibly have that you need?" She waved one hand around the one-bedroom cabin. "This is all I have in the world besides my truck. A camp in the middle of the bayou."

Helena looked at her with sad eyes that seemed to go straight to her soul. "That's not true. You're alive. You can touch things, move things. I can't. And you're the only one who can see me."

Maryse narrowed her eyes at Helena. "What do you mean you can't touch or move things? You got here, and the only way to get to my place is by boat."

Helena's eyes lit up. "I know. That's been the only interesting part about death so far. I stood at the bank thinking about how to get over here. Finally, I decided to borrow one of the small aluminum boats parked at the dock, but no matter how hard I tried, I couldn't get a grip on anything. My hands just passed right through everything like it wasn't even there."

"So how exactly did you get here?"

Helena beamed. "I walked on water. I finally figured what the hell, if Jesus did it, I would give it whirl. So I stepped off the pier onto the bayou and voilà—I could walk on water."

Maryse stared at her in dismay. This was the start of the

Revelation . . . she was positive. If Helena Henry could walk on water, Maryse was absolutely sure He was on His way back to claim His own.

Well, that sealed it. Church this Sunday was no longer an option. She had some serious praying to do.

Chapter Two

Maryse stopped at the office with the intention of making a quick in-and-out stop. The state was trying to determine if the orchid *cypripedium kentuckiense*, known to regular folk as the Southern Lady's Slipper, was reproducing as a poisonous hybrid. All she needed to do was get the picture the state had sent her and head for the bayou where things were safe, sane, and normal.

Except that the office wasn't empty.

A man sat at her desk, his back to the door. A man she'd never seen before. A man with a lot of nerve, since he was trying to log in to her computer.

Apparently, the hacking effort had him totally engrossed because he didn't seem to hear her come in. Maryse pulled the door shut with a bang and got a small satisfaction out of making him jump. "Who the hell are you and what are you doing in my office?" she asked.

The man turned around in the chair, and Maryse felt her breath catch in her throat. He was gorgeous. Long black hair pulled into a ponytail, dark eyes, and skin with that deep brown coloring that implied Creole or Native American. He smiled at her, and she blinked. Even his teeth were perfect.

He rose from the chair and extended his hand. "I'm Luc LeJeune."

Maryse stared at him a moment more, then shook his

hand. "And you're doing exactly what in my office, trying to break into my computer?"

Luc glanced back at the computer, then looked back at her. "Oh, that. Well, you see, I'm a zoologist for the state. I'm going to be working here with you for a while . . . maybe a couple of months, and this is the only computer in the office I could find."

Maryse's head whirled. "Working here? There's barely room for me." Technically, there were two offices, but one was her lab, and by God, she wasn't giving it up. "There's only one bathroom."

Luc smiled again. "I don't mind sharing as long as you leave the seat up."

Good looking and funny too. God help her. "This is not going to work," Maryse said. "There is one desk in here, one computer. There's no way we will both fit."

Luc shrugged. "Guess we're going to have to. I have a job to do, and this is where the state sent me. Based on the time you showed up here today, I assume you spend most working hours in the bayou. Either that or you're really not a morning person."

Maryse bristled. "I'm fine in the morning, Mr. LeJeune. *This* morning I was attending a funeral for my mother-in-law. Not that it's any of your business."

Luc glanced at her bare left hand. "You're married? That's a shame. This assignment was starting to look interesting."

"No, I'm not married. Well, technically, I'm married, but not really."

Luc looked at her in obvious amusement. "You're not really technically married? I'm fascinated. What's the story?"

She paused for a moment, deciding on an answer. "I'm getting a divorce."

"You don't sound convinced."

Maryse sighed. "Look, Mr. LeJeune, I don't really care to discuss my personal life with you, I don't care to share my office with you, and I sure as hell don't care to leave the seat up on the toilet. Now, if you don't mind removing yourself from my desk, what I do care to do is use my computer so that I can manage a bit of work today before the daylight is gone."

Luc slid the chair to the side and grinned, aggravating her even more. "All yours."

Maryse pulled a metal chair up to the computer since the rude zoologist apparently had no intention of giving up her comfortable leather chair. First thing tomorrow morning, she was calling the state about this. There was no way she was going to have that man snooping around her research, using her computer, looking over her shoulder.

Like he was doing now.

Luc LeJeune had rolled his chair back toward her and now the arm of her leather chair was almost touching the arm of the cheap metal thing she currently sat on. In the cool, air-conditioned office, she could feel the heat from his body as he shifted toward her, his arm and shoulders not even an inch from hers.

She lifted her arm away from his warmth and leaned forward in her chair and slightly to the side in order to block his view of the keyboard. Then she tapped in her password. The screen flickered, and she opened her mailbox and started scanning for the picture she needed. Leaning back again in her chair, she clicked to open the e-mail she'd been searching for.

"So who was your mother-in-law?" Luc asked. She could feel his breath on her neck.

Silently willing her hormones into submission, she

frowned. "*Ex*-mother-in-law. And why would you want to know? You're not from Mudbug."

Luc shrugged. "My grandparents used to live on the bayou in the next town. They have friends in Mudbug. I figure your mother-in-law might have been someone they knew."

"*Ex*-mother-in-law, and her name was Helena Henry."

Luc let out a laugh. "You're the one who married Hank Henry? Wow, that sucks. No wonder you're not technically married. Hank's been gone for, what, a year now?"

Maryse gritted her teeth and worked to control her voice. "Two years actually, but I'm sure that's about to change."

Luc studied her for a moment, then frowned. "So the wicked witch is dead. Ought to make things interesting."

Maryse clicked on the picture she was looking for and sent it to print. "What do you mean?"

He shrugged. "She was filthy rich, right? Always interesting when someone with that much money dies."

Damn. His words brought her right back around to Hank's likely reappearance and Helena's definitive one. She grabbed the printout from the printer and was about to shut down the computer when the office phone rang. She reached for it, but Luc got there first, sliding the headset just out of her grasp.

"Luc LeJeune," he answered and gave her a lazy smile.

Maryse turned back to the computer, determined to ignore him, but his next words caught her attention.

"Yes, sir," Luc said, his voice the epitome of respect. "She just walked in. Can I ask what this is concerning?"

Maryse jumped out of her chair and grabbed the phone from Luc. She covered the headset with one hand and glared at him. "When I need someone to screen my calls, I'll hire a secretary." She moved her hand and turned her back on Luc. "This is Maryse Robicheaux."

"Ms. Robicheaux," an ancient, very proper-sounding voice spoke. "My name is Randolph Wheeler. I'm the attorney for Helena Henry's estate."

Unbelievable. Helena was planning on collecting Hank's debt even from the grave. Maryse gritted her teeth and tried to modulate her reply. "If you'll give me your mailing address, Mr. Wheeler, I'll be happy to mail the last two payments to you tomorrow."

There was a pause on the other end of the line, then Maryse heard the attorney clear his throat. "I apologize, Ms. Robicheaux, but apparently there's a misunderstanding here. I'm not calling to collect anything on behalf of the estate. Quite the contrary, actually. My call is to notify you that you've been named in Helena Henry's will and your presence is requested at the reading tomorrow."

Maryse sank into her chair, stunned. "Helena named me in her will? What the hell did she leave me—more debt?"

There was another pause and Maryse could feel the attorney's disapproval coming across the phone line. "Ms. Robicheaux, I'll be happy to cover all of that tomorrow. The reading will begin at one o'clock at my office in New Orleans. The street address is 115 Morgan. Do you need directions?"

"No," Maryse said, her aggravation slowly giving way to disbelief. "I'll be there."

"Then I'll see you at one o'clock." The lawyer disconnected.

Maryse dropped the phone from her ear and sat completely still. What the hell? Life had offered her far more surprises lately than she'd ever asked for, and none of them the pleasant kind. Whatever Helena had left her couldn't be good.

"So," Luc said, "the old bat left you something. Cool."

Maryse stared at Luc, momentarily surprised that she'd completely forgotten he was in the room. "I seriously doubt anything to do with Helena Henry will ever be called cool." She reached for her mouse and closed her e-mail.

She'd been given more to worry about in this single day than a person should have in an entire lifetime, and more than anything, she needed to get out in the bayou and away from people. If there was any chance of getting a grip on her racing thoughts, the bayou was the only place it would happen.

She grabbed her printout off the desk, shut down her computer, and jumped up from her chair before Luc realized he still didn't have access to her PC. "I've got work to do," she said as she headed out the door. "We'll settle this whole office thing tomorrow afternoon, but I wouldn't get too comfortable if I were you."

Luc LeJeune watched as Maryse slammed the office door shut behind her. Things hadn't gone exactly as he'd planned. He had intended to waltz into the office, charm the woman who worked there, get the information he needed, and get the heck back to DEQ headquarters in New Orleans before he remembered why he hated small towns.

But Maryse Robicheaux might prove to be more of a problem than the Department of Environmental Quality had originally thought.

He turned to the computer, his fingers posed to start an intensive search of her personal files, when he realized the password box was flashing at him again. Damn it. She was sneaky. He'd give her that. And if he hadn't been pressed for time on this case, he might have even been amused. He yanked his cell phone from his shirt pocket and pressed in a number.

"Wilson," the man on the other end answered.

"Hey, boss, it's LeJeune."

"Yeah, LeJeune, you romance that botanist into giving up her secrets?"

"Not exactly."

There was a pause on the other end. "What . . . you losing your touch?"

Luc counted to five before answering. Given his reputation among the bureau as a ladies' man, he probably had that one coming. "No, I'm not losing my touch, but our research department needs a swift kick in the ass. This is no lonely, single scientist living like a hermit on the bayou."

"No? What part's wrong?"

"For starters, she's married—to the local cad, no less— and he ran out on her years ago. To top it off, the cad's mother died recently. The woman was filthy rich, and the reading of the will is tomorrow. Which means this town is probably about to be a clusterfuck of money-grabbing relatives—the least of which is going to be the disappearing husband, since he was an only child."

"So what's the problem?"

"The problem is this woman is so distracted she barely noticed me, except to be angry about my being in her space. She doesn't want me in the office and made that perfectly clear. I don't think this is going to be as easy as we originally hoped."

"Well, easy or not, it's still your job. We need to know if that woman's up to something. Do what you have to—pick locks, read diaries, whatever—just don't put it in your report. Either she's part of the problem or she's not. We need that information sooner than later."

Luc looked across the tiny office to the locked door. "There is another room here that's locked. I guess I need to get in there and see what she finds so important that she'd deadbolt an interior door."

"Sounds like a plan," his boss said. "And, LeJeune, don't take rejection so personally. Even a guy like you can't have them all."

Luc flipped his phone shut and glanced at a photo on the desk of Maryse and some other woman standing in front of a bar in downtown Mudbug. Her wavy brown hair was longer now, but the body was still the same—toned, tight, and tan. He knew he couldn't have them all. Hell, he hadn't had them all, and apparently this was going to be another one of those times.

But damned if he wasn't going to try.

Maryse rolled out of bed the next morning wishing her life belonged to anyone but her. She fed Jasper before he started wailing for his morning tuna, then walked over to her closet and peered inside, wondering what the heck you wore to a will reading. Business, casual, formal wear? Knowing Helena, and from the pompous sound of her attorney, it was probably somewhere between business and formal. And since her only good suit was still at the dry cleaners, courtesy of cleaning the funeral home floor the day before, her choices were seriously limited.

She sighed as she flipped through T-shirt after T-shirt and realized her wardrobe needed some serious updating if she ever planned to do anything but toodle around the bayou in her boat. God forbid she ever had a date. She would be one of those women who "didn't have a thing to wear."

At the thought of dating, Luc LeJeune flashed to mind. Oh, no. She blocked out the thoughts of his tanned skin and muscular build and dug into the back of the closet for something, anything but ratty old jeans. No way was she allowing any thoughts of Luc LeJeune to leak in, especially while she was standing in her bedroom, half-clothed.

Luc LeJeune was the hottest guy she'd seen in forever, and her body's reaction to him had confused and scared her. Sure, it had been a long time since she'd been with a man . . . okay, more like two years since there hadn't been anyone since Hank . . . but that was no cause to go jumping on the first good-looking man she saw. Especially when she couldn't afford distractions. Especially when a good-looking man was what had gotten her into the situation she was in right now.

Which brought her back to Helena.

She hadn't seen the ghost since her visit to the cabin, and Maryse hoped things stayed that way. Maybe there was a delay in transitioning to the other side, and she'd simply gotten the raw end of Helena's transfer. Surely God wouldn't let Helena roam the Earth alive *and* dead. He was supposed to be benevolent.

She frowned and yanked a cocktail dress from the back of her closet. Okay, so a will reading probably didn't rate a party dress, but she simply didn't have anything in between. Sighing, she tossed the dress onto the bed. At least it was black. It was as close as she was going to come to business attire and would have to do. She dropped down, dug around the back of the closet floor, and pulled out a pair of shiny black satin shoes. Yuck. But the only other options with heels were her rubber boots or her funeral pumps, and they were navy.

She rose with the shoes and tossed them next to the bed, then threw on a T-shirt, jeans, and tennis shoes. She figured she'd have just enough time to send off the samples she'd collected yesterday and still be able to rush home for a quickie shower before changing for the will reading. With any luck, Luc LeJeune would be out in the bayou studying rat droppings or whatever else he was there to do.

Ten minutes later, she was in her truck and headed to the office. She always drove just a little too fast down the windy gravel roads back in the bayou, but there were rarely other cars on this particular stretch, and the gravel certainly wasn't going to hurt her well-worn-in truck. Usually, her speed wasn't a problem.

Until today.

As she approached a sharp turn in the road, she pressed the brakes, but there was no response. Trying not to panic, she lifted her foot and pressed again. Nothing. The pedal just squished to the floorboard as the truck kept hurtling toward the ninety-degree turn.

Now frantic, she turned the wheel, hoping to make the turn, and threw the gear shifter into park. The truck lurched, and, despite the seatbelt, her forehead banged into the steering wheel. The truck tilted to one side at the very edge of the road, and for a moment, Maryse thought she had pulled it off. Finally inertia won out, and the truck slid off the road into the bayou.

Huge sheets of water splashed up and over the cab, making visibility nil. Maryse covered her aching head with her arms and hoped like hell this was a shallow section and not inhabited by any of the bayou's more aggressive creatures—particularly the meat eaters.

It only took seconds for the water to clear, but it seemed like forever. Almost afraid to look, Maryse lowered her arm and surveyed the damage. The truck was submerged in the bayou almost up to the hood. From the groaning of the metal and the increasing water level, Maryse knew immediately that the truck was sinking further in the thin bayou mud.

Water began to spill in through the cracks in the floor-board and the door, and Maryse figured now was as good a time as any to make her exit. As she cranked down the window, she was grateful she hadn't been able to afford the fully loaded truck with power everything. Sometimes the old-fashioned way is the best way, she thought as she grabbed her keys and her purse and crawled out.

She cautiously moved into the water, hoping she wasn't stepping on anything dangerous. As it took her weight, her foot sank into the mud up to her calf. She tugged on the foot to remove it from the vacuum created by the mud hole and took another step with the same result.

By the time she got to the bank, one shoe was missing—lost forever to a bayou sinkhole—and the other was so full of the stinky, gooey muck that it felt like her leg weighed a hundred pounds. She flopped onto the bank and groaned when she felt the jolt through her head.

"Ouch," she said, and gently rubbed her forehead. There was definitely a knot, but a quick body inspection didn't reveal anything bleeding profusely. Just minors cuts and what would probably develop into some lovely bruises over the next couple of days. She looked over at her truck and sighed. The water was over the hood now and pouring into the cab. Definitely a total loss. Her insurance rates were going to go through the roof.

What in the world had happened? She'd just had her truck in for its scheduled maintenance a couple of weeks before. If there had been a problem with her brakes, the dealership would have let her know. Hell, if there had been a problem with the brakes, the dealership would have been delighted to charge her more money.

She tugged her cell phone from her wet jeans pocket, but it was just as she'd feared—totally fried. Looking back at the road, she considered her options. It was probably five miles or more back to her cabin, which put her around two miles from the office. Maybe Sabine could give her a ride into New Orleans. She pushed herself up from the ground, swaying for a moment as the blood rushed to her aching head.

Unbelievable. She'd totaled her car and had a raging headache, and she hadn't even had the pleasure of being drunk to accomplish it. Disgusted, she shot one final look at her sunken truck and stepped onto the road with one muddy tennis shoe and one muddy bare foot. The gravel immediately dug into the sensitive skin on her bare foot, and she grimaced. All this and then a will reading—probably complete with a ghost.

The day just kept getting better.

Luc pushed his Jeep faster down the gravel road to the office. He had planned on arriving early, hoping Maryse might make a stop in before her appointment in New Orleans, but a faulty alarm clock put him thirty minutes later than he had hoped. He tried to tell himself that his desire to catch Maryse at the office was part of the case, just doing his job, but the truth was the woman intrigued him.

How in the world had such an intelligent, attractive woman allowed herself to get hooked up with the likes of Hank Henry? It simply boggled the mind.

As he approached a large curve in the road, sunlight glinted off something ahead of him, and he squinted, trying to make out where it was coming from. As he neared the turn, it was all too clear. Maryse's truck was buried in the bayou just off the curve, the sun bouncing off her side window.

He slammed on his brakes and threw his Jeep in park before it had even come to a complete stop. Panicked, he jumped out and rushed to the edge of the water, trying to make out whether a person was inside the truck, but he couldn't see a thing. He was just about to wade in when he saw a trail of flattened marsh grass followed by muddy footprints.

Thank God. Maryse had definitely made it out of the truck. His tension eased a bit now that he knew she was alive, but then his thoughts immediately turned to injury. The truck was totaled, and any number of things could have happened to Maryse during the wreck or wading through the bayou afterward.

The office was a couple of miles away, and since he hadn't passed her on his way from town, he had to assume she'd started walking in that direction. He rushed back to his Jeep, threw it in drive, and tore down the road to the office, scanning the sides of the road as he went, just in case she'd stopped to rest, or worse, collapsed.

He'd gone about half a mile when he rounded a corner and saw her walking on the road ahead of him. She turned around to look, and the relief on her face was apparent, even from a distance.

"I thought I'd scared you away yesterday," she said, as he pulled up beside her.

Luc shook his head. "I love a challenge. I thought I'd head in to the office early—practice putting the seat down on the toilet."

"Well, three cheers for work ethic," she said. "I was beginning to think I'd be walking the rest of the day."

He stepped out of the Jeep and gently gripped her arm with one hand, checking her up and down. "Are you all right? Are you hurt?"

"I'll be okay," she said. "I banged my head on the steering

wheel, so I have an enormous headache, and walking on a gravel road with a bare foot wasn't exactly fun. But I don't think there's anything serious."

He reached up to her face and moved her bangs to the side. She definitely had a goose egg, and from the size of it, he didn't doubt the severity of her headache. It was going to take more than Tylenol to fix this one.

"What happened?" he asked.

Maryse shrugged. "I don't really know. The brakes just failed, and I couldn't make the turn."

Luc felt his heart beat a little faster. "Have you had the truck serviced lately?"

"Yeah, that's the weird thing. I just had it in for a sixty-thousand-mile service. They checked everything." She paused for a moment. "Or at least they said they did."

Luc nodded, trying to keep his facial expression normal, but his senses were on high alert. This accident sounded fishy. "We need to get you to the hospital," he said. "Someone should take a look at that knot. Just to be safe."

Maryse shook her head, then put on hand over her forehead and groaned. "No time. I have to be at this will reading this afternoon. I still need to send some samples to the state, change clothes, and pick up my spare cell phone. The old one took a dip with the truck."

"The samples can wait. I'm pretty sure this rates a sick day."

"Maybe, but the reading won't wait, and I can't exactly go looking like this. If you'll just drop me off at the dock to my cabin, I'd really appreciate it."

"It's not a contest, Maryse. You don't have to be present to win. I'm pretty sure the attorney can tell you about it afterward."

Maryse gave him a withering stare. "Can you arrange to

have my wayward husband served with divorce papers, too? I have to find Hank, and Helena's death may be my last chance. There's more at stake here than some inheritance. Besides, knowing Helena, she probably left me more debt or a pig farm or bubonic plague."

"Fine. But as soon as you've showered and changed, I want to take you to the hospital."

Maryse frowned. "I've already told you there's no time. It's a headache. I'll have it checked out after the will reading."

"What about your truck?"

"It's not exactly going anywhere. It can wait until this evening."

"You've got insurance?"

She gave him a dirty look. "Of course I have insurance. I also have smoke detectors and contribute to my 401(k)."

Luc held in a smile. "If you give me your insurance card, I can take care of the tow."

"I can take care of the tow myself. I'm fairly certain no one's going to steal it."

Luc threw his hands up in exasperation. "Are you always this stubborn?"

"Are you always this bossy?"

He stared at her for a moment, then grinned. "Yeah, pretty much."

"Well, you've just run into a brick wall."

No shit. He looked at her and shook his head. "At least let me drive you to your appointment in New Orleans. I need to run an errand there today anyway, and you can pick up a rental car in the city a lot easier than getting one delivered to Mudbug."

She narrowed her eyes at him and stared for a couple of seconds, and Luc knew she was wondering what his angle was. He hoped to God she didn't find out until he was gone, because if Maryse was this prickly when she thought he was trying to help, he'd hate to see her reaction if she knew he was actually in Mudbug investigating her.

"Okay," she said finally, "you can drop me off at the attorney's office."

Luc nodded, and she pointed a finger at him.

"But I want to be very clear," she said, "that the only reason I'm accepting your offer is because I'm down to one source of transportation and I don't think I can get my bass boat all the way to New Orleans—at least not by one o'clock."

Luc couldn't hold back a grin. "You make me feel very special, Maryse. I'm so glad you're going to allow me to chauffer you around."

Maryse shook her head. "Don't get any ideas. Just because I'm catching a ride with you doesn't mean I've changed my mind about sharing an office."

"Now, what in the world makes you think I would get any ideas?"

Maryse frowned and walked over to the passenger side of the Jeep. "I know your type, LeJeune. Technically, I'm still married to him. Guys like you are always full of ideas."

As she climbed inside his Jeep, Luc took a peek at her firm, round bottom, every curve clearly outlined in her wet jeans. Maryse was dead wrong about him. He wasn't full of ideas—he was overflowing with them.

Chapter Three

Maryse stepped carefully out of her bass boat, making sure one of her shiny, satin heels didn't slip between the boards of the dock. Luc sat at the dock in his Jeep and stared at her with a mixture of amusement and disbelief. Okay, so it probably wasn't an everyday sight, but did he have to laugh? She glared at him as she climbed up in his Jeep. "What? You've never seen a woman in a dress before, LeJeune?"

Luc shook his head. "Mostly I see women out of dresses, and I've absolutely never seen a woman wearing fancy clothes in a bass boat."

"You would if you lived in Mudbug."

Luc smiled. "Aren't you a little overdressed for a will reading?"

Maryse shrugged. "It was either this or jeans."

"You need to get out more."

"Just drive," Maryse said, and reached over to turn the radio on—loud. Then she leaned back in her seat and closed her eyes, shutting out all images and sounds of Luc LeJeune. God knows she had enough to think about. She was about to come face to face with Hank Henry for the first time in two years. It was probably a good thing she was wearing a dress. It wouldn't be as easy to kick his ass in high heels.

Luc pulled up in front of the attorney's office fifteen minutes early, and Maryse felt her back stiffen as she picked up her purse and prepared to step out of the Jeep. Turning to

Luc, she gave him what was probably a grim smile. "I really appreciate you giving me a lift. And I'm sorry if I was a big bitch earlier."

Luc smiled. "You weren't that bad."

Maryse felt a momentary burst of disappointment. "I'll try harder next time."

Now Luc laughed. "I don't have any doubt about that. Now get inside and claim your pig farm and your divorce and anything else you've got riding on this reading."

Maryse smiled for real this time, stepped out of the Jeep, and glanced over at the attorney's office. Luc pulled onto the street, waving as he drove off. Maryse sighed and tore her gaze from the Jeep, trying to refocus on the will reading and everything that went along with it. Luc LeJeune was Hank Henry all over again . . . good-looking, charming, a professional flirt, confident beyond belief, and probably had a list of conquests that rivaled Alexander the Great. He was everything she was trying to avoid in one neat, gorgeous, well-defined package.

Taking a deep breath, she turned and walked to the attorney's office, hoping the will reading would be quick and painless. She was due a break after the horrific funeral, and besides, locating Hank was the most important thing on her mind. She pushed open the door to the office and stepped into a cherry-wood nightmare. Antique furniture covered every square inch of the tiny lobby. The place was so stiff that even the threads in the Persian rug were rod straight. Chintz pillows graced the corners of every chair, the narrow couch, and the loveseat. The only plus was the room was empty. Apparently she was the first to arrive.

At the reception window, Maryse checked in with a pinched-faced elderly woman wearing horned-rimmed glasses. Once the woman confirmed her identity, Maryse turned to consider her options and decided on a chair in the far corner of the room with a clear view of the doorway. That way she'd be sure to see Hank, just in case he showed up to collect his bounty. She'd put her attorney on speed dial in her spare phone, and he had a deputy waiting nearby ready to pop in and serve Hank the all-important papers. Everything was in place except her missing husband. As usual.

She removed the chintz pillows from their perch at the back of the chair, arranged them in the middle of the seat, and sat on top of them. Probably not what the decorator had intended, but she didn't really care. The chair was bound to be uncomfortable as hell, and she'd already put her body through enough strain today. She glanced at her watch for at least the tenth time in so many seconds and heard the office door open.

She sucked in a breath, wondering who was going to walk across the entryway, and did a double take when three women walked in—one of them a nun, in full habit, robes and all. The other two were in their sixties and wore the dark clothes and bad makeup of Helena's generation, so she figured they had to be family.

But what was the deal with the nun?

Surely she wasn't a relative. Being related to Helena Henry would be enough to convert a religious person to atheism. The other two women presented their IDs to the receptionist, then proceeded to cackle over the reading.

"She better have left me her porcelain angels," the first woman said. "I've been wanting those for years."

"Well, I don't give a rip about those angels," the second woman said, "but I desperately want her family quilts. Do you have any idea how much those quilts are worth? They're practically a part of history."

The other woman nodded. "Why do you think I want the angels? One just like them brought five hundred dollars last week on eBay. Think what we could get at the auction."

"Well, all I can say is it's about damned time she died. I could have used a trip to Bermuda last year."

Definitely Helena's family.

As the two hens finished their business and moved away from the window, Maryse leaned forward in her chair, straining to hear what the nun was saying. Sure enough, she was here for the will reading. This was getting stranger by the minute. Maryse picked up a couple of magazines and was trying to decide between *Law Review* and *Law Today* when the door opened again and Harold walked in . . . followed by a fuming Helena.

Maryse scrunched down low in her chair, hoping Helena wouldn't notice her, but the ghost crossed the room and sat on the chair next to her. Harold checked in, gave Maryse a suspicious look, then took a seat across from her.

Helena glared at Harold. "Asshole," she said. "Do you know he had the nerve to drive over here in my new Cadillac with one of those floozies he was seeing?"

Maryse stared at her, a bit surprised. "What floozies?"

"Did you say something?" Harold asked, frowning.

"No," Maryse said quickly, "Just clearing my throat." She leaned to the side and held the magazine up in front of her face. "What floozies?"

Helena didn't bother to lean or whisper, but then she didn't really have to. "Damn man was always getting a piece of something or other on the side. Started almost as soon as we were married, although I didn't really know about it until after Hank was born. Cut him off right quick, I did. Not about to catch something from one of Harold's floozies. Probably rot my crotch out."

Maryse considered briefly the type of woman that would sleep with Harold Henry and decided Helena had probably made a wise decision. "So why didn't you divorce him?"

"No way! Oh, granted, Harold couldn't get half of my holdings—everything was inherited, so even the income drawn off it was solely mine. But when we were married, we had a prenup that gave Harold a boatload of money if I ever asked for a divorce."

Maryse lowered the magazine and realized that everyone in the lobby was staring at her. She gave them a smile and pulled her cell phone from her purse. "Sorry, I just remembered a call I need to make." She pretended to push in some buttons, gave a fake greeting to the nonentity on the other end of the line, then turned sideways in her seat and leaned in toward Helena. "So what would have happened if he left you?"

"He wouldn't have gotten a dime. It had to be my decision or he got nothing. Why do you think he's hung around all these years, cavorting with floozies, hoping I'd divorce him?"

Maryse cringed, with little doubt in her mind that Harold had probably paid dearly for his indiscretions. Good God, was a free ride and a luxury sedan really worth living with an angry, embittered Helena every day?

"And the payoff is for what exactly?" Maryse asked. Rich people were very confusing.

"Hmmpf. Apparently for being so useless he couldn't work and wouldn't be able to support himself. You have to understand. I married Harold when I was nineteen. I didn't get control of the trust until I was twenty-one. Since no one thought our marriage would last, the lawyers insisted on something to protect my inheritance. Then Harold insisted on something to protect himself, since he was about to deploy to Vietnam and figured that would give everyone too much free time to change my mind."

Maryse absorbed all this. "So how much money are we talking about?"

Helena stared at Harold in obvious disgust. "Upwards of half a million. So I figured no way. I had ultimate control of the estate upon death, so I decided Harold would just have to suffer living with me if he wanted to maintain his lifestyle."

Maryse leaned closer and whispered. "So what exactly did you leave Harold then?" After all, he was at the attorney's office with the rest of them, so that had to mean she'd left him something, despite her griping and complaining.

Helena smiled. "You'll see. You'll all see. Especially Harold."

Oh hell. This couldn't be good. And here she was wearing high heels and a dress and sporting a headache set to turn into a migraine at a moment's notice. Running was definitely going to be out of the question.

She was just about to push Helena for more information when a tall, thin man stepped into the reception area from the back office. He had not a hair on his head but seemed as though he was trying to make up for it with a long, flowing gray beard. His posture was as stiff as his suit, which had probably been purchased somewhere around the time he started growing the beard.

"If you will follow me, please," he said, and Maryse immediately recognized the pompous voice as the attorney who had phoned her. "We're ready to begin."

Maryse tossed her cell phone back into her purse as everyone in the waiting area rose and followed Father Time down the hall and into a small office at the back of the building. The others had already taken their seats, so

Maryse perched on the edge of a particularly hideous gold lamée–covered chair, positioned right between Harold and the nun. The two hens were on the couch directly behind them. Everyone stared at the attorney, Wheeler, like they were waiting for him to pull a rabbit out of a hat. Or in her case, Hank Henry. *Where the hell was Hank?*

Wheeler took a seat behind a cherry-wood desk that occupied half of the room and gave them a sickly smile. "Thank you for coming. There were several people or agencies named in Helena's will, but this group represents those she wanted to be present for a reading. The remainder will receive notification by certified mail."

Maryse frowned, smelling a setup. She glared at Helena, but it did no good. She was too busy trying to strangle Harold from behind, but her fingers kept passing through his neck.

"What about Hank?" Maryse asked, unable to help herself. Damn it, that man was not going to get away with being married to her forever. If he didn't turn up soon, she was definitely going to pursue having him declared legally dead—again. And if she ever got her hands on him, it wasn't going to just be a declaration.

Wheeler reached over to the phone and pressed the speaker button. "Hank," he said, and frowned, "is joining us by phone. He felt his presence here wouldn't be prudent."

"Prudent, my ass!" Maryse jumped up from her seat, glaring at the phone. "You listen to me, you sorry piece of—"

"Uhmm," Wheeler cleared his throat and gave her a clear look of disapproval. "I'm sure that Mr. Henry would be more than happy to arrange a meeting with your attorney to discuss your unfinished business. However, your personal life has no place here."

Maryse glared at Wheeler, then at the phone, then at

Harold and Helena for producing that pile of pond scum. She also made note that the pond scum had not uttered a word during the entire exchange. "Fine, then let's get on with it. Obviously, I have some business to do with my own attorney and the sheriff's department. I can't hang around here all day."

Wheeler nodded, and Maryse took her seat. He picked up an expensively bound stack of paper from the top of his desk and said, "All the words I read from this document are Mrs. Henry's. They have not been edited or altered by this office or any of my agents."

Here we go. If Wheeler was already claiming absolution and hadn't even read the first sentence, this was going to be a doozy.

The attorney cleared his throat and began, "I, Helena Henry, being of sound mind and bad attitude, do hereby make the following bequeaths upon my death . . ."

Harold leaned forward in his chair eagerly. Helena moved to stand behind Wheeler, looking like an excited five-year-old. Maryse slouched back in her chair and waited for the insults to fly.

"All of my real estate holdings in New Orleans, Baton Rouge, and Lafayette, as well as the income they produce, I leave to the St. John's Orphanage in New Orleans. I also deed to them free and clear the building they occupy, which is mine to give."

The nun gasped and from the shade of white that washed over her face, Maryse thought she was going to pass out. Maryse grabbed a notepad from Wheeler's desk and fanned the woman. Helena owned an orphanage? And she was giving them real estate?

Maryse glanced sideways at Harold, but he looked as

confused as she was and more than a little annoyed. Maryse guessed the real estate was worth a lot.

The nun finally waved at her and managed to squeak out a "Thank you." Maryse put the notepad back on the desk and looked expectantly at Wheeler. God help her, this was starting to get interesting.

"My home and all the furnishings within, I leave to the Mudbug Historical Society, upon the condition that it be maintained as a historical tourist site, with a limit of four rooms available for rental as a bed and breakfast. All rental profits will go toward the maintenance of the property. In addition, I also leave the historical society my real estate holdings in downtown Mudbug. The rental income on those properties should more than offset any occasional shortfall in the maintenance of my home. Any remaining profits from the rentals are to be remitted to the Mudbug School District."

Looked like Harold better start packing. Maryse looked over at Helena, who gave her a huge smile.

Wheeler flipped the first page over and continued to read. "To my son, Hank Henry, I leave the sum of one million dollars in trust, upon the condition that he obtain respectable employment and remain clean, sober, and gambling-free for a term of five years—"

"Ha!" Maryse shouted at the speakerphone, where muffled cursing emitted. "Hank can't remain clean, sober, and gambling-free for five minutes."

"That will be enough, Ms. Robicheaux," Wheeler said and shot her a disapproving look. "Actual fulfillment of the terms will be determined by Randolph Wheeler, or his succeeding associate."

Good thinking on Helena's part putting in that

succeeding associate clause. Wheeler would probably be dead in five years. Heck, if he had to spend his time checking up on Hank, Maryse only gave him a couple of weeks.

She glanced over at Harold, but he just shook his head at the entire exchange. He looked a bit disappointed but not really surprised.

"To my cousins, Sarah and Rose," Wheeler read, and Maryse heard the two behind her shifting on their couch, "I leave the remainder of my silver and china. You've been stealing it on holidays for years, so this way it will become a matched set again."

There was a sharp intake of breath from the nun, and the movement behind them ceased completely. "By the way," Wheeler continued, "none of the china is real. It's all a very clever reproduction."

Maryse winced and tried not to laugh as she glanced back at the two putrid faces behind her. *Rough one.*

"To my husband, Harold, I leave the Lower Bayou Motel. You've spent so many nights there with other women that I felt you should call the place home. It's been operating in the red for the last eight years, owes back taxes since 1986, and is covered with deadly asbestos. Nothing but the best for you, dear."

Maryse smiled as the nun gave Harold a disapproving stare. She probably hadn't been closed up in a room with this many sinners since Lent. The look on Harold's face was absolutely priceless. Even Wheeler had smirked when he delivered the last sentence.

Harold glared at everyone, then waved at Wheeler. "Get on with it. Get to the good stuff."

"Of course, Mr. Henry," Wheeler said, obviously holding back a smile. "My final asset of this distribution, the property secured by state lease known as the Mudbug Game Preserve and Wildlife Center, as well as the annual fees paid by the government for said lease, I leave to my daughter-in-law, Maryse Robicheaux Henry."

"That's bullshit!" Harold jumped from his chair, reached across the desk, and grabbed Wheeler by his throat. The two cousins squeezed onto one side of the couch, and the nun made the sign of the cross. Maryse scanned the desk for a sharp implement to defend herself with but didn't see a thing. Good God Almighty, Helena *owned* the game preserve? Maryse stared at the ghost in shock, but Helena only smiled and clapped, obviously enjoying the show.

"What the hell do you think you're doing?" Harold continued to yell. "Helena can only leave that land to family. Those are the rules of the trust, and Hank is her only son!"

Wheeler pried Harold's hands off his throat and smoothed his collar back down. "That may be the case, Mr. Henry, but Hank is not her only relative. Helena is perfectly within her rights to leave the land to her daughter-in-law, as long as the marriage lasted a minimum of two years."

"She can't cut me and Hank out of everything," Harold argued, "and you know it."

"Actually, sir," Wheeler said, "she *can* cut you and Hank out of everything and *you* know it."

Harold stared at Wheeler for a moment, then whirled around and narrowed his eyes at Maryse. "I don't know what you and Helena cooked up, but I won't stand for it. Hank is the rightful heir to that property. You're just the dumb piece of ass he made the mistake of marrying."

Maryse felt the blood rush to her face and her pulse begin to race. "You forgot dumb, *landowner* piece of ass. And believe me, the mistake was all mine."

A bright red flush crept up Harold's neck and onto his

face. He clenched his fists, and for a moment, Maryse thought he was going to hit her. Harold glared for what seemed like forever and finally spit out, "I wouldn't start spending the money just yet. And I'd watch my back if I were you." With that, he stalked out of the office.

Helena winked at Maryse and hurried behind him, probably wanting a ringside seat when Harold told his floozies about his "big" inheritance. "I'll see you later, Maryse," Helena shouted over her shoulder as she left the office.

Maryse frowned. *Not if I see you first.* She turned back to Wheeler. "Some show, huh?"

"I'm sorry about that," Wheeler apologized to everyone. He handed the nun an envelope. "There are additional instructions concerning your inheritance inside of the envelopes. It will take a couple of days to push everything through probate, then you can collect your bequeaths."

The cousins glared at Wheeler and left the office, not bothering to take their envelopes. The nun thanked Wheeler and headed out wearing a dazed expression. It was no wonder. Her orphanage had just inherited the bank, and she'd probably heard more cussing in the past half hour than she had in the past forty years.

Wheeler watched as the nun closed the door behind her, then blew out a breath and slumped into his chair. "There are requirements of your inheritance that we need to discuss, Ms. Robicheaux, but I hope you don't mind if we go through them tomorrow. This entire exchange has exhausted me, and I have another appointment after this one."

"I understand. I'm feeling kind of tired myself."

Wheeler reached behind his desk and brought up a huge document bound in expensive leather. "This is all the instructions and restrictions that accompany the land inheritance. This land has been in Helena's family for well over a hundred years, so a lot of the old rules were established long before my time and yours. You need to review this document in its entirety as soon as possible."

He pushed the document across the desk to Maryse, and she lifted it, momentarily surprised by the weight.

"If you have no objection, I can meet you in Mudbug first thing tomorrow so we can go over the most relevant points. I'll give you a call this evening to arrange a place to meet. In the meantime, the only thing you need to know is that you can't leave town."

Maryse stared at him. "What do you mean I can't leave town?"

"It's one of the restrictions of the original estate. You must remain in Mudbug for a probationary period of one week. That's why I'm going to meet you there tomorrow. Once the probationary period is over, you're free to go anywhere, of course." He reached into his desk and handed Maryse an envelope. "There's a set of documents inside that detail Helena's agreement with the state for the lease of the preserve. The annual payment from the state is due next week, which means you'll be receiving a check for fifty thousand dollars."

Fifty thousand dollars a year! Maryse sucked in a breath and stared at Wheeler in surprise. "You're kidding me."

Wheeler smiled. "Not in the least, Ms. Robicheaux. Helena left you her most prized possession. It wasn't an easy decision for her. You should feel honored."

Maryse shook her head, the strangeness of the past two days washing over her. "But why?"

"One day, the land will be worth quite a bit of money . . . to developers and others. Helena was afraid that if it fell into the wrong hands, it would be immediately leased out to a chemical company or the like and the town she grew up in and loved would cease to exist. She held firm on the belief that you wouldn't allow that to happen, regardless of the money involved."

Maryse began to understand. If a chemical company leased the land, they'd close off the bayou, inserting sludge ponds for their runoff and new manufacturing facilities for their products where there was once marsh. The tides would shift, and with the tides, the shrimp, fish, and all other bayou commodities that Mudbug residents made a living off of would disappear. If those commodities ceased to exist, so would Mudbug.

Helena had given her a great gift, but how could she have been so sure that Maryse wouldn't sell out? Had Helena really had that much faith in her integrity, or was the only other choice so bad that she gambled on the second?

Maryse thanked Wheeler, lugged the giant leather book onto one hip, and made her way out of the building. As she stepped outside, she scanned the parking area for her truck before remembering it was sinking in the middle of the bayou.

Great. She yanked her cell phone from her pocket and pressed in 411. She was just about to hit the Talk button when Wheeler's receptionist rushed outside and let out a breath of relief.

"Oh, thank goodness, you're still here," the receptionist said. "I completely forgot to give you this." She handed Maryse a rental car agreement and a set of keys. "A very nice young man dropped these off while you were in the reading. He said to tell you not to worry about your truck. He arranged to have it towed to a friend at the dealership."

"He what?" Maryse asked, no doubt in her mind who the nice young man was.

The receptionist smiled at Maryse. "You're so lucky to

have such a gentleman looking out for you. It's the red Honda Accord parked across the street." She gave Maryse a wave and walked back into the office.

"Gentleman my ass," Maryse said, even though no one was around to hear. She had no idea what kind of game Luc LeJeune was playing, but it was about to come to an end.

Chapter Four

Maryse raced back to her office, eager for two things: first, to confront the sneaky, bossy Luc and second, to study her lab supply book cover to cover to figure out exactly what she could buy with her lease money. This money could make a huge difference in her success, and it couldn't have come at a better time. She was starting to doubt her personal quest for a medical breakthrough altogether. Better lab equipment would aid in her research *and* her morale.

If only Blooming Flower had told her what plant she'd used in her medicine before she died. But the Native woman had been tight-lipped about revealing any of her secrets. With a little more time, Maryse knew she could have won the woman over, but time ran out. As it always seemed to where Maryse was concerned.

Maryse sighed. Despite her misgivings about anything associated with Helena, it was hard not to be excited about what she could do with the money. Just knowing that the alternative could have meant the end of Mudbug made her heart catch in her throat. But things had turned out for the better.

At least she thought it was for the better.

She tried to focus on the highway in front of her, but her temples were pounding in time with her heartbeat. Maryse was beginning to suspect that the bossy Luc was right and she needed to see a doctor. The aspirin she'd taken only thirty minutes ago hadn't done a thing. In fact, her headache was worse.

Yet another delay was annoying, but she refused to be one of those stubborn people who ignored all the signs until it was too late. Like her dad had. With a sigh, she pulled off the highway at the far end of Mudbug and headed for the hospital.

The emergency room was fairly quiet, and a nurse told her that a doctor should be able to see her almost immediately. She followed the nurse down the hall to a lab where a man in a green lab coat took an X-ray of the lump on her head. Then the nurse escorted her to an available room and said the doctor would be in shortly.

Maryse sat on the end of the hospital bed, the paper runner crinkling beneath her, and tried not to worry, especially since worrying tended to make the lump pound harder. It was just a bit of a goose egg. No worse than the ones she got as a kid playing around the bayou. Still, why did they always ask you to sit on those uncomfortable beds? Why couldn't you just sit on the chair in the corner like a normal person?

She was just contemplating a move to the corner chair when the door opened and Dr. Breaux walked in, followed closely by a much younger, cuter man who was smiling directly at her.

"Hello, Maryse," Dr. Breaux said. "This is Doctor Warren."

Maryse tried not to ogle.

"Doctor Warren transferred here from New Orleans last week. He'll be taking over some patients for me as I move into semi-retirement, so I want to introduce him to as many people in Mudbug as I can."

Dr. Hottie stuck out his hand, and Maryse shook it, the

ache in her head suddenly not quite so painful. "Nice to meet you," she said warmly.

Dr. Warren cocked his head to one side and laughed. "You don't remember me, do you?" He still held her hand in his. "Advanced Chemistry, Mrs. Thibodeaux . . . *Christopher* Warren."

Maryse studied the man again, mentally running through the entire seating chart of high school chemistry. "Holy crap! Christopher?" She stared in surprise, the image of the thin, dorky, pimply-faced adolescent rushing back to her in a flash. "I would never have recognized you."

Christopher smiled. "Late bloomer."

Maryse laughed. "Better than not blooming at all, I guess."

"Uhmm," Dr. Breaux cleared his throat. "All class reunion business aside, we have three other patients waiting."

Christopher immediately snapped back to professional demeanor. "Of course, Doctor Breaux." He gently brushed the bangs away from Maryse's head and took a look at the offensive lump. "Got a doozy of a goose egg there."

"Is that your official medical opinion?" Maryse joked.

Christopher smiled. "Absolutely. Are you saying you're already unsatisfied with my services?"

Maryse struggled to maintain her composure. Was he flirting? Surely not. Two men in one week was so far beyond her average it wasn't even in the ballpark. Realizing she'd never answered, Maryse said hurriedly, "Oh no, that's not what I meant. I never thought it was that bad, but everyone kept insisting I have it checked out so . . ."

Christopher nodded. "That's always a good idea with a head injury, no matter how slight it seems."

He stuck the X-rays on a machine and flipped on the light. Dr. Breaux stepped over, and they analyzed the gray blobs and mumbled to each other. As Christopher studied the X-rays, Maryse studied him. Okay, so he wasn't exactly her type. Christopher was too pretty, too turned out, too GQ. Maryse liked her men a little more rugged. Five-star restaurants weren't exactly her usual fare—just give her a guy who could drive a bass boat and shoot a gun. Christopher looked too refined for shooting anything but photos with his phone.

But he's a doctor.

Maryse couldn't help but think of all the possibilities a successful relationship with a doctor might bring. There was so much she didn't know about the body's chemical reaction to medication, so much she needed to learn but only so many hours in the day. And far more importantly, a man like Christopher was probably a much safer bet than a ladies' man like Luc. God knows, she'd already made that mistake once and wasn't interested in being a two-time loser.

She took a look at his perfectly manicured hands, then glanced at her own chewed nails. She remembered Christopher from high school, the quiet, brilliant kid who hid in the back of the classroom trying not to draw any attention to himself. That was probably the only reason Maryse had noticed him . . . because she was busy doing the same thing but without the benefit of being brilliant.

He had helped her with her homework a couple of times, never actually looking her in the eye, his neck flushed with red the entire time. Christopher Warren had been a nice kid and had probably become a nice man. And maybe, just maybe, if she had another man around, she wouldn't spend so much time thinking about Luc.

Her mind made up, she flashed Christopher her best smile as he turned around to look at her. "Am I going to live?" she asked.

He returned her smile and nodded. "I'm afraid so, but with one whopper of a headache for a couple of days. I can prescribe you something stronger than aspirin for that, but otherwise, I just want you to take it easy until the swelling goes down. Try not to jostle your head and it will heal a little faster. If it lasts more than a week, I'll need to see you back here." He looked over at Dr. Breaux for confirmation.

"Doctor Warren is correct," Dr. Breaux said. "The X-ray doesn't show anything to cause alarm, but you should watch the lump over the next couple of days and come back in if it gets worse." He patted Maryse on the shoulder and nodded to Christopher. "I'll leave you to the prescription writing. That way I don't have to pull out my glasses again." He smiled at both of them and left the room.

"Alone at last," Christopher said, and smiled at Maryse.

Okay, he's probably flirting.

Christopher pulled a prescription pad from his pocket and began to write, then handed her the slip of paper.

She took it without looking and asked, "Can I get this filled at the hospital pharmacy?"

He flashed her a broad grin. "I rather doubt it. That's my phone number."

Definitely flirting.

"If your head isn't killing you in a couple of days," Christopher continued, "I'd love to take you to dinner. We can catch up on the post–high school life events, and I'd love to hear about the work you're doing here. Botany, right?"

Maryse nodded.

"Besides," Christopher continued, "any woman who wears a cocktail dress for an emergency room visit has got to be an interesting date. Call me whenever you feel up to it." He handed her a second slip of paper. "This is for your headache, and yes, the pharmacy should have them in stock."

Maryse held in a groan when he mentioned the cocktail dress. She hadn't even thought about how strange she must look. Heck, the whole day had already been so strange that now the dress seemed such a small matter. But hey, if it got her date offers from cute doctors, then maybe she'd have to reconsider Sabine's shopping suggestion. She took the second sheet of paper, and Christopher lingered a bit, making sure his fingers brushed against hers. She waited for a spark, for her skin to tingle, but had to admit that aside from wondering what brand of lotion he used to keep his hands so soft, she really didn't get much out of it at all.

"I'll give you a call," she promised, and stuck the slips in her purse.

He gave her arm a squeeze and walked out of the room. Maryse leaned over slightly to study his behind as he walked away. *Not as good-looking as Luc's.* With a sigh, she hopped off the table and made her way down the hall to the pharmacy. It didn't mean a thing. Most men in the world didn't have a butt as nice as Luc LeJeune's. Besides, butts weren't everything. One day she'd be too old to see it, and her arthritis too bad to squeeze it, right?

She was insane—there was no doubt in her mind. Apparently, she was more attracted to men who wouldn't stick around long enough to leave a scent on the sheets than men who would probably not only leave a scent but help with the laundering. Christopher was good-looking, successful, and seemed to be just as nice now as he had been in high school.

But even as she ran through Christopher's list of attributes, a mental picture of Luc flashed through her mind— leaned back in her office chair, looking at her with that slow, sexy smile, his jeans rippling in all the right places. Stopping in the middle of the hall, she closed her eyes, silently willing the scene to go away. Then she pulled the slip of paper with Christopher's number from her purse. No more playboys, regardless of how sexy their butts were. She was going to learn to walk on the safe side.

For once in her life, she was going to do the boring, responsible thing.

Maryse was relieved that Luc's Jeep was nowhere in sight when she pulled her rental up at the office. She was simply out of energy for confrontations. Ten or so a day was probably a national limit or something. She let herself into the office and went straight to her lab, unlocking the deadbolt with a key from her personal set. Then she pushed open the lab door and went straight for her catalog on the desk in the far corner.

She was two hours and at least thirty flagged items into her catalog when she glanced down at her watch and realized the time. Tapping her pen on the desk, she thought about her options—head home or into town for an early dinner with Sabine. She had just settled on early dinner when the office phone rang.

She checked the display and felt her heart speed up when she recognized the number for the lab manager at the university in New Orleans. "Aaron," she answered, "I didn't expect to hear from you so soon. I don't suppose you have any good news for me?" She waited expectantly, wondering if he was about to give her a way to spend some of her newfound riches.

"As a matter of fact," he began, and Maryse could feel him smiling over the phone, "I have excellent news. You know that one batch you threw in for the hell of it—Trial 206?"

"Yes."

"Well, it passed tests one and two with flying colors. I'm moving to test three this afternoon and possibly four tomorrow. Can you get me more? I might not have enough to carry through the remaining trials."

Maryse let out the breath with a whoosh and held in a shout. "That's fantastic! Let me check that number." She unlocked her desk drawer and pulled her notebook from inside, then flipped the pages past failure after failure until she reached the possible success, Trial 206.

Then she groaned.

"Is something wrong?" Aaron asked.

"No," Maryse hedged, "not exactly. But thanks to a couple of drunken fishermen and an out-of-control barge, Trial 206 might not be as easy to obtain as it was before. Those idiots took out the entire group of plants. I'll have to find another location. I know I've seen them somewhere else, but offhand, I can't recall where exactly."

"Don't sweat it, Maryse," Aaron said. "You're way ahead of the game. Even if you have to propagate your own plants, it would only take a few more months, right? Maybe you should check on seeds just in case."

Maryse tapped her fingers on her desk. "You're right. I'll get out my seed catalog and see what I can work out. In the meantime, I'll try to remember where I saw that other batch. Let me know how far you get with what you have. I'll also contact every nursery I can find and see if they happen to have a full-grown bloom."

"Sounds like a plan," Aaron said. "Chin up, Maryse. This is only a momentary delay, and this is the best run yet."

Maryse thanked him and hung up the phone, excited and frustrated all at the same time. She'd only thrown that specimen into testing for the hell of it. At the time, she hadn't been paying too much attention to whether that particular batch was a hybrid, like so many others in the bayou were. Without another look at it, she couldn't know for sure. And now she didn't even know where to find another. Her "momentary delay" was suddenly looking pretty major.

"Wow," Luc said, striding into her lab. "This is some setup for a botanist." He walked over to her desk and picked up her notebook, scanning the pages. "What are you doing in here, exactly?"

Maryse grabbed the notebook from his hands and shoved it in a drawer, locking it afterwards. "What I do in here is none of your business. I rent this space from the state, so it's off limits to anyone I haven't personally invited in. That list starts with you."

Luc gave her a lazy smile. "Aww, c'mon, Maryse. I thought we had come to some sort of working arrangement."

Maryse narrowed her eyes at him. "You mean an arrangement like you towing my truck and sending me a rental without asking? The kind of arrangement where the big, strong man takes over because the helpless female couldn't possibly handle things?"

Luc stared at her for a moment, and if she hadn't been so aggravated, his confusion might have been amusing. "I was only trying to help. My buddy works at the dealership, so I called in a favor. He's not charging you for the tow."

Maryse stared back at him, feeling just a tiny bit guilty but not about to admit it. "Look, Luc. I'm not trying to be a bitch, but I'm used to doing things for myself. I don't like people making decisions for me."

Luc shrugged. "Whatever. But maybe if you let other people make decisions for you, your life wouldn't be such a mess. Exactly how many people told you not to marry Hank Henry?"

Maryse felt the blood rush to her face. "That is none of your business, and you're not furthering your cause by insulting my intelligence. There were a lot of reasons I married Hank, none of which I need to discuss with you." She shook her head. "I simply don't understand what you get out of being in this backwoods place harassing me. Isn't there a more lucrative assignment calling you in this great state? Not that I've actually seen you out working on anything."

Luc gave her a smug smile. "I'm the nephew of the district operations supervisor, so I've got family at the top of the food chain. I pretty much get to do whatever I want."

"Then why on Earth would you want to be here?"

"It was either this or some forgotten forest in the middle of nowhere north Louisiana. This is close to my apartment in the city and the retirement home my grandparents live in now. Don't even try to get me pulled from this assignment. It would take a hurricane to remove me from this marsh."

Maryse gave him a matching smile. "Yeah, well, say hello to Hurricane Maryse. As of this morning, you're standing on my property, so your food chain just became extinct."

He gave her a puzzled look, but Maryse couldn't really blame him. It was a strange statement. "What do you mean, 'your property'?"

"Apparently, all of this land belonged to Helena Henry. The entire preserve. She leased it to the state for their studies and to keep it protected, but it was hers to own and hers to give. And this morning, it was willed to me."

Luc stared at her in obvious shock. "Helena Henry owned this land? And she willed it to you?"

"Yep. Which makes this my office that I'm leasing to the state that I'm leasing part of back to myself." Maryse paused for a moment, the absurdity of that business transaction just hitting her.

"So you're leasing from yourself," Luc said, "and you'd like me to respect your privacy. Is that about right?"

Maryse blinked, surprised Luc had caught on to everything that fast. "Yes."

Luc nodded. "I have no problem with that. Sorry, I never meant to make you uncomfortable. I guess I'm just used to dealing with a different kind of woman." He extended his hand. "Truce?"

Maryse hesitated for a moment, then rose from her seat and placed her hand in his, trying to ignore her body's response to his strong hand clasped around hers. She released his hand and stuck her own in her jeans pocket, silently willing the tingling to stop.

Luc smiled and exited her lab, closing the door behind him.

Maryse stared at the closed door for a moment, then sat on her desk. What was it with that man? No matter how hard she tried to stay angry at him, he always managed to diffuse the situation and leave her wondering how he would look naked. Luc LeJeune was definitely a walking hazard to her mental and emotional health. Just when she thought he was a complete and utter cad, he managed to turn the tables on her by saying something unexpected, and an apology had been the absolute last thing she had expected.

I'm used to dealing with a different kind of woman.

Yeah, Maryse would just bet he was. The sexy, self-confident kind of woman that Maryse would like to be but didn't have a clue where to start. And given her current situation, it didn't look like she was going to find time to research it anytime soon.

In addition to everything else she had on her mind, Luc's

comment about his uncle had left her a bit unsettled. If his uncle was really as highly placed with the state as he claimed, Luc might still be able to make trouble for her if he thought she wasn't doing her job.

She'd just have to be careful—make sure she didn't let her personal research and the small matter of Helena Henry get in the way of her job any more than it already had, at least during work hours. Which meant the first item on her list was figuring out a way to avoid the ghost during working hours anyway. If the will reading had been any indication, anything involving Helena was bound to be trouble.

Maryse shook her head as her mind roamed back over the events of the morning. What a fiasco. Then, with a start, she remembered where she'd seen that other group of plants and groaned.

Directly across the bayou from Helena Henry's house.

Luc heard the lab door slam behind him and turned in his chair. Instead of the aggravation he'd expected, Maryse had that look of intent concentration mixed with excitement that you get when you have a great idea but are still trying to work out the details. She didn't even acknowledge him as she pulled on her rubber boots and hustled out of the office without so much as a wave or a backwards glance.

Luc sighed. So much for his powers of sexual attraction. He'd gotten women in bed with less than a handshake and an apology before, but Maryse Robicheaux was a force to be reckoned with.

Of course, with the day she'd had, Luc couldn't blame her too much for being distracted. She'd gone from a wrecked truck to inheriting a game preserve, and, technically, it wasn't even quitting time.

Still, he'd thought they'd moved beyond suspicious. But

if the scene in her lab was any indication, Maryse's defense system was back in full force. But why? Was it really because he'd had her truck towed, or was it something else entirely? Granted, he sometimes had trouble remembering all that women's independence stuff. Not that he didn't like strong women—hell, he'd been raised by the strongest of women, his grandmother. But he was also Choctaw, and it was ingrained into them from a young age to take care of their responsibilities—especially to their women.

She's not your woman.

Okay, so he knew it was true, at least in the real sense of the sentiment. But until the DEQ was satisfied that his work in Mudbug was done, Luc felt responsible for Maryse, and if she was in some kind of trouble, then he felt obligated to help. In fact, if Maryse was the informant he sought, then it was his *job* to help. All kinds of trouble could be headed her way if the chemical company got wind that someone was airing dirty secrets to the DEQ.

He studied the locked lab door. That notebook . . . he hadn't gotten a good look at the page, but he'd seen enough to know that it wasn't filled with regular writing. Those symbols were chemicals equations, but high school chemistry was such a distant memory he'd never be able to scratch the surface of what exactly she had written, not even with all day to consider it. But he'd be willing to bet his department had someone who could decipher whatever Maryse had been so quick to hide.

He rose from his chair and studied the lock for a moment. It was one of the best, but not completely unbeatable. Reaching into his jeans pocket, he pulled out his cell phone and hit a speed dial.

"Wilson," his boss answered on the first ring.

"It's LeJeune. I need a set of B&E tools down here. Something that can get past a pretty high-tech padlock."

"What's wrong, LeJeune—the woman wearing a chastity belt?"

Luc counted to three, then replied. "Hilarious. She's renting office space from the state that she's turned into some sort of chemistry lab. I need to get in there and see what she's working on."

"She's running lab experiments?"

"That's what it looks like to me. Place is full of really high-tech equipment. We're talking a lot more than just a microscope and some test tubes."

"Why would a botanist need a chemistry lab? There's nothing in her job description to require it. From what I've read, she's supposed to just collect the samples and then they're analyzed someplace else. You think she's the informant?"

Luc studied the locked door for a moment. "Maybe, but it doesn't feel right. It's sort of an elaborate and expensive setup to turn someone in for polluting the water."

"Then maybe she's working with them. Did you ever think of that? Maybe she's testing for them, hoping the water gets back to an acceptable place before someone discovers their dumping sites."

Luc turned from the door and stared out the big front window at the bayou. "At this point, I guess anything is possible, although, I have to say, she doesn't really fit the profile of a criminal. And there was another incident today that might cause us some trouble."

"What kind of incident?"

"Apparently, that mother-in-law of hers owned this preserve and leased it to the state. Well, you'll never guess who she left it to."

"Good grief, LeJeune, and you think this botanist is pure as the driven snow? How the hell did the mother-in-law die?"

Luc rubbed his jaw with one hand. "I don't know exactly."

"Well, you best be finding out. This all smacks of a cover-up, and your unassuming botanist may be the biggest ringleader of all. You're letting a nice set of T&A cloud your judgment."

"You know better, boss. I'm checking out everything."

"Hmm. I'm certain you are. LeJeune, do you have any idea how uncomfortable it is to have the whole damned EPA up your ass? Because that's what I have right now, and according to my wife, I've never had much ass, so it's getting crowded down there and I'm more than a little uncomfortable. You don't want me uncomfortable, do you?"

Luc closed his eyes for a moment, not even wanting to think about another man's ass. "No, we wouldn't want that."

"Good!" Wilson disconnected, and Luc pressed the End button on his phone. What a friggin' mess. The call had brought up a possibility Luc hadn't even thought of, and it didn't please him in the least. Was his boss right? Was his attraction to Maryse coloring his judgment? What if she *was* protecting whoever was making illegal dumps in the bayou? Then again, maybe his initial read was right, and she wasn't involved at all.

He took another look at the locked door and sighed. No matter what, Maryse Robicheaux was up to something, and the way she shot out of the office led him to believe that she was off to do something important and personal. After all, she had taken the day off work. Glancing at his watch, he realized it had been ten minutes since Maryse had fled the office. He flipped his cell phone open again and punched some buttons.

A map of the Mudbug area filled the display, and Luc watched as a small blinking dot came into view, moving rapidly across the bayou that stretched alongside downtown. So whatever couldn't wait had taken her into the bayou, and he'd be willing to bet everything he owned that whatever she was doing didn't have anything to do with her job as a state botanist.

But he was about to find out.

Maryse pushed down the throttle of her bass boat and zoomed across the bayou. Even though she'd been awake for hours, there was still that tiny thought lingering in the back of her mind that she'd wake up any moment and find the whole thing had been one big dream—parts of it a nightmare.

Of course, that theory already had two strikes against it. The first being that she completely lacked the imagination to even dream something this weird, and the second being that even if she had dreamed up a haunting, the last person she would have put in the starring role was Helena. And now, against her better judgment, she was headed down the bayou to a stretch of bank within easy view of Helena Henry's house. Not that Maryse knew where Helena hung out, exactly, but her house seemed to make the most sense. And the last thing Maryse needed today was another dose of Helena.

In fact, the more she thought about it, the more avoiding Helena seemed like the best plan. Maryse spent most of her days in the bayou, and even though Helena claimed she could walk on water, and quite possibly run, she probably couldn't keep up with a boat—not in ghostly high heels, anyway.

Of course, her cabin posed a bit of a problem. Helena had already "dropped by," so that wasn't safe at all. There was always the Mudbug Hotel, but it probably wouldn't take Helena long to get around to that one either, given that the hotel owner, Mildred, had essentially raised Maryse after her mother died.

She turned the steering wheel and guided her boat into a large offshoot of the bayou that ran parallel to downtown Mudbug. The bayou was lined with cypress trees on one side and historical homes on the other, Helena's estate being the largest, of course. Maryse could see the white, imposing monstrosity as soon as she made the turn. She wondered for about the millionth time what God could possibly be thinking by sending a scientist a ghost.

She'd always figured He had a sense of humor, but this was ridiculous.

Cutting her boat over toward the cypress trees, she let off the throttle and tried to find the tiny shoots of greenery she needed for the trials. They'd been here just last week, she could have sworn it, but no matter how hard she looked, the plant in question seemed to evade her. She had just leaned over the side of the boat to finger something that looked reasonably close to the plant in question when she heard shouting behind her.

Maryse groaned, afraid to look. She turned around and confirmed this world was definitely going to hell in a handbasket.

Helena Henry was walking on water.

Chapter Five

The bayou tide was moving in a slow roll out toward the Gulf. But Helena Henry was a force of her own, inexorably making her way against the current. Every move forward put her a little farther downstream, and then every five steps or so, she'd jog a bit upstream, huffing like she was about to keel over.

If she hadn't already been dead, that is.

Maryse stared at Helena and frowned, not certain whether to be more worried about another visit with the ghost or the fact that her physical fitness level apparently wouldn't get any better in death. Perhaps she should start eating better and working out more. Or at least working out more—giving up beer was out of the question.

It took another couple of minutes for Helena to make it across the bayou and climb over the side of Maryse's boat. She slumped onto the bench, dragging huge breaths in and out.

"Are you all right?" Maryse asked.

"Of course not." Helena shot her a dirty look. "I'm dead."

"Damn it, I know that. I just thought . . . I didn't know . . . never mind." The whole situation was simply too mind-boggling for thought.

"Sort of an ass-ripper, huh?" Helena said. "You'd think

you'd get a better body if you're destined to roam the Earth as a spirit."

Maryse shook her head. "You don't know any such thing about your destiny. Maybe the line's too long at the Pearly Gates—maybe there was a thunderstorm on Cloud Nine and all the flights are delayed." *Maybe Hell's full and they're waiting for an opening.*

"Maybe I'm stuck here until I figure out who killed me," Helena said.

Maryse sat back on her seat with a sigh. "We've already had this discussion, Helena. I'm not an investigator and don't want to be. In fact, I don't want to be involved in this at all. You've already got Harold gunning for me—not that I'm complaining about the inheritance—but my point is my plate is not just full, it's overflowing. I'm not about to get myself deeper in the hole by doing whatever you had in mind."

Helena grinned. "I was thinking we'd start with a little B&E."

"Oh, no." Maryse shook her head. "I am not breaking into anything. I know you might find this hard to believe, but you're not worth going to jail for, game preserve or no."

"Oh, c'mon, Maryse. You never want to have any fun. Besides, technically, I own the house we'd be breaking into."

"Not anymore you don't. The historical society does."

"But no one's there. I've already checked. It won't take ten minutes at the most."

Maryse shook her head again, her jaw set. "No way."

Helena studied her for a moment. "If you just do this one little break-in, I promise to go away for at least a day."

Damn. Helena was playing dirty. A whole day ghost free was *very* tempting. But would she keep her word?

"It's too much of a risk," Maryse said finally. "What if someone sees me? There's no way I could explain being inside your house when you're dead. Everyone would think I was stealing or something."

Helena laughed. "You . . . Ms. Goodie Two-Shoes . . . stealing? Not likely." She narrowed her eyes at Maryse. "I might have a cell phone number for Hank somewhere inside and perhaps even a last known address."

Maryse was instantly angry. "You told me you didn't know where Hank was. I always knew you were a royal bitch, Helena, but keeping me from getting a divorce after the way Hank treated me is low, even for you."

"Now, don't get your panties in a knot." Helena put up a hand in protest. "I didn't know where Hank was until today. He called a few hours ago, and Harold wrote down his information on a tablet next to the kitchen phone." She shrugged and looked away. "I guess he's still trying to figure out how to get some money and clear his worthless butt with the locals."

Maryse stared at her for a moment, but Helena wouldn't meet her eyes. Was that actually remorse . . . sadness she saw in Helena's expression when she talked about Hank and her money? Was it possible that Helena had been hurt by Hank's disappearing act, too?

Letting out a sigh, she pulled up her anchor, not even glancing at Helena. She looked both ways up the bayou to make sure it was clear, then started her boat and crossed the bayou to Helena's dock.

"Dock on the left side," Helena instructed. "That way the boathouse covers you from one direction and the cattails will hide you on the other." She gave Maryse a gleeful smile and clapped her hands like a five-year-old.

Oh goodie. All they needed were party hats and a cake.

Maryse edged the boat in between the dock and an enormous growth of cattails, then checked the bayou again. Still clear. And Helena had been right about the docking spot. The boat was almost completely hidden.

Of course, that in no way solved the problem of walking up the pier and across the backyard to the house, but hey, who was she to complain? She'd never even had a traffic ticket, but she was about to commit a crime with a woman who couldn't testify on her behalf and certainly couldn't be thrown in the clink along with her.

Helena hopped out of the boat, skipped across the remaining water of the bayou to the shore, then turned around and waved for Maryse to follow. Casting one final glance around, Maryse pulled off her rubber boots, stepped onto the dock, and hurried down the pier and across the yard behind Helena.

She expected Helena to go to the back door, but instead, the ghost trailed off to the side and ducked around behind a row of azalea bushes. Maryse pushed aside a bit of the dense foliage and followed her. There was a small path, about a foot wide, between the bushes and the house. When they reached a narrow window, Helena stopped and pointed.

"You're small. You should be able to fit through that."

"Excuse me? You want me to climb in a window like a thief? Why don't you have a key hidden outside somewhere?"

"Because I didn't want anyone to break in, silly. C'mon, the window is low enough for you to climb in, and the latch on this one has been broken for months."

The window was about four feet from the ground. God knew she wasn't an acrobat, but she could probably make it work. At this point, she'd stick her head in a lion's mouth for information on Hank. She reached up and pushed on the window, sliding it up until it wouldn't go any farther.

She placed both of her hands on the window ledge and looked over at Helena. "I am so leaving this house through a doorway. Got it?"

Helena nodded. "Whatever you want to do. Just hop on in there and open the side door for me.

Maryse stared at her. "Let me get this straight. I have to do circus moves through a window, but you get to stroll in through the door. Why don't you walk through a wall or something?"

"Oh, sure." Helena pouted. "Go picking on my weaknesses when I'm at a low point."

"You can't walk through walls?"

"Not exactly. Well, I did once, but I haven't perfected it yet. Last time I tried I almost knocked myself out. If you hadn't left your patio door open yesterday, I wouldn't have gotten into your cabin."

Maryse shook her head. "There is something incredibly wrong with all of this, but I don't have time to sort it out now." Before she could change her mind, she pulled herself up to the window and shoved her head and shoulders through. She lost her momentum about midway through, and she kicked her legs trying to edge through the narrow opening. Finally, she crossed the balancing threshold and tumbled through the window headfirst into a stack of dirty laundry.

"Yuck." She pulled herself up from the floor and brushed a really tacky pair of boxers from her shoulder. "You owe me huge, Helena," she yelled out the window.

"Yeah, yeah, just open the damned door."

Maryse picked her way through the dirty laundry, careful not to step on anything. Tennis shoes didn't protect you from being grossed out, and Maryse knew if any of Harold's boxers had touched her bare skin, she wouldn't be able to look at a Calvin Klein ad for a long time.

The side door had a single deadbolt that Maryse slid back before she pushed the door open. Helena strolled inside like this was all completely normal and jumped over the stack of laundry and into the kitchen. "This way, and hurry. Harold should be home anytime now. He'll be needing to pack."

Maryse crept down the hall and into the kitchen, catching a glimpse of Helena as she disappeared around a corner. "You kind of left out that part about Harold coming home, Helena!" She rounded the corner and saw Helena at the top of a humongous circular stairway, beckoning to her from the second floor.

"It's in my bedroom."

Maryse glanced out the front window at the driveway. Clear. She blew out a breath and followed Helena up the stairs, wondering what exactly "it" was and why it was in the bedroom.

At the top of the stairs, Helena pointed to a closed door. "That's my bedroom. I need to look in my safe."

"Your safe? I'm risking an arrest over your pearls or something?"

"No, no! Just please get in there and open the safe. I'm afraid things aren't going the way I'd planned."

"Sort of an understatement considering you're dead, huh?" Maryse pushed the door open and stepped inside. "Where's the safe?"

Helena pointed to an oil painting on the wall across from the bed. It was an original of Hank, probably around age three and long before he'd become a burden on society. That incredible smile was already in place, even on such a small child, and Maryse felt a tingle all over again as she looked at the man she'd married.

Holding in a sigh, she lifted the painting from the wall, exposing the safe behind it. She glanced at the combination lock, then looked at Helena. "Well, do you have dynamite or are you going to give me the combination?"

"Fourteen, three, forty."

Maryse twirled the dial and heard a click when she stopped on the last number. She looked over at Helena, who nodded, then pulled the lever to open the safe. She'd barely gotten the door open before Helena was standing almost on top of her, trying to peer inside.

"Damn it!" Helena ranted. "That son of a bitch didn't even wait until my body was cold before he took the cash."

"What did you expect? You didn't leave him anything from your estate. He's probably out pawning your silver right now."

Helena sighed. "You're right, but that's not what I'm worried about. Pull out that stack of papers in the back."

Maryse reached inside, removed a stack of envelopes, then looked at Helena.

"Flip through them," Helena instructed. "I'm looking for one from Able & Able."

Maryse shuffled through the envelopes one at a time, studying the return addresses. When she reached the end of the stack, she looked over at Helena. "There's nothing here with that name on it."

"Double damn!" Helena paced the bedroom up one way and down the other. "I knew it. There's no telling how long that worthless husband of mine has been pilfering from my safe."

Maryse studied Helena, a bad feeling washing over her. Should ghosts really be this worried about things they couldn't control? "What exactly was in that letter, Helena?"

Helena stopped pacing and looked at her for a moment, her expression wavering as if on the verge of saying something important. Finally, she shook her head and looked away. "Nothing to concern yourself with. At least not yet. If it becomes an issue, I'll let you know."

"You'll let me know? I have news for you, Helena. All of this is an issue for me. I don't believe in ghosts. I don't believe in breaking and entering, and furthermore—"

Before she could complete the sentence, a tiny red light in a small box on the backside of the bedroom door started to blink. Had that been there before? She didn't remember seeing a blinking light when she'd entered the room. Surely she would have remembered.

"Uh, Helena," Maryse said and pointed to the box. "What exactly is that red light?"

Helena whirled around to look at the light, then spun back around, a panicked look on her face. "It's the alarm. Harold must have set it when he left. It's on a delay, but we don't have much time left before it goes off."

Maryse tossed the stack of envelopes back into the safe, slammed the safe door and whirled the dial, then hung the picture on the wall as quickly as she could. She'd stepped one foot outside the bedroom door when the sirens went off. The shrill shriek of the alarm deafened her for a moment, and Maryse froze.

"Run!" Helena cried and ran down the staircase.

Maryse took the steps two at a time, passing Helena on the way, and almost fell as she hit the foyer floor. The scream of police sirens was far too close for comfort, and Maryse struggled to pick up the pace. Skidding on the polished wood, she dashed around the corner and onto the textured tile in the kitchen, where her shoes had a much better grip and she picked up some speed. She ran into the laundry room, shoving down the window where she'd entered the house. Then she rushed out the side door, locking it before she slammed it behind her.

She made for the huge hedge of bushes that separated Helena's yard from her neighbor's and ran as fast as she could to the dock. She jumped in the boat from shore, banging her knee against the metal bench, and stifled a yell. Limping over to the controls, she started the boat, threw it into reverse and shoved down the throttle.

The boat shot out from between the dock and the cattails, and she changed it to drive and forced the throttle all the way down again, causing the boat to leap out of the water and slam back down onto the bayou, jolting her so hard her teeth hurt. She looked back at Helena's house and blew out a breath of relief when she didn't see police or any curious neighbors observing her departure.

Her knee was throbbing now, and Maryse could feel a tiny trickle of blood down the front of her leg. Her aching head would probably never be the same. As soon as she rounded the bayou out of view of Helena's house, she'd stop and assess the damage. She slowed a bit, so as not to look suspicious, and twisted on the bench to look back at Helena's house. The police were just pulling into the driveway, and she breathed a sigh of relief that she'd be well out of their line of sight before they got out of their cars.

She turned back around and almost panicked when she realized she was headed directly toward an anchored boat.

She threw the throttle in reverse and the engine whined in protest. The boat jerked one direction, then another, and as every muscle in her body strained to hold her inside the bouncing vehicle, Maryse knew she was going to pay for this tomorrow.

Miraculously, the boat stopped just inches from the other vessel. Maryse sank down on the bench, trying to catch her breath.

"Quite a stop you made there," a voice sounded from the other boat. "Do you do everything as fast as you drive a boat?"

That voice was too familiar and wasn't one she wanted to hear. She raised her head a tiny bit and saw the smiling face of Luc LeJeune. Just what she needed—an opportunity for Luc to file a reckless endangerment charge against her with his uncle. This day just kept getting better.

"Hi, Luc." She tried to force her voice to normal. "I was having a bit of engine trouble. I thought I might have a little trash collected down there. Figured I'd blow it out."

Luc looked at her, still smiling, not believing a word of it. "Uh huh. Hey, what's that noise around the bayou? It sounds like an alarm? Cop cars have been racing along the highway to get here."

Maryse looked behind her even though she knew she couldn't see around the bend of the bayou to Helena's house. It bought her a moment, and in that moment, she was hoping to come up with a better answer than "I didn't hear anything."

"I don't know," she said. "I didn't hear anything." So much for the moment.

Luc studied her, a curious expression on his face. "Really? That's odd, because the sirens and everything are pretty loud. Of course, if you were working on your engine, you might not have heard it over the motor." He gave her another smile that clearly said, "you're full of shit and up to something and I know it." "What happened to your knee?"

Maryse looked down at her leg, just realizing that she'd been massaging the top of her kneecap. A patch of red was seeping through her jeans, and given that it was growing in size, she probably couldn't pass it off as an old stain.

"I banged it on the bench when I was working on the engine. I didn't even notice it was bleeding. Must have a sharp edge somewhere. I'll get the metal grinder after it tomorrow."

"After the bench or you knee?" Luc asked, clearly amused.

Maryse sighed. "The bench. Look, I need to get going. I have a lot of things to do tonight."

Luc waved one hand across the bayou, as if to say "What's stopping you?"

"I'll see you at the office tomorrow," he said as she backed her boat away from his.

Managing a weak smile, she turned the boat and headed down the bayou toward the station. She was halfway there when she realized she'd locked Helena inside her own house, and she hadn't gotten the promised information on Hank.

Damn it! Things were out of control, and she had to get a grip on them fast or she was going to end up costing herself everything. Breaking and entering? What had she been thinking? All that drama for a fractured kneecap and a reinjury to her throbbing head, and she still hadn't gotten what she'd gone in for, which was information on Hank.

She'd hoped after the will reading that the situation with Helena would resolve itself and she could go back to her regular life, minus Helena Henry, of course. But it looked like things were far more dire than she'd initially thought, and her options were limited.

What she needed was professional advice, and the only

two people she could think of to give it were her priest and Sabine. One of them had to know of a way to help Helena pass or cross or whatever it was that she needed to do.

And if anyone would know how to make that happen, it would probably be Sabine.

Luc watched as Maryse headed up the bayou in her boat, wondering what in the world was going on with that woman. He'd stepped right in the middle of something strange and for the life of him couldn't figure out what.

He'd followed after she left the office, the GPS he'd installed on her boat made finding her among the hundreds of bayous an easy task. But when he'd initially arrived at the location the equipment had specified, he wondered if there had been a malfunction. Her boat was nowhere in sight, even though the tiny gray monitor clearly showed a blinking red light not fifty yards in front of him.

Then the alarm sirens had gone off, and seconds later, he'd spotted Maryse running along a group of dense hedges, away from the house with the sounding alarm. He glanced down at the bank and saw a tiny tip of her boat peeking out from the cattails, suddenly realizing why she'd shown on the equipment but not to the bare eye.

She'd made a leap into her boat from the bank that Indiana Jones would have been proud of, and it probably explained the injury to her knee, but it didn't explain why a seemingly rational woman would break into a house in broad daylight. Before she could catch him spying, he'd hustled around the corner and anchored directly in her flight path.

He pulled his cell phone from his pocket and pressed in a number. His buddy and fellow agent answered almost immediately.

"LeJeune here. Brian, I need you to check on something for me."

"Go ahead," Brian said.

"There's a house in downtown Mudbug along the bayou where an alarm just went off. The police responded, so I know the alarm system is linked to an outside provider. I need to know who owns that house."

Luc heard tapping and knew Brian was working his magic on the computer. It took less than a minute to get the answer.

"The house belongs to a Helena Henry," Brian said. "You want me to pursue anything further?"

"No," Luc said. "That's it for now. Thanks." He flipped the phone shut and shoved it in his pocket.

Maryse had just broken into her dead mother-in-law's house. He was certain. And even though it probably had nothing to do with his case, he couldn't help wondering what the woman had gotten into. The information on Maryse from the DEQ research department didn't allude to anything remotely dangerous or illegal. Truth be told, on paper she was probably the most boring human being he'd ever read about. In person, well, in person obviously things were a bit different.

Luc smiled. He couldn't wait to find out why.

Fifteen minutes after she'd risked a criminal record, Maryse docked her boat and left the office before Luc could show up and start in with any more embarrassing questions. It was fast approaching supper time, and since she'd completely forgotten lunch, Maryse was on the verge of starving. She had thirty minutes to snag a clean pair of jeans and make the drive into Mudbug. Sabine would just be closing up shop for the day, so the two of them could grab some burgers, and Maryse could fill Sabine in on her ridiculous day.

She made the drive in twenty minutes flat, which was fast even for her. But then, being haunted tended to create a sense of urgency. As she parked her rental in front of one of the restored historical buildings along Main Street, she spotted Sabine through the plate-glass window of her shop, Read 'em and Reap. She was dressed to the hilt in her psychic getup—a floor-length, midnight-blue robe with stars and moons on it and a matching head wrap with a huge fake sapphire in the center. Her long earrings and dozens of bracelets glinted in the sunlight. With her jet black hair—dyed, of course—and black nails and lipstick, the picture was complete. And completely frightening.

Maryse smiled for a moment, unable to help herself. From the outside, two more different people had never been made than she and Sabine, and she was certain that more than a few Mudbug residents wondered how in the world they had ever become such close friends. But then people in Mudbug could sometimes be a little obtuse.

Those two poor little girls with no mothers. Maryse could still remember overhearing her first-grade teacher saying that to the principal their first day of school. They were different from the other kids and knew it. And Sabine didn't even have a father, just an aging aunt who had taken her in but couldn't tell her much if anything about her parents.

Now they were both short two parents. Sabine's parents from a car accident when Sabine was still a baby, and Maryse's parents lost to cancer.

Maryse frowned and tapped her fingers on the steering wheel. She hated being pitied and had felt the difference in the attitudes of the teachers and other kids even then. As much as Maryse missed her parents, and Sabine wanted to know something about her own, neither of them wanted the pity of people who would never understand. Pity was for those who couldn't do anything about it. She and Sabine had spent their lives trying to fill those gaps, and damn it, one day the holes their parents left were going to be filled.

Sabine's tarot cards were fanned out before a distraught, middle-aged, overweight woman with more jewelry than Sabine and hair that was entirely too big. There was a shiny-new, white Cadillac Deville parked in front of Sabine's building, so Maryse figured she better wait a minute until Sabine delivered the happy news to whatever rich idiot was currently seeking her "professional" advice.

Immediately, Maryse chastised herself for judging others and their beliefs. She'd always been the typical scientist, not believing in anything she couldn't put her hands on, and now she had a ghost stalking her. It had taken her years to buy into the unnatural ability of Raissa, Sabine's mentor, but the other psychic had been right about so many things that even Maryse had to admit Raissa had talents that couldn't be explained. God had been the only exception to her self-imposed rule of proof, and she still wondered whether if she hadn't been raised in the church she would have questioned His existence as well.

And despite all that, here she was—smack in the middle of a paranormal nightmare. She was about to tell her best friend, who believed in the existence of damned near any-thing, that Helena Henry was haunting her. For Sabine, who'd been trying to convince her of the supernatural since the first grade, this moment would be beyond value—just like one of those stupid commercials.

One lost tarot reading for closing the shop early—$15.
Three glasses of wine and a burger at Johnny's—$20.
Hearing your best friend, aka The Disbeliever, say she's
being haunted by a ghost—Priceless.

She shook her head and sighed, feeling so far out of her
element it wasn't even funny. About that time, Cadillac
Woman broke into smiles, and Maryse figured Sabine had
wrapped up the good news. She hopped out of her rental
and started across the street before she could change her
mind.

Chapter Six

As Maryse stepped inside Read 'em and Reap, Sabine looked up in obvious surprise.

"Maryse, is everything all right? What in the world happened to your head?" Sabine jumped up from her chair and rushed over to inspect Maryse's forehead.

"I wrecked my truck this morning." She held up a hand to stop the barrage that was about to ensue. "I've already been to the doctor, and I'm fine. It's just a bump and a hellacious headache. A couple of uneventful days and I should be good as new." Of course, she had a ghost of a chance at stringing together a couple of uneventful days. Literally.

Sabine stared at her for a moment, then narrowed her eyes. "Something's wrong."

"Of course something's wrong. This whole day was wrong."

Sabine shook her head. "I know that look."

"What look?" Maryse was already having second thoughts about telling Sabine about Helena. What if Sabine thought she was crazy? What if she *was* crazy?

"That 'I don't want to discuss it' look that you always get when you need help and don't want to ask." Sabine paused for a moment. "I'm almost afraid to ask, but did Hank show up for the reading?"

Maryse sighed. "I should have known I couldn't hide anything from you. But I don't want to talk here. I can't drink taking the pain medication, but I was thinking a burger and a painkiller might loosen me up enough for the subject I need to cover."

Sabine nodded. "Let me lock up and shed the robes. I'll meet you at Johnny's in a few." She grabbed a set of keys off her desk. "Get the corner table."

"Sure." Maryse headed out of the shop and into the hot, humid Louisiana evening. The sun was still beating down on the concrete, heat vapors rising from the street. The smell of boiled crawfish from Carolyn's Cajun Kitchen down the block filled the air and made her remember that it had been forever since breakfast.

She hesitated for a moment as she crossed the street to Johnny's bar, wondering again if she was making the right decision. If she told Sabine about Helena's ghost, she was leaving herself wide open for lectures on all kinds of unexplained phenomena—Bigfoot, the Loch Ness Monster, UFOs. She wasn't sure she was ready for a lifetime of hassle.

She bit her lower lip and cast a nervous glance back at Read 'em and Reap. On the flip side, there was the one huge advantage of letting her friend in on it—Sabine knew darn near everything about the supernatural, and anything she didn't know, she could find out. If anyone could make Helena go away, it would be Sabine. And getting rid of Helena was the number one priority, even if it meant going to near-death-experience meetings or looking at those blurred photos of God-knows-what that Sabine was always trying to push off on her as real.

Seeing no better alternative, she pushed open the door and entered the bar. A couple of fishermen sat at the old driftwood bar and waved a hand in acknowledgment when she walked in. Other than that, the place was empty. She made her way to the table in a dim corner, far from the bar, and took a seat. The owner and chief bartender, appropriately named Johnny, shuffled over to her a minute or so later.

"Sorry to hear about your mother-in-law," he said, brushing aside a stray strand of thinning, silver hair from his forehead.

"Really?" Maryse stared at him.

Johnny fidgeted for a moment, then gave her a grin. "Well, hell no, actually, but 'sorry' sounds a lot more polite. Did Hank show up for the funeral?"

"Not a chance. I figure he won't come around until he gets the money to pay off the local law enforcement."

Johnny nodded. "Sounds about right. I swear to God, that has got to be the most useless human being ever produced." He gave her an apologetic look. "Sorry, I know you married him and all."

She waved one hand in dismissal. "You haven't offended me. I was young and stupid. I don't blame myself for being taken in by Hank Henry. I'm certainly not the only one who was."

"That's for sure. I think he owed damned near everyone in town before he skipped out."

No shit. "Yeah, that's what I hear." It was all she could say about the situation without exploding.

"Well, what're you drinkin'?" Fortunately, Johnny saved her from dwelling on all Hank's debts.

"Could I get a club soda and a glass of white zin for Sabine? She'll be here in a minute."

Johnny nodded and clasped her shoulder with one hand. "You let me know if you need anything, okay? I promised your daddy I'd look after you, and I intend to keep that promise." He gave her a grin. "Can't have the old bastard coming back to haunt me, can I?"

Maryse gave him a weak smile. "Guess not," she managed as Johnny shuffled back to the bar to get the drinks.

Given a choice between Helena Henry and her dad, she'd have taken the "old bastard" any day. He'd been as hard as every other commercial fisherman in Mudbug and hadn't given an inch on anything, but at least he'd been honest and fair.

It couldn't have been easy on him, raising a girl on his own after her mother died, but he'd done the best he could, and she didn't think she'd turned out too bad. Except for the major slip of marrying Hank, she had a pretty good track record. And let's face it, if her dad hadn't come back from the dead to stop that wedding, she was pretty sure he wasn't ever returning.

Clenching her fists in frustration, she mentally cursed Hank Henry for about the hundredth time that day. If he hadn't got a hold of her at the absolute lowest point in her life—just after her dad had passed—would she have fallen for his act?

She liked to believe the answer was no, but the reality was that Hank Henry had charmed the pants off darn near every girl in town at some time or another. But none of them had been stupid enough to marry him. She frowned at her shortsightedness and shook her head as Sabine slid into the chair across from her, the bracelets on her arm clinking together like wind chimes.

"Did you order drinks already?" Sabine asked and brushed the bangs from her eyes.

"Yeah, I got you a glass of wine."

Sabine gave her a grateful look. "Thanks. It's been one of those weeks."

Maryse smiled. *Oh yeah, honey. Wait until you hear about my week. Yours has to look better after that.* "I haven't had the best week myself. In fact, that's what I wanted to talk with you about."

"I was worried when I didn't hear from you this afternoon," Sabine said, "but then I didn't really know how long the will-reading would take. Is that the problem . . . something to do with Helena's will?"

"Sorta." Maryse inclined her head toward Johnny, who was on his way across the bar with a tray of drinks, and Sabine nodded in understanding. She waited until Johnny had delivered the drinks, did his old-man flirting routine with Sabine, and shuffled back behind the bar before she got down to business.

"Hank didn't show, but the reading was very interesting," Maryse said and proceeded to tell Sabine all the events of the morning, from her truck wreck to the list of equipment she was going to buy with her lease money.

Sabine hung on every word, laughing at some points and gasping at others. "Good Lord!" Sabine said when Maryse finished her tale. "What a day. Makes my entire life look simple and boring."

"And that's not all. In fact, as screwed up as all that is, that's not even what's really worrying me."

Sabine stared. "You're kidding me. There's more?"

Maryse took a deep breath and pushed forward. "This is going to sound ridiculous, but I have to ask you a question. And I need you to answer me in all seriousness."

"Wow. This must be heavy. You know I'd never hedge things with you, Maryse. Ask me whatever you need to. I'll give you an honest answer."

Maryse studied her friend for a moment. Finally, she took a deep breath and said, "I need to know why a ghost would appear to someone when other people can't see it."

Sabine stared at her for a moment, then slowly blinked.

"Well, based on everything I've ever read or heard about, unless you're a conduit, a ghost will appear if you have something to do with them."

"A conduit—you mean like that kid in *The Sixth Sense*?"

"Exactly. Conduits are able to see a lot of ghosts, even if they've never met them before."

"Okay. So if someone sees a ghost and they're not a conduit, why would the ghost appear to them?"

Sabine scrunched her brow and gave her a hard look. Maryse gave her friend points for not reaching across the table to take her temperature. This had to be the very last thing Sabine would have expected from her.

Finally, Sabine cleared her throat and continued. "The commonly accepted theory on hauntings is that unless the ghost is stuck in a certain place, like a house or something, it's out walking about because of unfinished business or because it doesn't know it's dead."

"Unfinished business—like a murder?"

Sabine's eyes widened. "Certainly being murdered might cause someone's essence to stick around this world. Justice is a very powerful emotion. It sometimes overrides even death."

Maryse nodded and considered everything for a moment. "So how does the ghost pick who it will appear to?"

Sabine shook her head, a puzzled expression on her face. "I don't think the ghost has any say. I think it's visible to someone who's supposed to help and that's it. If the ghost got to pick, then it would just appear to whoever killed it and slowly drive the murderer off the deep end. It couldn't be much fun being hounded by a ghost."

Maryse nodded. *You think?*

Sabine reached across the table and placed her hand on

Maryse's. "Where is all this going, exactly? This kind of stuff is so far beyond your usual fare that you're really starting to worry me. I mean, first you want to attend that horrible woman's funeral, then that weird inheritance, and now this?"

Before she could change her mind, Maryse leaned forward and looked Sabine straight in the eyes. "What would you say if I told you that I've seen Helena Henry—walking, talking, and still very dead?"

Sabine stared at her for a moment, obviously waiting for the punch line. When one never came, she removed her hand from Maryse's, completely drained her wineglass and sat it back on the table, her hands shaking slightly. "Helena Henry appeared to you?"

Maryse nodded and told her all about her first sighting of Helena at the funeral and her subsequent visit to her cabin, then the disastrous will reading. She left off the breaking and entering part of her day. Sabine already had enough to absorb.

"Murdered?" Sabine sat up straight as she finished her tall tale.

"That's what she says."

Sabine inclined her head and tapped a long, black nail on the table. "Well, if she says it's so, it probably is. I mean, what would be the point of lying now? Besides, if she's still hanging around, then there's obviously a problem."

"That's great to know and all, and very unfortunate for Helena, but why do I have to be involved in this? Why me?"

Sabine gave her a small smile. "Hardly seems fair, right? The most horrible human being you've encountered in your entire life, and now she shows up after death. What are the odds?"

"I don't even want to know. I just want to get rid of her."

Sabine turned her palms up and shrugged. "I don't think you can get rid of her until you figure out who killed her. It sounds like that's the problem."

"But I don't *care* who killed her."

Sabine shook her head and gave her a sad look. "That's not true, and you know it. You're the fairest person I know. Don't tell me it doesn't bother you that Helena was murdered. I'm not buying it."

"Unbelievable. I barely tolerate the living and now I have to be associated with the dead?" Maryse sighed and slumped back in her chair. "Okay, so maybe the fact that she was murdered bothers me . . . a little. But what am I supposed to do about it? I'm not the police. I'm a botanist. Studying plants does not exactly equip one to solve a murder."

"I don't think you were selected because of your crime-solving skills," Sabine said, her expression thoughtful.

"Then why would the forces of the universe select me at all?"

"I don't know. But you must be tied into everything. Maybe it's something to do with the game preserve."

Maryse groaned. "Are you sure?" This just kept sounding worse.

"I don't see any other explanation. Maybe the next time you see Helena, you ought to ask her."

"Yeah, right, like she's been forthcoming so far," Maryse said. "Besides, Helena was as shocked as I was that I could see her. I'm sure of that. So if she's visible to me for a reason, why didn't she say so?"

Sabine narrowed her eyes. "Helena may not have expected your ability to see her, but she knows good and well what she's gotten you into. There's something she's not telling you, and you can bet if it involves Helena Henry, it's not going to be pretty."

Maryse woke up the next morning in the Mudbug Hotel with a headache to beat the band. It had been late by the time she had finished explaining the entire Helena disaster to Sabine, and even longer before Sabine had managed to absorb it all. Once her friend had been able to breathe normally again, she'd given Maryse tons of good advice both *for* Helena and how to get rid of Helena. It was around midnight when they'd left Johnny's, and the late hour coupled with the fact that Helena might be at her cabin waiting had sent Maryse straight to the hotel for the night.

Maryse pulled on her clothes, trying to figure out how to leave the hotel without running into Mildred again. Exhausted as she'd been, she hadn't gotten to bed without sharing the saga of her wild day—well, everything except Helena. That was a bit too wild even for Mildred. And right now she didn't really feel up for any more lectures or discussion.

Her hopes were dashed when she found Mildred in the lobby instead of her office. The hotel owner was standing in the front lobby peering between the front window blinds. Her gray hair pointed in fifty different directions, and her long red nails made a sharp contrast with the bright white blinds.

"What's so interesting?" Maryse asked, and Mildred jumped, then cast a guilty look back.

"Nothing."

"You were concentrating pretty hard on nothing." Maryse stepped over to the window and lifted a slat to look outside. Downtown wasn't exactly bustling yet; it was still too early, but it was easy to see what had caught Mildred's attention. Luc LeJeune was bending over the newspaper machine outside of the café, and the hotel offered the perfect rear shot angle.

Maryse looked back at Mildred. "You really ought to take another look. He's bending over now."

"Really?" Mildred yanked the cord on the blinds, and they flipped open, allowing both of them a full view of the street. The hotel owner looked across the street just as Luc stood and turned, allowing her a full front view. She clutched one hand over her heart. "Lord have mercy. That has got to be the best-looking man I have even seen in person."

Maryse held in a sigh. Like she needed any more reminders of just how attractive Luc was. "Mildred, I'm surprised at you."

Mildred turned to stare at her. "Are you kidding me? Only a woman with no pulse or the taste for women could look at that man and not wish to be younger, hotter, and in *really* good shape." She looked back out the window as Luc walked toward the café door. "The things I could do with that."

Now Maryse did sigh. She didn't want to think about doing things to "that" and damned sure couldn't afford to think about Luc doing things to her.

Mildred turned from the window and stared at Maryse with a critical eye. "It's official then—you died two years ago when that stupid Hank left, and you've been a walking corpse ever since." Mildred shook her head. "I know you've got a lot going on. Hell, you babbled for an hour after you staggered in here at midnight high on pain killers. The will, the money, your missing husband. Things are really weird, and I get that, but Maryse, when a woman fails to appreciate a man like that, well, she might as well hang up her bra."

"It's not that I failed to notice him. It's more like I already know him, and his type, so the new has worn off the butt-looking festival."

Mildred's eyebrows rose. "You know him?"

Maryse shrugged. "Yeah. He's a zoologist for the state, and he's set up shop in my office. Apparently we're going to be sharing space for a while."

Mildred reached into her shirt pocket, pulled out her inhaler, and took a quick puff. "You're sharing an office with Adonis? No wonder you're exhausted."

"It's not like that. It's work, and he's a total playboy and sorta annoying. Besides, I'm still married, remember?"

"Hmmpf. Some marriage. I'm thinking God would probably give you a pass on finding someone else since He hasn't bothered to produce Hank in the past two years. Maybe since you never manage to leave the bayou, God just brought a man to you."

Maryse rubbed her temple, thinking this conversation was way worse than the one she'd originally been trying to avoid and the biggest reason she preferred not to leave the bayou. "I'm sure that's it, Mildred. God sent me a man. Anyway, I really need to get going. I've got a ton of work to do today, so if I could just get some coffee and some aspirin, I can get on my way."

"The aspirin are in the cabinet, same as usual, but my coffeepot broke yesterday, and I haven't had time to get a new one." Mildred paused for a second, then smiled. "Hey, I've got an idea. We could step across the street to the café and have coffee and a muffin. I haven't had more than a ten-minute phone call from you in months. You can grace me with a half hour of your presence."

Bullshit. Maryse knew good and well why Mildred wanted to have breakfast at the café, and it had nothing to do with Maryse's less-than-stellar visitation record. Not that Maryse could really remember the last time she'd spent any quality time with Mildred, but that wasn't the point. Even though Mildred was trying to be sneaky and deceitful and conniving, Maryse couldn't say no to the woman who had dated her dad for over twenty years and practically raised her.

Maybe Luc would be so engrossed in his newspaper and his breakfast that she could slip in and out without a huge production. "Fine," Maryse said finally. "But we have to make it fast. I really do have a ton of stuff to do today."

Mildred practically ran to her office to grab her purse and some aspirin for Maryse, then rushed them both out the door. They had barely stepped inside the café when Maryse heard Luc call her name. So much for slipping in and out.

Mildred paused for a millisecond, but when it was clear that Maryse wasn't going to move, the hotel owner turned and headed straight toward the smiling zoologist. She stopped at Luc's table, Maryse in tow like a petulant teenager. "You must be Luc, the new zoologist," Mildred said. "I'm Mildred, and I own the hotel across the street. Maryse has been telling me all about you."

Maryse felt a flush run up her neck, and she fought the desperate urge to flee from the café as if on fire. Luc looked over at her and smiled. "All about me, huh? I didn't think you'd noticed."

Maryse waved a hand in dismissal and tried to sound nonchalant. "She's exaggerating. I barely know anything to tell, much less all."

Mildred slid into the chair next to Luc and motioned for Maryse to sit across from them. "Well," Mildred said, "we've got some time. You can tell us all about yourself over breakfast." Mildred waved at the waitress for coffee, then turned back to Luc. "So, are you married?"

Maryse downed the aspirin with a huge gulp of water and willed herself to disappear.

"No," Luc said.

"Girlfriend?" Mildred pressed.

"Not even close." Luc grinned.

Mildred narrowed her eyes at him. "You're not gay, are you?"

"Hell, no!"

"Thank God," Mildred said under her breath, but Maryse was certain Luc heard every word by the way his lips quivered with a smile. Maryse searched her mind for a way to stop the freight train of humiliation when Mildred rose from the table. "I just remembered I need to finish the books from last night," the hotel owner said.

Maryse stared. "You close the books every night at nine."

Mildred waved a hand in dismissal but didn't meet Maryse's eyes. "I went to bed early last night. There was a special on Lifetime I wanted to catch." She gave Luc a broad smile. "It was a pleasure meeting you. I'm sure Maryse will enjoy working with you." Then before Maryse could say a word in protest, Mildred spun around faster than a large woman ought to be able to and hustled out of the café, the door banging shut behind her.

Maryse counted to five, then looked over at Luc. "I'm really sorry about that. Mildred is . . . well . . . Mildred."

"I like her, although her subtlety could use a little work."

Maryse sighed. "That *was* subtle."

Luc laughed. "So I guess the Lifetime story doesn't hold?"

"Not even close. Unless it's forensics, cop shows, or a hockey game, you won't catch Mildred anywhere near a television. She likes her entertainment a bit violent."

Luc shook his head. "Wow. With friends like that . . ."

Maryse reached for the cup of coffee as the waitress slid it across the table and dumped a ton of sugar in it. "She's more than a friend. Mildred dated my dad after my mom died. She pretty much raised me."

"How old were you when she died?"

"Four."

Luc gave her a sympathetic look. "That's tough."

Maryse shrugged and stirred her coffee. "I had Dad and Mildred, so it was okay."

"Yeah, but it's not the same. My dad died when I was eight. I had tons of uncles and my grandfather, and my mom was super, but there's always that feeling that it's incomplete."

Maryse stopped stirring and looked at Luc. "Incomplete. That's the perfect word."

"Yeah, well." Luc shrugged and picked up his knife and the butter.

Maryse watched him as he buttered his toast, his eyes not meeting hers. It wasn't fair. No man should be this sexy and be in touch with his emotions. And no man should be able to touch her heart in the way he just had.

"So do your dad and Mildred still date?" Luc asked.

"No," Maryse said, her voice catching in her throat. "He died of cancer a little over two years ago."

Luc stared at her for a moment. "I'm sorry. I can't imagine burying both parents so young."

"I really should be going," Maryse said, and rose from the table. "I've got a ton of things to catch up on this morning."

Luc looked up at her and nodded. "I won't be in the office till later. I've got to run some errands in the city."

Maryse felt a momentary surge of disappointment but quickly squelched it. "Okay, then. Guess I'll see you later."

She turned and walked out of the café, cursing Mildred for engineering her exposure to yet another facet of Luc LeJeune. Like she needed to find anything else about him attractive.

She shook her head as she crossed the street, mentally tabulating her list for the day. All she had to do was check on her truck, talk to the insurance company, meet Wheeler about the inheritance, get in eight hours of work for the state, avoid a ghost, locate a plant that she had absolutely no idea where to find, and figure out a way to wash Luc LeJeune from her mind.

Piece of cake.

Luc stood in the dealership garage in New Orleans, staring at the heap of mess that used to be Maryse's truck. He knew what he was about to hear from the Service Manager—had been thinking about it pretty much since the accident, but for the life of him couldn't make the facts add up. Someone had tried to hurt Maryse and used her truck to do it, but he didn't know why.

He was still having trouble believing Maryse could be his informant. It just didn't fit what he knew about her, although some of her actions were a bit suspect. But if it wasn't the chemical company trying to shut her up, then who was? If that ridiculous will reading had been before the accident, he'd say someone was out for the inheritance. Most likely Harold or Hank.

So his next guess was it had something to do with what she was working on in that lab of hers. All he had to do was get the proper tools, find a window of opportunity to break into the lab without being discovered, steal that notebook, make copies, and find someone to decipher it before things got any worse.

Piece of cake.

"You occupy space here much longer," a voice broke into Luc's thoughts, "I'll get you a set of coveralls and put you to work."

Luc looked over at his high school buddy, Jim, the Service Manager, as he walked across the garage to stand beside him. "Damn shame," Jim said and pointed to Maryse's vehicle. "The truck's got high miles, but the lady that owned it has taken care of it nice. It was in great shape before that crash."

Luc nodded. "You checked into the scheduled maintenance?"

"Yeah, pulled it off the computer first thing. Lady had that truck in here just a week ago for regular maintenance and everything checked out fine. I talked to the tech that worked on it, personally, and he said everything was in top shape."

"So why did a well-maintained, reasonably new vehicle lose its brakes?"

Jim pulled his hat off with one hand and rubbed his temple with the other. "You ain't gonna like the answer."

Luc looked at him, the inevitability of his friend's words already weighing heavy in his mind. "Someone cut the lines."

Jim nodded. "Yep. Almost clean through. They left enough so that the brakes would work for a couple of miles, then they would go to nothing almost immediately."

"So they fixed it so she'd think everything was working fine and hopefully build up enough speed before noticing anything was wrong, which is exactly what happened." He gave the truck one more look, then nodded to his friend. "Thanks, Jim. And if you don't mind, can we keep this between us for now? And remember, I'm a zoologist. No one can know what I'm really up to."

"Hell, I don't know what you're really up to, but I get what you're saying." Jim looked at the truck again and scratched his head. "What do you want me to tell the insurance company—or the lady?"

"Make something up that they'll both buy." He clapped his friend on the shoulder. "Something that doesn't have anything to do with attempted homicide."

Jim swallowed and looked at Luc, his expression grave. "You're gonna protect her, right? I don't really know her, but every time she's been in, she's always been so nice and friendly. This is a nasty piece of business, and I just can't imagine something a girl like that would be mixed up in that could get her killed."

Luc gave the truck one more look and shook his head. "She may not know herself."

Chapter Seven

Maryse made a mad run to her cabin, hoping to get in and out before anyone could discover her—namely Helena. She'd showered and changed the Band-Aids on her scrapes the night before at the hotel, so all she really needed was a fresh set of clothes. But her hopes were dashed as soon as she opened the door. A very irritated Helena Henry sat on her couch, staring at the wall in front of her.

"Where the hell were you last night?" Helena started bitching before she could even get the door closed. "I had to crawl through an open window to get in here, and the damned thing closed after me. I've been stuck in here all night with no way to get out. Do you have any idea how boring it is when you can't read a book or turn on the television? I spent hours reading the labels on cleaning supplies that happened to be turned in the right direction."

Maryse's head began to pound, and she walked into the kitchen to get a glass of water and one of Dr. Christopher's little pills. Mildred's aspirin weren't going to do the trick at all.

Helena rose from the couch and trotted after her. "And why in the world does your kitchen look like the cabinets spit up their contents?" She waved one arm over the counters, cluttered with utensils, pantry items, and cleaners. "Your housekeeping is an atrocity."

Maryse tossed one of the pills in her mouth and took a

huge gulp of water, wishing she had the nerve and the time to take two of them and just go to sleep right where she stood. "We don't all have the luxury of ten thousand square feet of space to store our stuff, Helena, and I'm not even going to get into the cost of hiring a maid. It so happens that I'm installing some extra shelves in the cabinets and building a pantry in the corner, which is why all my stuff is on the counters. If I'd have realized I was going to have uninvited guests, I would have worked quicker. I'm sorry to offend your delicate sensibilities with my less-than-stellar housekeeping."

"Hmmpf. Got a mouth on you this morning, don't you? Who pissed in your corn flakes?"

Maryse stared at her. "You. *You* pissed in my corn flakes. You almost got me arrested yesterday, Helena, and Lord only knows what Harold's plotting to do to me now that I inherited the land."

Helena waved a hand in dismissal. "You weren't even close to being arrested. And Harold's too big of a pansy to do anything to you. He's all talk and no action—believe me, I ought to know." Helena looked over the contents of the counters again. "Shelves, huh? Well, at least that explains the power tools on the counter. I was really starting to wonder what you ate in here. Still, place like this out in the middle of nowhere, you ought to at least leave a radio or the television or something turned on when you're gone."

Maryse considered Helena's night dilemma and smiled. After all, Helena had bored everyone to tears for years in Mudbug running her yap. It seemed only fair that she be the one bored for a change. "It may surprise you to know, Helena, that I'm an adult and sometimes I don't sleep at home. Since I have nothing of value to steal, my cat spends his nights prowling the bayou, and the mosquitoes aren't as picky about their entertainment as you, I really see no reason to leave appliances running while I'm gone."

Helena glared but didn't bother to ask where Maryse had spent the night. "Well, since you've decided to show up today, we need to have a talk. Things might be a bit worse than I originally thought, and I need you to check up on something for me at the library."

Maryse shook her head. "I don't have time for any of your shenanigans today. I'm two days behind at my job, I have a meeting with Wheeler this morning to discuss the 'rules' that come with this land inheritance, and I have a whole list of personal things to take care of on top of everything else." Maryse walked into her bedroom and yanked some clean clothes out of the closet, Helena trailing behind her.

"You know how to use a computer, right?" Helena asked. "One of those women down at the beauty salon said you can find the answers to anything on the Internet. I figured we could find out about all this ghost stuff. You know, I'd really be a lot more help if I could touch things."

"God forbid," Maryse said and pulled on a clean T-shirt and jeans. "You've been too much help already. What I need is for you to ascend or rise or whatever and let me deal with the fallout by myself."

"But this is important," Helena griped. "You can think up new names for stinkweed some other time."

Maryse grabbed her keys and left the cabin, Helena close behind. "Sorry, Helena," she said as she walked to the dock and stepped into her boat. "I know my job may seem like nothing to you, but it's important to me, and I'd like to keep it. Besides, since naming stinkweed is what has paid your son's debts all these years, you don't really have any room to complain."

Helena stepped into the boat before Maryse could shove

away from the pier and plopped down on the bench up front. "Fine, I'll just wait until this evening."

Maryse shook her head, wondering where in the world she was going to hide this evening. It had just become a top priority.

At the dock, Helena took one look at the rental car and looked back at Maryse. "What's with the car?"

Maryse opened the car door and started to get in, but Helena rushed in before her, crawling over the center console like a child. Maryse stared at the big pink butt glaring at her from the center of the car and sighed. Not a sight you ever wanted to see in life, much less this early in the morning and with a head injury.

There was a moment of concern, when Maryse thought Helena wasn't actually going to make it all the way to the other side, but finally the ghost twisted around and plopped into the passenger seat. Maryse slid into the driver's seat and tore out of the parking lot.

"Did you sell your truck?" Helena asked.

"No. I didn't sell my truck. I had a wreck yesterday."

Helena sat upright and turned in her seat to stare at Maryse. "What happened?"

Maryse shrugged. "I don't know. The brakes just failed for some reason, and I took a dip in the bayou. The truck's probably totaled."

Helena's eyes grew wider and looked Maryse up and down. "Are you all right?"

"I'm fine. Just banged up a little and pissed off that I'll have to buy a new vehicle when the other one was still in great shape." She studied Helena for a moment. "Why this concern all of a sudden?"

Helena sat back in her seat. "Have you read the instructions for the land inheritance yet?"

Maryse stared at Helena as if she'd lost her mind. "Are you kidding me? I just got it yesterday. Do you really think even if I had absolutely nothing else to do at all that I would rush home, break open a bottle of bubbly, and read the Encyclopedia Inherita? Jeez, Helena, I appreciate you leaving me the land and all, more than you'll ever know, but it's not the only thing I have going on."

Helena pursed her lips and stared silently at the dashboard. "I know you've had a lot thrown at you here lately, and you're not going to want to hear this, but I think it's really important that you understand all the rules. It's been so long since I've gone over them, but I keep thinking there's something I ought to remember."

"And that's why I'm on my way to meet with Wheeler. He should know everything about your inheritance, right?"

Helena shook her head, deep in thought. "Maybe. I hope so."

Maryse pulled in front of the café and parked the car. "Well, he better, because I bet that book is longer than the Bible and just as hard to interpret. I'm not trying to slack off on my responsibilities, Helena. I want to make sure I maintain control of the preserve, but there's no way I can finish something like that and even hope to understand it without some serious time and probably a translator."

Helena sighed. "You're probably right. That document is as old as the land and so is the language it was written in."

"Finally, we agree," Maryse said and hopped out of the car. "I'll get the basics from Wheeler and fill in the blanks as time and brainpower allow." She pushed the car door shut and walked a good five steps down the sidewalk when she heard Helena yelling.

"Damn it, Maryse," the ghost shouted from inside the car. "You know I can't open the door. I could suffocate in here."

Maryse walked back to the car and opened the passenger door to allow the angry specter out. She wasn't even in the mood to argue the suffocation comment and that whole "you're already dead" thing. She shook her head as Helena climbed out of the car. "You have got to learn how to walk through walls, Helena. I am not going to squire a ghost around town. Do you have any idea how weird this would look if someone was watching?"

"About as weird as you talking to a car door," Helena shot back, then huffed up the sidewalk to stand next to the café door.

Maryse steeled herself for her appointment, now complete with a ghost, and let them both into the café.

Wheeler was already there, perched in a booth in the corner and looking as out of place as a Coors Light distributor at a Southern Baptist convention. Maryse crossed the café, signaling to the waitress for a cup of coffee, and took a seat across from Wheeler, intentionally sitting too close to the edge to allow Helena to sit next to her. Helena glared, then took a seat next to Wheeler, who shivered for a moment, then looked across the café.

"Must be a draft in here," Wheeler said.

"Probably," Maryse agreed as the waitress slid a cup of steaming coffee in front of her for the second time that day. "I'm not trying to rush you or anything, Mr. Wheeler, and I really appreciate you coming all the way down here to talk to me, but if you don't mind, could we go ahead and get started? I have a very busy day and not enough daylight to get everything done."

Wheeler nodded. "Absolutely. This shouldn't take too much time. The basics for the land ownership are very straightforward."

"Really? Then why the enormous book?"

"The book is as old as dirt and written in circles. Plus, there are a lot of rules that simply don't apply anymore. Things to do with rice farming and possible exceptions for owning herds of cattle. Things you would never consider in the first place."

"Okay. Then give me the skinny."

Wheeler looked at her for a moment, probably not having a clue what "the skinny" was exactly, but finally decided she must mean the rules. "Well, the first item is one I covered briefly yesterday—you can't leave Mudbug for a period of one week, starting yesterday. If you take even a step outside the city limits and anyone has proof, the land will revert to the secondary heir."

"And who is that?"

"Hank. There is really no other option."

Maryse nodded, not really surprised. "And why this rule at all? I have to tell you, Wheeler, it sounds kinda weird."

Wheeler cleared his throat. "I agree that it probably sounds a little strange in this day and age, but back when the rules were written, health care wasn't what it is today and the country was at war. If a son inherited the land and was called off to war before he could decide on an heir and draw up the paperwork, his death might leave the estate in limbo indefinitely. And the state wasn't exactly diligent in ensuring the proper family maintained their estates. A lot of property was simply stolen by the state or passed on to political supporters."

"I see. So the one-week period is supposed to give me time to select an heir and have the paperwork drawn up so that the land can't hang in limbo with the state deciding how to settle it."

"Exactly. Selecting an heir is one of the first things I need you to address. Since you don't have children, you're not limited by the trust in any way as to who you chose, except that it has to be an individual and not a corporation." Wheeler paused for a moment. "You know, now that I think about it, you're the first person outside of the bloodline to inherit the land. Amazing it was held that way for so long."

"That is rather odd," Maryse agreed. "Why hasn't anyone sold it before now? Surely there have been offers, and I'm willing to bet that in a hundred years someone needed the money, even if Helena didn't."

"The land is held by the trust, not really the individual. The person who inherits gets limited control of the land and is the beneficiary of any income received off the land."

"And the trust doesn't allow for the sale of the land." Maryse felt the light bulb come on. "So then why would it matter who inherited at all?"

"Well, the original trust documents were prepared long before anyone considered the possibility that companies and individuals might enter into long-term leases, essentially giving the same benefits to the lessee as buying. Helena felt you wouldn't entertain those sort of offers, so she selected you."

"Lucky me," Maryse said, and smiled. "So you need me to select an heir, and it can be anyone I want, unless I have kids at some point and then things have to change. Is that the gist of it?"

"That's correct. If you have no objection, I'll be happy to draw up that paperwork for you as soon as you give me a name."

Maryse pulled a pen from her pocket and proceeded to write Sabine's name on a napkin. She pushed the napkin across the table to Wheeler. "I know it's not very official, but I figure you just need the name, right?"

Wheeler folded the napkin and placed it in his suit

pocket. "That will do. I'll draw the papers up and make sure to get them signed and filed before the end of the one-week period. From that point forward, if anything were to happen to you, the land will be safe and secure in the hands you've selected."

Maryse straightened in her seat and stared at Wheeler. "From that point forward?" She narrowed her eyes. "So God forbid, something happens to me in the next week, what happens to the land?"

"It passes to the next heir—Hank."

"That's it," Helena shouted and jumped up from her booth. "That's the part I couldn't remember that I thought was important."

Maryse stared at Wheeler in dismay. "You're telling me I have to outlive Helena by a week or the land goes to Hank, no questions asked?"

Wheeler nodded.

"Unbelievable. And it never occurred to anyone that this rule might leave the first to inherit with a much shorter life span than originally intended?"

Wheeler shook his head. "I don't think they were thinking in those terms. It was simply a different world back then. And while I understand your concern, I really don't think you have a lot to worry about. Certainly, it's possible the land could be worth a good bit of money to developers at some point, but that's not the case at the moment. The state is the only interested party as things stand right now. Ten, twenty years down the road, things could change, especially if New Orleans continues to push its boundaries, but what you're suggesting is an awfully big risk for a payoff that might not even happen in a person's lifetime."

"But you said the land was Helena's most valuable asset."

Wheeler nodded. "Sentimentally, it was, and as I said,

long-term the land will probably be worth more than any of us can imagine."

"I guess you're right," Maryse said, but one look at the pensive Helena, and Maryse wondered if there was something that Wheeler didn't know. Something that Maryse didn't want to know. "Is there anything else?"

Wheeler pulled some documents from a folder on the table. "I need some signatures for the paperwork for the state to ensure they make the check out to you rather than Helena, and there's a couple other documents needing signature . . . mostly just legal posturing, but required nonetheless."

Maryse pulled the stack of paperwork over toward her and spent the next fifteen minutes signing her name as Wheeler pointed out the correct spots. Finally, she passed the last document back to Wheeler, who placed them all neatly back in his folder. "Well," Maryse said, "if that's everything, I guess I'll be on my way."

Wheeler nodded and rose from the booth. As Maryse rose, he extended his hand. "Thank you for meeting me this morning, Ms. Robicheaux. I'll call as soon as I have those papers ready for your signature. I can meet you here again if that's convenient."

"That's fine," Maryse said, and shook Wheeler's hand. "Just let me know." She turned from the booth and left the cafe, Helena trailing behind her. Maryse loitered a bit on the sidewalk, waiting for Wheeler to leave. She needed to talk to Helena and wasn't about to give the ghost a ride again. Hanging out with Helena all day simply wasn't on her list of things to do. Finally, Wheeler made it to his ancient Cadillac and pulled away.

Maryse glanced inside the café to make sure no one was looking and turned her back to the huge picture glass.

"Okay, Helena, spill it," she said. "You've got this pained look on your face, and I have the bad feeling that you're about to say something else I'm not going to like."

Helena lowered her eyes and shuffled her feet. "I'm just concerned about the one-week clause. That's all."

Maryse stared at her. "Why? You heard Wheeler. It'd be too risky for Hank or Harold to try anything when the land isn't really worth much right now."

Helena bit her lower lip and raised her head to Maryse. "You remember that envelope I had you look for in my safe? The one that was missing?"

Maryse nodded. "How could I forget?"

"Well, it had some documents from a survey of the land."

Maryse closed her eyes in frustration. "So what did it say, Helena? Where are you going with this?"

Helena clenched her hands together and stared at Maryse. "It might have said that the preserve was full of oil."

"What!" Maryse cried, then glanced around making sure no one had seen her yelling into empty space. "Oil? Exactly how much oil might that letter have said was in the preserve?"

"It might have said there was billions of dollars worth . . ."

Maryse stared at Helena, horrified. "Billions, as in I don't even know how many zeros, billions?" Maryse felt a flush rise to her face. "Jesus Christ, Helena! You heard Harold threaten me at Wheeler's office. He probably took that letter before the will reading. He expected Hank to inherit the land. That's why he's so mad."

"Now, let's not get excited."

"Excited? Are you crazy? You've made me a moving target. One without a lot of places to hide given that I can't leave Mudbug. Do you really think Harold wouldn't take a shot at me over billions of dollars? He may be lazy, but he's not that lazy."

Helena took in a deep breath, and Maryse could tell that despite her protests, Helena was worried. Great. Just great.

"It's only six days counting today," Helena said. "We can come up with a plan."

"What kind of plan? Maybe locking me in a Kevlar box for a week? Even the bayou has a limited number of hiding places."

Helena shook her head. "I don't want you camping in the bayou. In fact, if you could not go into the bayou at all for a while that would probably be better. As long as you're surrounded by people, it will be much harder to get to you. And you do have a secret weapon."

Maryse narrowed her eyes. "What secret weapon?"

Helena pointed to herself. "Me. Think about it, Maryse. I can look out for you without anyone suspecting. I can warn you if anything is out of the ordinary."

Maryse stared at her. "Yeah, because everything else that's happened this week has been normal. You're not a weapon, Helena. You're the angel of death, and I don't want you anywhere near me. You've done quite enough."

Maryse jumped into her rental and tore out of the parking lot before Helena could fling herself on the trunk or anything else ridiculous the ghost may come up with. Six days. Unbelievable. Not quite a week, and it seemed ages. Suddenly, still being married to Hank seemed like such a simple problem.

She turned onto the gravel road and headed toward the office. She had to get her head on straight. Had to come up with a plan. Maybe she'd just have a heart attack right here and now and save Harold the trouble. A second later, she slammed on the brakes and brought the car to a stop in the middle of the road. The thought that had hit her was so horrible, so awful that she couldn't even breathe.

If Harold killed her, she might be stuck in limbo like Helena. Even worse, she might be stuck in limbo *with* Helena.

For all eternity.

Six days was looking shorter by the minute.

Luc eased the thin tool into the deadbolt on the door to Maryse's lab. Since he'd hacked her e-mail and found out about her appointment with Helena's attorney, he knew she would be late coming in. Unfortunately, the guy bringing him the tools got stuck in a traffic jam in downtown New Orleans, so he was getting started a good hour later than he'd planned.

He leaned in close to the door, listening for the tell-tale click that would let him know he was successful. It took a couple more seconds before he felt the tool give and heard the barely audible sound of the locking mechanism turning. He slipped the tool in his pocket to use inside on the locked drawer where the notebook was stashed, and grabbed a second tiny rod from the black carrying case that housed his breaking and entering tools. He'd need that one to relock the drawer and the door once he was done.

He closed the case and crossed the room to slip it inside his gym bag. If Maryse came back sooner than expected, the last thing he needed was for her to see the tool set and start asking questions. It wouldn't take a genius to figure out what the thin blades were for, and Maryse was no dummy. The case secure, he slipped into the lab and worked his magic on the drawer. A minute later, he pulled the notebook from inside and headed out of the lab and straight for the office copy machine.

He flipped page after page, copying as fast as the antiquated machine allowed. The front office window gave him a clear view of the road and the dock, which was good since he was never quite sure what mode of transportation Maryse might use. Either way, he should see her in enough time to get everything back to where it belonged. He hoped.

Ten more pages or so, he thought as he turned the notebook over and over again and prayed that the copier would hold out. He was only a couple of pages from the end when the copier whined to a stop. What now? He studied the copier display screen and groaned. The thing was jammed, and if that display was any indication, it was jammed all over.

He put the notebook on the table behind him and opened the feeder tray. As he pulled a sheet of paper lodged halfway in the feeder, he looked out the window. Shit, shit, shit! There was no mistaking the red rental car turning the corner. And it was coming fast.

Chapter Eight

Luc grabbed the notebook and ran into the lab. He shut the notebook in the drawer, then poked his tool in the lock, hoping it worked its magic. The lock clicked almost immediately and he rushed to the door, repeating the process on the deadbolt. He hurried over to the copier and pulled the documents off the tray and shoved them into his gym bag.

His pulse racing, he glanced out the window just as Maryse pulled to a stop in front of the office. Yanking open the panels of the copier, he prayed that he got the paper removed before she could offer to help. If any of the jammed pieces were partially copied, he was busted, pure and simple. There was no logical way to explain what he was doing with her personal property—or how he had broken into her lab to get it.

He flipped open drawers and panels and yanked the lodged paper from inside, cramming it into his pockets as he went. He was down to the last tray when he heard the office door open. He glanced into the tray at the offending paper and held in a stream of cursing. The paper was jammed in the rollers, crinkled like a Japanese fan, but if you flattened out the folded rows, Maryse's handwriting still showed on the document clear as day.

"Problems?" Maryse asked as she tossed her keys onto her desk.

Luc rose from the copier and shook his head. "Nothing out of the ordinary for a machine this old. Just a paper jam."

Maryse nodded. "It does that all the time. Let me take a look. I've gotten to be a real pro at fixing that piece of junk."

Luc waved one hand, desperate to fend her off. "No, that's all right. I'll get it."

Maryse stared at him a moment. "What's your problem, LeJeune? Would my fixing the copier somehow be an affront to your manhood?" She walked over to the machine and gave him a shove. "Move out of the way. I don't want to listen to you banging and cussing over here for the next thirty minutes. There's a trick to getting paper out of this spot."

Luc clenched his fists in a panic, searching for something, anything that would stop her from reaching into that panel, but he came up with absolutely nothing. His only hope was that she wouldn't take a close look at the paper while removing it and he could somehow get it away from her immediately following removal.

Maryse squatted down in front of the copier and looked at the offending paper. "You got it jammed in good. Usually you've got to unscrew this top piece to get the paper out, but after I went through that process for about the hundredth time, I got smart and installed a pin to hold it in place. See?" She pointed to a long, thin, metal pin slotted through the panel and into the roller.

Luc glanced at the pin and nodded, certain he hadn't taken a breath since she'd walked in the door.

"So all I have to do is pull the pin out," Maryse said and proceeded to remove the pin while holding her hand under the top panel. "And, voila, the tray drops and the paper is easily removed." She gently worked the paper out of from between the roller and the panel and held it up in front of him, the tell-tale text facing her direction and just below eye level.

All he could think about was keeping her from looking at that paper, and the only way he knew to throw someone like Maryse off track was to give her something bigger to focus on. Before he could change his mind he yanked the sheet of paper from her hand, ignoring the surprised look on her face, and stepped so close to her that he could feel the heat coming off her body.

"Mechanically inclined women really turn me on," he said and leaned in to kiss her before she knew it was coming and could formulate a retreat.

As his lips touched hers, a spark hit him deep in his center, and the panic he felt began to subside. When she didn't pull away, he kept his mouth on hers, gently parting her lips for his tongue to enter. He involuntarily pressed into her, his arousal firm against her leg.

The instant other parts of him made contact, Maryse jumped back and stared at him, her face full of surprise and confusion. "What the hell is wrong with you, LeJeune? Are you bucking for a hostile work environment complaint?"

She stared at him, obviously waiting for an answer, but he couldn't come up with a single excuse that would fly. "I'm sorry," he finally said. "I just got carried away."

She gave him a wary look as she backed away and grabbed her keys from the desk. "Well, don't let it happen again." Without so much as a backward glance, she walked out of the office, slamming the door behind her.

Luc watched as she jumped in her boat and tore down the bayou. As the boat rounded a bend and disappeared, he slumped back against the wall next to the copier. What the hell had he been thinking? Maryse's threat was very real— behavior like that could get him a legal complaint and completely blow his cover.

He looked down at the piece of paper, still clenched in his hand. At least he'd gotten the paper without her seeing it, and that had been the whole point, right? But as he shoved the papers in a file and headed out of the office to take them to a scientist in New Orleans, he couldn't help but think he'd gotten way more than he bargained for.

Maryse pushed down the throttle on her boat and grimaced every time the bow beat against the choppy surface of the bayou. At the rate the boat was moving, she could probably have run faster, even with her injuries.

And running is just what you're doing.

That thought brought her up short, and she eased up on the gas and gritted her teeth as the boat bounced to a slower, less-jarring crawl. She'd gone to the office with the intention of actually getting some work done. Then Luc had pulled his playboy routine, and she'd panicked like a schoolgirl.

Jesus, you'd think she'd never been kissed. She was a married woman, for Christ's sake. Well, not really married, but married enough that she shouldn't have been so disturbed by a kiss.

But she was. And that really, really stuck in her craw.

Professional ladies' men like Luc LeJeune had no business putting the moves on women like her, especially when she wasn't exactly in her best fighting shape. She cut the gas on the boat and coasted to a stop. Sinking down on her driver's seat, she looked out over the bayou and took a deep breath, trying to clear her mind of the fog of Luc's kiss, but her evil brain brought it all back to her in amazing Technicolor.

Luc's lips, masculine and soft all at the same time, pressed against her own. All she could think of was how those lips would feel other places. When he'd slipped his tongue in her mouth, she'd almost melted on the spot. She couldn't allow herself thoughts about that tongue going other places. There were just some lines you didn't cross because you knew there was no returning afterward.

Her skin was still hot from his touch, so she stripped down to her sports bra, hoping the bayou breeze would cool her overstimulated skin. It was unnerving to be as old as she was and have this much loss of self-control. Even Hank hadn't stirred her up this way, and he'd been a pretty good playboy himself.

Luc LeJeune had all the makings of trouble. More trouble than Hank. More trouble than she needed in this lifetime and certainly more trouble than she needed right now.

Before she could change her mind, she yanked her cell phone from her pocket and pulled out the small slip of paper tucked inside the case. She pressed in the numbers and waited while the phone rang over and over, finally rolling to voice mail.

"Christopher, this is Maryse Robicheaux," she said when she heard the beep. "If you're still interested, I'd love to take you up on that offer for dinner. Just give me a call."

She flipped the phone shut, shoved it in her pocket, and eased her boat up the bayou. She was going to put Luc LeJeune out of her mind, even if she had to throw herself at another man to accomplish it.

Maryse docked her boat at her cabin early that evening in somewhat of a mild panic. Her workday had gone well for the state—she'd finally found that elusive Lady Slipper hybrid they were looking for, but she hadn't located the plant she needed for her trials. She'd just about been ready to try yet another area of the bayou when Christopher had returned her call. Not only did he want to take her to dinner, but he wanted to take her to dinner that night. At Beau Chené, a first-class restaurant just on the edge of Mudbug.

As she yanked open her closet doors, she tried not to think that this was the second time in less than a week that she probably didn't have anything nice to wear. After all, Christopher had already seen her one and only cocktail dress when she'd gone to the emergency room.

She pushed the clothes from one side to another, frowning the entire time. There had to be something that would work. Anything. She paused for a moment, and her brow crinkled in unpleasant memory. There was an outfit that Sabine had made her buy one year for a Christmas party. It was clingy and sparkly and she'd hated it at the time, but if she could find it, it would work perfectly for Beau Chené.

After going through every inch of her closet and each drawer of her dresser, it looked as though a hurricane had blown right through her tiny bedroom. She plopped onto her bed with a sigh. The tiny crunch of plastic when she flounced her entire body weight on her mattress brought her mind into focus, and she reached beneath the bed to tug out a plastic storage container. She pulled off the lid and heaved a sigh of relief as the offensive garment, complete with way-too-high and incredibly uncomfortable heels, lay resting inside.

Her problem of something to wear was solved. Her problem of something to say was still in the hopper.

Twenty minutes later, she stepped out of the shower and saw Helena perched on her toilet. Maryse bit back a scream and quickly wrapped a towel around her chest as she shook the water from her hair. "Damn it, Helena, I know you can't knock, but you could at least yell or something. One of these days, you're going to give me a heart attack. Then where would that leave us?"

Helena glared, the showgirl makeup still as thick and dark as it was the day she was buried. In fact, everything about her was exactly as it was in the casket. Bummer. If Helena found out who gave the funeral home that outfit *and* figured out how to move things, someone was in a boatload of trouble. Maryse almost felt sorry for them.

Then she took another look at the putrid pink polyester. Well, maybe not sorry.

Helena huffed. "You're one to talk about leaving us in a bad situation. Based on the way you took off today, I figure you don't give a damn anyway, so why should I?"

"Because it would be a pleasant change?" Maryse started to brush out her damp hair. "You know, you caring about something besides yourself? Who knows, you might have centuries to figure it out." Maryse gave her a fake smile, fully expecting Helena to fly off the handle—or in this case, off the toilet—but Helena only looked at her with a sad expression on her face.

"I do care about other people . . . or did care . . . or hell, I don't know how to explain it now that I'm dead. It feels like I still care, but I don't know if that's possible. Is my soul still here?"

Maryse studied her for a moment, not sure how to answer, but Helena looked so troubled she couldn't stand holding out on her any longer. It was time to let the ghost in on her paranormal connection. "I told Sabine about you."

Helena stared at her in obvious confusion. "That nut at the psychic place?"

"She's not a nut . . . well, not exactly . . . She's just not like other people."

Helena raised her eyebrows.

"Okay. So she's a bit of a nut, but no one I know can tell you more about the paranormal, and that includes ghosts. You ought to be thankful I'm checking on things for you. And you shouldn't judge those who want to help."

Helena looked surprised. "She wants to help?"

"Sure, she wants to help." *Wants to help me get rid of you, anyway.* "Got all weepy when I told her about the situation." *Or maybe that was the six glasses of wine.* "Anyway, she thinks that you still have your soul and that's why you're still here. You can't transcend, or whatever, until your soul is put to rest. In your case, she feels that's by figuring out who murdered you."

Helena considered this for a moment, then nodded. "Kind of what we already figured except for the soul part, right? Hey, she didn't mention anything about how I would be able to touch things, did she?"

"As a matter of fact, she did. I asked specifically since it's a hell of a lot more useful for you to be able to move things than me. I'm not pulling a repeat of that stunt at your house."

"And what did she say?" Helena asked eagerly. "How do I do it?"

Maryse shook her head. "Sabine doesn't really know how to tell you to do it. She's never actually been dead or talked to a ghost. But her best guess was you had to will it to happen and assume it would. You couldn't go into it thinking it wouldn't work."

Helena frowned. "Will it to happen? That's it? If it was that damned easy, don't you think I'd have already done it?"

"You're doing it right now. You're sitting on my toilet. Why didn't you fall through if you couldn't come into contact with solids? And last time I checked, regular people did *not* walk on water."

Helena stared down at the toilet and scrunched her brow. "Why, I never thought of that. So it's a matter of faith, then?"

Maryse shrugged. "Guess so. You just have to figure out a way to think of touching things as naturally as you do sitting or walking on them."

Helena sighed. "Faith . . . that's a low blow. I was the most cynical person on the face of the Earth." She gave Maryse a small smile. "Guess I still am."

Maryse shook her head and picked up her blow dryer, directing the hot air toward her short waves. "Well, you're going to have to find a way to believe, because I'm not breaking and entering again, no matter how long you have to wander around here."

Helena waved one hand in dismissal. "Yeah, yeah, Miss Goodie Two-Shoes, so I'll practice tomorrow. Tonight, I have important business to discuss with you."

"Tonight, I have a date with Dr. Christopher Warren." She plunked the dryer down and pointed a finger at Helena. "And you will not interfere." Maryse walked into the bedroom and began to dress.

"But it's important," Helena whined, and flopped onto the bed, jettisoning throw pillows onto the floor when her weight connected with the springy mattress. Maryse glanced at the pillows and shook her head. Helena was never going to get it.

"Look," Maryse said as she wriggled into the tight, short black skirt, "I don't doubt in the least that what you have to say is important, to you anyway. And I know there are things we need to do, but the problem is I'm still trying to have a life. And while it may not seem like a great one to you, it's the only one I've got. I'd like to get some enjoyment out of it, if that's even possible."

Helena started to respond, but Maryse held up a hand to stop her. "Which means two things: One, I have to take care of my job, and it is a full-time venture. Two, I will not cancel a date with the most eligible bachelor in town."

"Bachelor is right. That cad's already dated half the women in New Orleans and probably bedded the other half without the prospect of dinner."

Maryse gave Helena a withering stare. "Oh, but your son was the pinnacle of honesty and ethics. Give me a break."

Helena frowned. "No. Hank was as useless as his father. I tried really hard with him but some things just can't be changed. Guess Harold's DNA won out."

"That's funny," Maryse said as she slipped the sparkly, low-cut blue top over her head and adjusted her bra. "I always got the impression you thought Hank was wonderful. If not, why did you defend him all those years? Why pay his bills every time he got in trouble? And most of all—why in the world did you make me pay you back for Hank's debts if you already knew how worthless he was? It's not like they were my fault." She walked over to her dresser and picked up a black eyeliner pencil.

Helena put her chin up in defiance. "I needed to test you."

Maryse dropped the mascara in the makeup tray and stared at her in disbelief. "Test me? What in the world for? To see how much I could take before I drowned myself in the bayou? Or were you itching for death then and thought I'd eventually strangle you?" The thought had crossed her mind more than once.

Helena shook her head and said in all seriousness, "I needed to test your character so I could decide what to do with the land. I couldn't just mess that up, you know."

Maryse turned from the dresser and frowned. "Okay, Helena, I can get that you had a big decision to make and not a lot of choices given your son's proclivity for uselessness, but you made my life miserable for two years. My life to some extent is on hold unless Hank shows up and does the right thing. You have to know that land or no land, I'm not happy to be in this position, and I'm certainly not happy to have you hanging around as a spirit. You were easier to avoid when you were alive."

Helena started to respond, but the phone rang. Maryse glanced at the display with a groan and flipped open the phone.

"Is anything wrong, Maryse?" Christopher asked. "You were supposed to be at the dock ten minutes ago."

Darn Helena. Now she was late for her date with the hottest catch in town. "I'm running a bit behind is all," Maryse said, not even going to answer the very loaded question about what was wrong. "I'll be there in two minutes." She flipped the phone shut, finished her makeup, grabbed her purse, and rushed out of the cabin, Helena in tow.

"You can't go out with him tonight," Helena begged. "There are too many important things we need to discuss and he's really, really wrong for you. I know."

"You don't even know him." Maryse tossed her bow line in her boat and eased down inside, one hand clutching her stilettos. "And like you're an expert at picking men. I'm not doing this tonight, Helena." She started the boat and threw the accelerator down as far as it would go. Giant sheets of water rose behind the boat and showered the land a good ten feet behind the dock, including the piece Helena stood on. Maryse looked back, hoping to see her doused, but the water passed completely through her and she stood perfectly still, staring forlornly at the boat.

Maryse prayed that whatever problem Helena had now wasn't worth skipping her date. Given her week, there was a lot to be said for anything remotely normal. Not that dating doctors was exactly the norm for Maryse, or dating at all for that matter, but damn if she wasn't going to give it a whirl.

At the dock, Maryse took one look at Christopher Warren and decided right then and there that she had made the right decision. He was definitely hot. His black slacks and black silk shirt were designer quality, and he wore them well, the clothes doing nothing to disguise a tight butt and perfectly toned chest and arms. His light brown hair glistened with natural blonde highlights and his pale green eyes focused on her as she made her way up from the dock.

Focus on your future. She paused for a moment to consider what smart children they would have and smiled. Christopher smiled back and leaned in to kiss her on the cheek. Maryse couldn't even think about enjoying it because at that moment she caught a movement out of the corner of her eye. Helena was walking across the bayou straight toward them, a determined look on her face.

Holy hell. Maryse took Christopher's hand and tugged him toward his shiny new Lexus. "We don't want to be late," she said in response to the somewhat puzzled look on his face. "And I don't want my hair to frizz in this humidity."

"Sure." He chuckled in understanding, vanity apparently a very good excuse for rudely rushing people. He opened the car door, and Maryse jumped inside, slamming the door before he could even reach the handle. He stared at her for a moment but finally turned and headed back to his side of the car and climbed inside.

He took his time getting the car started, then burned at least a minute inspecting his hair in the rearview mirror. Maryse kept a wary eye on Helena's approach the entire time. If he didn't get them the heck out of there, this was going to get ugly. Helena might not be able to open the car door, but she wouldn't hesitate to plop herself right on the hood.

"I'm starving," Maryse said, trying to hurry him along. "What time is our reservation?"

Christopher took the hint and put the car in gear, pulling slowly out of the parking lot just as Helena stepped onto the dock. Maryse half expected her to break into a run as they pulled away, but she guessed even ghosts had their limits. Or maybe it was too hard to run in pointy-toe heels and a polyester suit. Either way, Maryse held in a sigh of relief as she saw Helena fading in the mirror.

"We don't exactly have a reservation," Christopher said, "but I called in a favor. They'll fit us in whenever we arrive."

Maryse's eyes widened. "Really?" The restaurant was usually booked weeks in advance. "That must have been some favor." She sank back into the soft leather seat with a smile. Beau Chené was the stuff dinner date dreams were made of. It was fabulously exclusive, ridiculously expensive, and had more class than the entire state of Louisiana. The fact that it rested just inside the Mudbug city limits was a mystery within itself, but who was she to complain?

The only other time she'd graced that establishment was a dinner with Hank, Helena, and Harold. Not exactly a pleasurable evening for such an impressive place. But this time was different. This time she was dining with an attractive, intelligent doctor. She was going to have a good time, even if it killed her.

She caught Christopher looking over at her and gave him a sexy smile. This was going to be a night to remember.

A night to remember turned out to be a gross understatement. The look on Maryse's face when Helena walked into Beau Chené and took a seat at their table was probably one Christopher would never forget. In any event, it was bad enough to cause him to jump up from his chair and rush to her side, as she grabbed her glass of ridiculously expensive champagne and tossed the entire contents back in one gulp.

"You're white as a sheet," Christopher said and placed one hand on her forehead. "What's wrong? You look like you've seen a ghost."

Helena hooted, and Maryse choked on the last bit of champagne, spraying it across the table. She was afraid Christopher was about to start the Heimlich maneuver so she waved one hand to ward him off. Taking a deep breath, she tried to calm down, but with Helena laughing like a hyena, it was damn near impossible. Finally, she gained control of her breathing, although her blood pressure was questionable, and apologized profusely to Christopher for alarming him.

"I don't know what came over me," she said, trying to come up with a believable excuse fast. "I've had a pretty stressful week, and I guess it just all caught up to me in one moment."

Christopher nodded and took his seat again, gently caressing her hand. "Probably an anxiety attack. I heard a little around town about your mother-in-law and the situation with your ex, or sorta ex. That along with your wreck would be enough to send anyone in a spiral, but this sort of problem rarely continues once the issues causing them are settled. In a week or so, you ought to be back to normal."

"Gee," Helena said, "I could have made that diagnosis."

Before she could stop herself, Maryse frowned. Christopher noticed her expression and squeezed her hand, trying to reassure her. "I promise it will go away," he said. "There's nothing really wrong. At least nothing a great dinner won't help. If you're still up to it, that is." He removed his hand from hers and began to pour more champagne in her glass.

"Please," Helena said, and smirked. "This guy couldn't cure a cold sore. What the hell does he know about anxiety? Besides, hooking up with an asshole like this is enough to cause high blood pressure."

"That's enough," Maryse said, and shot Helena a dirty look.

Christopher stared at her, a confused expression on his face, but stopped pouring the champagne at half a glass. Great. Not only had Helena ruined a great dinner, Maryse wasn't even going to be able to drink enough to forget her misery.

"Would you like to order an appetizer?" Christopher asked and placed the half-empty champagne glass in front of her. "I hear the rum-soaked shrimp are delicious."

Before she could answer, Helena jumped in. "Ha! He's just trying to get you into bed and thinks now is a great time because you're vulnerable. Look how desperate he is to get alcohol into you—first the champagne, now the shrimp. What a louse."

Maryse finally reached the boiling point and she knew she was about to lose it. Helena's return from the dead, her wreck, that awful will reading, breaking and entering, Sabine's warning about Helena, and her unwanted and unprecedented attraction to Luc LeJeune swam violently in her mind like angry piranha. "Did you ever stop to think that someone might like me for some other reason than sex?"

The diners at the tables surrounding them grew silent, and it occurred to Maryse that not only had she not whispered as she'd originally intended, but speaking out loud to a ghost that no one else could see did not bode well for her date that everyone could see. Christopher stared at her in shock, his face beginning to flush.

"For the record," he said, keeping his voice low and controlled, "I wasn't thinking of sleeping with you at all. I mean, I thought about it, but that's not what this dinner is about." He shook his head and looked closely at her. "Maybe we ought to head home. You're obviously not feeling up to this yet."

Maryse clenched her hands and held in tears of embarrassment and anger, afraid to even look at Helena lest she do something even more foolish, like try to stab her to death with the butter knife or choke her with the two hundred-dollar champagne she'd barely gotten a taste of. "Maybe that's a good idea," Maryse agreed, since the only other alternative was dinner with Helena—something she obviously couldn't manage with any decorum or taste.

Feeling guilty, Maryse reached across the table to place one hand on Christopher's arm. "I'm really sorry about this, and I swear, I didn't think your intentions were anything but honorable. I just don't know what's come over me."

"That's all right," he said, giving her a curt nod, and Maryse knew he was miffed. "We'll call this one a night and try again some other time when you're feeling more up to it."

Meekly agreeing, Maryse plucked her purse off the chair, rose from her seat, and attempted to follow Christopher out of the restaurant without making eye contact with any of the curious patrons. Aside from marrying Hank, this had to be the single most mortifying moment of her life.

As she jumped into the car, hoping to erase the night from her memory and start all over, Helena walked through the car door and sat in the back seat. "Cool, huh?" the ghost said. "I figured out that walking-through-walls thing when I got to the restaurant."

Great. Just fucking great.

Maryse looked out the car window and watched Christopher tip the valet. "You had to follow me to the car, too?" she hissed. "Haven't you caused me enough trouble already?"

"Oh, please," Helena said, and gave Christopher a disgusted look. "I was only trying to stop you from making the biggest mistake of your life."

"The biggest mistake of my life was marrying your son."

Helena stared at her for a moment, then shrugged. "Okay, then the second biggest mistake of your life."

Maryse turned around in her seat and glared at Helena. "And why in the world would taking up with a good-looking, successful doctor be a mistake? Can you tell me that? I've known Christopher since we were kids, and all I ever wanted was a healthy relationship with a man. I got cheated the first time around."

Helena snorted. "Healthy relationship? You're barking up the wrong tree, honey. You might have known him as a kid, but one of you has changed. And it's not you. First of all, that doctor does not have 'relationships.' He has conquests. How do you think I knew where you were eating? I used to eat here several times a week, and your perfect doctor was always here with a different woman."

"I don't believe you," Maryse said. "Besides, what's wrong with dating other women? He didn't come back to Mudbug until a week or so ago. I could hardly ask for anything exclusive before we even reconnected."

Helena rolled her eyes. "You weren't interested in anything exclusive. You just wanted to get laid. You're not even wearing underwear."

Maryse felt her blood boil. "I never wear underwear!" she shouted, at the exact same moment Christopher opened the car door.

Maryse whipped around in her seat, trying not to groan. She could feel Christopher staring at her, but he didn't move. Finally, he sank into the driver's seat and started the car. As he pulled out of the parking lot, he leaned over and whispered, "Good to know."

Maryse just nodded and tried to smile, although she was certain it came out more like a grimace. She turned slightly and glanced at the backseat, hoping at least for the opportunity to give Helena the finger behind the headrest, but the backseat was empty.

What should have been the perfect date with the perfect man was ruined. Even worse, instead of fantasizing about her night with Christopher, the only thing she could think of was Luc LeJeune's kiss. It was all his fault she'd gotten into this mess to begin with. Maryse sank back in her seat with a sigh, feeling sexually frustrated for the first time in, well, forever.

And there wasn't a single battery-operated device in her nightstand to handle the job.

Chapter Nine

Unless Helena learned to fly, Maryse figured it would take her at least an hour to get to Maryse's cabin. Relieved to be rid of the ghost and frustrated that her date with an eligible doctor had ended with her thinking of Luc LeJeune, Maryse reached for the tequila bottle and poured herself a shot. She gritted her teeth as the bitter liquid burned her throat. She was a lousy drinker. A cold beer was one thing, hard liquor was another.

She poured another shot but couldn't get it past her lips. Disgusted with herself, Helena, and her night, she walked into the kitchen and began to make a peanut butter sandwich.

She didn't even care whether Christopher called her again. Which was good, because despite the intriguing underwear comment, he probably wasn't interested in being embarrassed in a fancy restaurant again anytime in this life. She took a bite of the sandwich and pulled a beer from the refrigerator.

She went back into the living room and plopped down on the couch, trying to ignore the fact that the reason Dr. Christopher held no appeal to her was because Luc LeJeune held entirely too much. Damn that man! Why did he have to go and kiss her? She was doing a fine job of pretending she didn't find him sexy as hell, and then he crossed that line. And once you crossed that line, there was no going back. Oh, she could pretend it didn't affect her, but she wasn't going to fool anyone—especially not Luc.

And all of this thrown at her when she really, really needed to be concentrating on finding that plant for the trials. Whatever Blooming Flower had brewed up for Maryse's dad had been working. The cancer was moving toward remission, and he hadn't experienced a single side effect—something that could rarely be said for the radiation treatment he'd refused. Then Blooming Flower had died without revealing her secret. The secret Maryse was still searching for. She took a long swallow of beer and flipped the remote to some boring talk show.

It was over an hour before Helena showed up. Maryse was about to go to bed when the ghost popped into the living room, walking straight through the wall and the television. For a moment, Maryse thought she was having a hallucination that someone had stepped out of the television set, but then her vision cleared a bit, and the pink polyester seemed to glow in the dim living room light.

"What took you so long?" she asked. "Couldn't catch a ride?"

"You know good and well no normal person's coming out into a swamp in the middle of the night."

Maryse glanced up at the clock on the wall. "It's only eleven. Hardly the middle of the night."

"When you're my age, eight o'clock is the middle of the night."

Maryse shook her head. Something else in life to look forward to. "Look, Helena, I'm a little drunk, and I'm tired. I'm in no mood to deal with you, especially after that stunt you pulled tonight. I know you might find this hard to believe, but I don't want to live alone on the bayou with only a cat for company the rest of my life. I'm an introvert, not a hermit. Snagging a doctor isn't exactly the worst way to go, regardless of whether you think I could have landed him or not."

"Hmm. You live like a hermit. When's the last time you got out of the bayou for anything . . . dinner, a movie, a night on the town? Maybe if you spent some time in the general population, you could meet a nice man. Something the doctor is not. He uses women."

Maryse waved one hand in the air. "I am not going to discuss this with you. It's simply none of your business. You never liked me anyway, so let me take my chances. What the hell difference does it make to you if I end up a two-time loser?"

Helena studied her for a moment, seeming to contemplate her next words. Finally, she sighed and said, "I never said I didn't like you. And besides, none of that matters now. We have bigger fish to fry, and I can't have a decent conversation with you if you're in such a snit."

"Well, then you're out of luck tonight." Maryse rose from the couch. "I'm going to bed. Are you staying?"

Helena sat on the couch and glared at the television remote. "Don't have much choice do I, if I want to talk to you. As long as I'm stuck here, will you at least change the channel?"

Maryse considered refusing for a moment. Hell, she considered turning the whole damned thing off and making Helena sit in the dark, but she just didn't have the energy to listen to the griping. "You know, you could have saved us both the hassle and stayed at the hotel. I'm sure there are at least twenty televisions on there with all kinds of things to watch."

Helena gave her a horrified look. "Oh, no—I already tried that one. Do you have any idea what those salesmen turn on when they are away from their wives? I can't believe Mildred allows that crap in her hotel. Good God, the things I've seen."

Some of the things Helena had seen were probably the same things Maryse could have been doing herself if her mother-in-law hadn't cheated her of the opportunity. But she thought it wise not to point that out. "Fine. What do you want to watch?"

"I heard down at the beauty shop that channel six is doing an all-night marathon of real hauntings," Helena replied, looking animated for the first time that evening. "That will be interesting. Maybe I could learn how to move things."

Oh goody. "Yeah, sure, and if things don't work out here with that little business concerning your soul, at least you'll know where to find friends."

Maryse awakened the next morning to the ringing of her telephone. She groaned and covered her pounding head with her pillow, trying to block out the shrill sound.

"Aren't you going to answer that?" Helena asked.

"No," Maryse replied without even looking out from under the pillow. "Go away."

"Sounds like someone needs coffee."

The phone finally stopped, and the answering machine kicked on. "Ms. Robicheaux," a polite voice began, "this is Mrs. Baker down at the insurance company. I just wanted to let you know that we finished processing the claim on your truck, and unfortunately, it is totaled. We'll be preparing two checks, one for the last payment due on your loan and the other for the balance due to you. If you don't receive that within ten days, please contact me at the office and let me know. Thanks and have a nice day."

Maryse pulled the pillow back and looked at the answering machine. Last payment? What the hell were they talking about? She owed another two years on that truck. Knowing she couldn't sleep until she sorted things out, she pushed herself off the bed and grabbed the phone off the nightstand to call her bank, happy to see that Helena had at least vacated the room.

When the branch manager picked up, Maryse explained what had happened and that she needed to verify the amount needed to pay off the loan on her truck.

"I hope you weren't injured in your accident, Ms. Robicheaux."

"I'll be fine. Just a little bumped around."

"Well, that's good to hear. Just one more second . . . ah, yes, you owe just a tad bit more than one payment on your truck. I can print the exact amount and fax it to you if you'd like."

Maryse rubbed her forehead, not sure she could stand all the confusion without at least taking an aspirin or fifty. "How can that be? I have two more years left on that loan."

"We've been splitting those extra checks every month and applying the money to your house and truck payments." The manager sounded confused. "Those were your instructions. I hope we didn't misunderstand."

"What extra checks?"

"Are you sure you're all right, Ms. Robicheaux?"

"I'm fine," Maryse replied, beginning to get a little irritated. "I'm just having trouble remembering everything. The doc says it will all come back in time."

"Okay," the manager said, but didn't sound completely convinced. "The first cashier's check was received in this office almost two years ago with instructions to apply it to your house. When you bought the truck, we received instructions to change application to half of the check on each of the loans. We've been doing that every month since."

"You've been receiving cashier's checks every month for almost two years?" A sneaky suspicion began forming in Maryse's mind—one she didn't understand in the least and wasn't even sure she wanted to. "Exactly how much are these cashier's checks for?"

"Five hundred twenty-five dollars. Are you sure you're all right, Ms. Robicheaux? This conversation is really starting to concern me."

"I have a doctor's appointment today," she managed to mumble. "Thanks." She hung up the phone and stared out the window over the bayou. She'd never sent the bank checks for five hundred twenty-five dollars, but she'd paid someone else that exact same amount every month for almost two years. "Helena!"

She stalked into the living room, but the ghost was nowhere in sight. It didn't take long to check every nook and cranny of a one-bedroom cabin, so it was only minutes before Maryse was certain the ghost had fled. And she'd bet it was during that phone call.

Maryse smelled a two-year-old rat. And she'd bet her truck payoff check that rat's name was Helena Henry.

Luc made it into the office a little early, but not for any reason except he just hadn't slept well. God knows, he wasn't attempting another break-in of Maryse's lab unless he did so in the dead of night. And given the woman's strange behavior, probably even that wasn't safe. Besides, he'd delivered the notebook to his buddy back at the agency. If anyone could get to the bottom of what Maryse was up to, it would be Brian.

He flipped his cell phone open just in case he'd missed a call but was once again disappointed by the blank display. Frustrated, he sat back in the chair and propped his feet on the desk. What the hell was he supposed to do now? Maryse was certainly easy on the eyes, so following her had been no hardship but had definitely been a study in bizarre. Still, it hadn't gotten him anywhere. From where he sat, the only thing Maryse was mixed up in was something to do with her in-laws and her missing husband, and he was no closer to finding the informant than he had been the first day here. If only the DEQ would let him branch out a bit and investigate some of the other residents, but his orders were clear—he was a zoologist and was to do nothing to make people think otherwise.

He rose from the desk and headed to the coffeepot on a corner table. At least making coffee was doing something productive. He dished the grounds up and was just about to fill the pot with water when his cell phone rang.

He reached into his pocket and, recognizing the agency's main number, he pressed the Talk button. "LeJeune."

"Luc, it's Brian. I got that information on the notebook."

Luc felt his hand tighten on the coffee pot handle. "And?"

"It was definitely chemical formulas—you were right about that."

"Okay, but for what?"

There was a slight pause on the other end. "We don't know exactly."

"Damn," Luc muttered. "Well, what *do* you know?"

"She's mixing up different plants, it looks like. Each combination is clearly identified by species and anything other than plants used to make the sample. They're all labeled with trial numbers, the way a big lab would do things."

"Okay, so she's trying to create something. Do we have any idea what?"

"Hell, it could be anything . . . weight-loss pills, hair products, a cure for insomnia . . . there's just no way of knowing unless we can see what she's testing this stuff on. You said there's no animals or anything like that in her lab, right? No refrigerators with little dishes with some of the mixture in it?"

Luc cast his mind back to his lab tour. "No, nothing like that. It's a tiny room. All that's there really is a couple of tables with the test tubes, burners, that sort of thing. I didn't see any evidence of testing on anything."

"Well, she's testing somewhere. All that effort is not for nothing. Have you gotten the trace on her phones yet? Maybe that will give you an idea where to head next, although I got to tell you, Luc, it doesn't look like this has anything to do with our case, and if the boss-man finds out, he's probably going to pull the plug on you."

"There's something going on with her," Luc argued. "Someone intentionally cut the brake lines on her truck."

"Unless it has something to do with our case, it's not your problem. Don't get involved, LeJeune. It always turns out bad."

Luc flipped his phone shut without answering. *Don't get involved.* Like it was that easy. He didn't understand his attraction to Maryse at all. Sure he'd dated plenty of women, but never for any reason other than a good time for a short time. Maryse pulled at him in a different way, and that made him very uncomfortable.

Usually women just hit him below the belt, and that was an easy fix, but Maryse challenged him on an intellectual level, and not just with his investigation. She was a complex woman, something he usually avoided like the plague.

But for the first time in his life, he found himself wanting to figure her out rather than run for the hills.

No matter his discomfort, he wasn't about to leave her unprotected if someone was trying to hurt her. She may not be part of his case, but that didn't mean she shouldn't have some help.

He finished filling the coffeepot with water and turned it on. Glancing at his watch, he realized Maryse should be at the office any minute, assuming she wasn't off on one of her many mysterious adventures. He turned on the computer and bypassed Maryse's sign-on screen using a hacker tip he'd picked up from Brian the day before. As soon as the operating system loaded, he double-clicked the internet icon and logged into his e-mail. Surely the phone trace was back by now—at least the last couple of days' worth.

He scanned the e-mail files, sorting through the usual spam that not even the government could manage to screen . . . improve sexual performance, new stock alert, penis enlargement . . . ah ha, phone tap results. He glanced out the window as he printed the file, happy to see the road was still clear of Maryse's rental.

This is it? One page for two phones? No matter how busy Maryse appeared, apparently it didn't involve much in the way of phone calling. He scanned the list, looking for something that stood out—the state office, the attorney in New Orleans, her friend in Mudbug, her insurance company—and, wait a minute, a laboratory at a university in New Orleans.

Jackpot.

That lab must be running the tests on whatever it was Maryse was cooking up. Another glance out the window let him know he was still in the clear, so he opened his cell and punched in Brian's number. "Brian, it's LeJeune. I need you to hack something for me."

"Okay," Brian said, "what's the case file number?"

Luc hesitated. "This one is off the record. At least for the time being."

"Oh, man, not your botanist in distress again? Do you know how much hell I caught over that stripper in New Orleans?"

"She wasn't a stripper, she was a performer, and you helped get her daughter back from the molester ex-husband who'd made off with the kid. Surely that was worth an ass-chewing."

"I guess. But one of these days, LeJeune, you might want to think about settling down with one woman instead of rescuing every one you come in contact with. And if you want my help with your Sir Lancelot routine, you're going to have to come up with something besides doing a good deed to convince me to risk that ass-chewing again. After all, I'm not privy to the same perks you're getting out of these deals."

Luc sighed, not about to admit that he was yet to receive a single perk from Maryse Robicheaux. In fact, it was exactly the opposite. The woman seemed to frustrate him on all levels. Something he wasn't exactly used to. "How about two tickets to this week's game?"

"How are the seats?"

"The best—they're mine."

"Throw in the use of your Corvette for the night and it's a deal."

"Absolutely not." Even Luc didn't remove his black, 1963 split-window dream machine from the garage unless it was a special occasion. "You know I only drive the Corvette when it's important."

"And you haven't seen the woman I plan on asking to the game."

Luc clenched his jaw. "Fine, but if you get so much as a scratch on her, I'll kill you, and you know I know how."

"Sounds reasonable. What do you need?"

"I need you to get some information for me. There's a lab at Tulane University in New Orleans where Maryse is sending her stuff for testing. I need to know what she's testing and why."

"Jesus, LeJeune! Do you really think the university is just going to hand over that kind of information just because I ask nicely? Her tests are protected information, especially if she's working on something she can patent."

"So get a warrant."

"Based on what, exactly? Hell, you won't even tell me why you want the information or give me a case number to support it. How am I supposed to convince a judge to go along with this plan of yours?"

Luc frowned. "Don't you have a friend, a contact, someone who could get you a line on the information?"

Brian sighed. "I've got a buddy who works in the science department. He might be willing to ask around. But he's going to need some time to do it with any finesse or it will look suspicious. Then someone might tip off your botanist."

"Yeah, okay. If that's the best we can do."

"And I mean real time, LeJeune, not an hour or two. This could take days, maybe even a week."

Luc looked out the window as the Maryse's boat raced up to the dock. He reached over to shut down the computer. "Just do your best. Make it as fast as you can, but tell your friend not to draw any attention to himself. I can't afford exposure."

"No problem. I'll call when I've got something."

Luc flipped his phone shut and watched as Maryse docked. Even from a distance, Luc could see her mouth set in a straight line, her upper body tensed. What now?

She entered the office without even a glance over, then poured a cup of coffee and stood staring at the wall while she drank. Luc stared at her back, then dropped his gaze to her behind, nicely tucked in a pair of old, tight-fitting jeans. "Do I dare even ask?"

"What?" Maryse spun around and looked at him as if realizing for the first time that he was in the room. "Oh, sorry. Good morning."

Luc raised his eyebrows and stared. Okay, it was even worse than he thought. She was being polite. "Good morning. Is everything all right with you? You seem a little . . . distracted."

"I'm just a little pissed and more than a little confused." She refilled her coffee, then dropped into her office chair with a sigh. "My life used to be so simple, you know? I did my job, had my side interests, one friend, one surrogate mother . . . no drama, no issues."

"Except for Hank," Luc pointed out.

Maryse nodded. "That's a given."

"And now you have other issues?"

"Jeez, LeJeune, haven't you been paying attention the last couple of days? My mother-in-law is dead, and Hank has yet to show up so I can serve him. The worse part is that's the least of my worries at the moment."

Intrigued, Luc leaned forward in his chair. "So what's the worst?"

"The worst is wondering what the hell Helena Henry has been up to all these years. I mean, the woman was the Antichrist of Mudbug. Even you had heard of her, and then she goes and leaves me the game preserve."

"Okay. But that's a good thing, right? I mean, if she'd have left it to Hank, he would have sold it off right away."

"Leased it," Maryse corrected. "The trust prevents an outright sale, but that's not the point." She picked up a pencil from the desk and started tapping it on the desktop.

Luc leaned back in his chair, giving her his full attention. "What else is there?"

Maryse looked over at him, her face full of uncertainty. "When Hank ran off, he owed money to a lot of the wrong kind of people. I had to borrow from Helena to pay them off." Then she told him about the payments she'd been making to Helena that had most likely been used to pay down her loans.

Luc sat back in his chair and stared at Maryse, now crystal clear on her confusion. "What the hell?"

Maryse shrugged. "I don't know. I mean, I have no friggin' idea. And it just makes me wonder how much manipulation has gone on behind my back. I get the feeling I was used, but I can't put my finger on how or for what purpose. There is no way Helena Henry paid that money on my loans to be nice. Helena doesn't know nice. Without an ulterior motive, she had no reason to get up in the morning."

"I agree. It sounds really strange, and given the source, I guess it would make me sort of nervous, too." He shook his head. "Too bad you didn't find out about the payments before the old bat died. You could have asked her yourself."

Maryse frowned and stared down at the floor. "Yeah, that is a shame."

Luc studied her for a moment. It was obvious from the way her eyes dropped to the floor that she was hiding something. But what? Given the weird situation she was in, it could be anything. In fact, Luc was surprised she'd even told him as much as she had. Obviously Maryse was in some mild level of shock if she was carrying on a personal conversation with him. Especially after that stunt he'd pulled yesterday, kissing her over the copy machine.

"I wish I had some advice," Luc finally said, "but I have to admit, I'm as stumped as you are. The whole thing is just too bizarre."

"Well, I'm not going to figure it out sitting around here." She gave Luc a small smile as she rose from her seat. "Thanks for listening. I know I haven't been the most pleasant person to be around, but I swear, I'm not usually this bad."

Luc shrugged. "You've got a lot going on, and I'm not the easiest person to be around, either."

Maryse laughed. "Yeah, you got that right. Anyway, I've got to get some work done today, whether my mind's in it or not." She pulled open a drawer in her desk and swore. "Crap, the map I need is at my cabin. I completely forgot I brought it home last week."

She pulled her sunglasses from her pocket. "Guess I'll be taking a detour before I work, huh? I'll see you later, Le-Jeune." She gave him a backwards wave and walked out of the office and down to the dock.

Luc watched as she threw the tie line into her boat and stepped down inside, pushing the boat from the dock as she went. What the hell was going on? Maryse was right—according to everything he'd ever heard, Helena Henry didn't do nice. And why charge her that outrageous interest, then pay her debts? Luc had no idea what Helena had been up to, but he had a feeling it wasn't much good. And he wondered just how much of a mess Helena's shenanigans had left Maryse in.

Something didn't feel right. And although he didn't like to talk about his feelings much, they were something Luc didn't ignore. He was much more intuitive than most—it's what made him so good at his job—and right now his senses were on high alert. Maryse Robicheaux was smack in the middle of something bad . . . he was certain.

And he was even more certain that she had no clue what it was.

He pulled his boat keys from his pocket and headed out of the office. If anything happened to Maryse, he'd feel guilty the rest of his life. She might not like him lurking around, but he saw no other way to figure out what was going on and offer her some protection. He'd just have to figure out a way to either watch her without being seen or come up with a reason for hanging around.

He had a five-minute boat ride to figure it all out.

Chapter Ten

All Maryse wanted to do was get the map and get into the bayou. With any luck, she'd be able to get some work done for the state *and* locate the plant she needed for the trials. But when she pulled her boat up to her cabin dock, Helena Henry was there, looking more upset than Maryse have ever thought possible.

"You can't go in there," Helena said, her face tense.

"Try to stop me. You still have some things to answer for, Helena, and don't think I forgot them just because you pulled a disappearing act this morning." Maryse stepped onto the dock and strode toward her cabin.

"No! Wait!" Helena hurried after her. "I think there's something wrong with your cabin."

Maryse stopped short. "What do you mean, something's wrong?"

"Your truck wreck got me to thinking. What if it wasn't an accident at all? So I've been watching your place as much as possible, figuring if the truck didn't work, then they might do something here. I made a quick trip to my house this morning after your phone call and hightailed it back here as soon as possible, but I was too late. I saw a man leaving as I walked across from the dock. He was carrying a duffle bag and got in a boat that was parked in that cove behind the cabin. Then he tore out of here something fierce."

"It was probably just kids. You know how teenagers traipse around the bayou."

Helena shook her head. "It wasn't a kid. This guy moved like an adult, his frame was mature—medium height and a ball cap."

Maryse stared at her. "Then who was it? C'mon, Helena, you know everyone in this town, same as me."

Helena shook her head again, the panic starting to show on her face. "I didn't see his face. And I couldn't catch up to the boat in time to read a license tag or anything. But he was up to no good. I know it. Why else would he dock in that cove and wade through the marsh to get up here when there's a perfectly good pier out front?"

Maryse glanced over at her cabin and bit her lower lip. Unfortunately, Helena was right—it didn't sound good. Suddenly, entering her cabin for a map didn't appear as easy as she'd originally thought. She looked once more at the cabin, then back at Helena. "So why don't you pop through a wall and take a look?"

Helena gave her a withering stare. "Don't you think I've already done that? I still can't move things. If he hid something in a cabinet or a drawer, I'd never see it. Not like I know what I'm looking for in the first place."

A sudden thought struck Maryse and she felt a chill rush over her. "Jasper was in the cabin this morning."

"Who the hell's Jasper?"

"My cat. I can't let anything happen to him."

Helena stared at her. "You mean that ragtag old tomcat missing an ear? That's what you're worried about?"

"I rescued that ragtag old tomcat from a fight with an alligator, and yes, I'm worried about him. He's family, whether you get that or not."

Helena shrugged. "You have strange ideas about family,

Maryse, but it doesn't matter either way. The cat took off out the kitchen window as soon as I walked into the cabin." She frowned and pursed her lips. "Maybe it's true what they say about cats seeing ghosts. He shot out of the room the first time I visited you, too."

As interesting as Helena's observation may have been some other time, Maryse just couldn't care about it at the moment. "You're sure he's not in there?"

"Positive," Helena said, and nodded. "He was halfway across the marsh when I looked out the window, but I'll pop in and take another look." She strolled up the path and through the wall of the cabin, then reappeared a couple of minutes later. "He's not there. I checked every nook and cranny."

"Okay. So what do you think I should do?"

"I don't know, but I don't want you going in that cabin. What if they left the gas on or something?"

Maryse considered her words and weighed her options. "You think he could have rigged something . . . like an explosion, maybe?" She ran one hand through her hair and tried to think. "Okay, if he rigged something to explode, then it would probably happen when I opened the front door, right? I mean, one look at my kitchen and anyone could see I don't cook, and besides, I had my gas turned off when I started construction on the cabinets."

Helena shook her head, clearly miserable. "I guess. I just don't know."

"Well, hell, that's the way it happens in the movies." She blew out a breath in frustration. "How should I know? We didn't exactly cover this sort of thing in college."

"Well, it wasn't covered in the society pages, either, so I don't know why you're getting all pissy with me. I'm trying to save your skinny ass from whatever that man cooked up."

Maryse clenched her jaw, not about to launch into why she was pissy with Helena. If not for Helena and her games, Maryse's skinny ass would be nice and safe. She took another look at the cabin. Mind made up, she drew her keys from her pocket and began walking toward the front door. Helena started to protest, but Maryse beat her to the punch. "I'm not going inside. I'm only going to unlock the door."

She crept up the path, feeling like a fool for sneaking up on her own home, and stopped at her front door, easing the key into the lock. It slid in silently, and she heard the barely audible click of chambers rolling inside the door as she turned the key to the left. Then she backed away from the cabin as quickly as possible and stopped at the dock next to Helena.

"What now?" Helena asked.

Maryse jumped into her boat and lifted the back seat to get into the storage box. "The latch on the front door is so old it doesn't hold anymore. Unless it's locked, even a good wind will blow it open."

"No wind today. Figures."

"No matter." Maryse reached into the box and pulled out a shotgun and a box of shells.

"What the hell are you doing?"

"Rubber bullets," Maryse explained. "I have to have them for the job. Not supposed to kill the critters, you know. They won't tear anything up, but it will be more than enough punch to open that door." Maryse grabbed the tie line for her boat and pulled it along the edge of the bank until it rested behind an overhang. "Better stand back," Maryse said as she loaded the gun. "I know nothing can touch you, but this might be scary if you're right about that guy."

Helena hesitated for a millisecond, then hopped into the boat next to Maryse. They stood on one side and peered over the edge of the bank. Satisfied with their position, Maryse lifted the shotgun over the bank and aimed it at the front door.

"You ready?" she asked Helena.

Helena covered her ears with both hands and nodded.

"Here goes," Maryse said, and pulled the trigger.

The shot seemed to happen in slow motion, although it couldn't have taken more than a second for the bullet to hit the door. The instant they heard the smack of the rubber on the wood, the door flung open, giving them a clear view of the inside of the cabin. Maryse was certain neither of them moved, or breathed, or even blinked, but as the seconds passed, only dead silence remained.

Maryse was just about to give the entire thing up as Helena's overactive imagination when the cabin exploded.

Maryse ducked behind the ledge and flattened herself against the dirt wall as flat as possible. If she hadn't been so frightened, she might have been amused to see Helena crouched there next to her as pieces of glass and wood flew everywhere—some hitting Maryse on her hands which covered her head, and some landing in the bayou behind them.

It took only seconds for the rain of glass and wood to stop, but it felt like forever. When the last piece of debris plopped into the water, Maryse waited another five seconds, then peeked over the bank and sucked in a breath at what she saw.

The cabin was completely leveled. Not a single wall remained, and even the bathtub was nowhere to be seen. That had her wondering for a moment since it was an old cast iron tub and had to weigh a ridiculous amount. She stared in stunned silence at the degree of damage, unable to make out anything, not even a wall. Absolutely everything had been torn apart by the blast.

Maryse swallowed the lump in her throat and tried to hold back tears when she caught a glimpse of something shiny hanging from one of the cypress trees. She strained her eyes to make out the object and realized with a jolt that it was a picture frame. Even with the metal twisted and black, she knew exactly what picture had hung in that frame.

Suddenly, Maryse's sadness and loss shifted to anger. Two years worth of anger, all bubbling forth at this exact moment. She screamed at the top of her lungs and pounded the embankment with her fists. Helena stepped back in surprise and fell off the back of the boat and onto the bayou where she rested on top of the water, rising and falling with the waves.

"This is all your fault!" Maryse shouted at Helena. "Like producing that sorry excuse for a human being you call a son wasn't enough—you had to rise from the dead, visible only to me, the person who probably despises you most, and then have the nerve to make me a moving target by leaving me some piece of land I was much better off without!"

Helena stared at her a moment, then looked down at the bayou, not saying a word.

"Look at this," Maryse cried, and waved an arm over the embankment at the disaster that used to be her home. "I have nothing left because of you. Everything I owned was in that house. And don't even talk to me about insurance because I don't want to hear it. How is insurance going to replace my mom and dad's wedding photo? How is insurance going to replace the Dr. Seuss books my mom read to me when I was a baby?"

Maryse bit her lip, trying to hold back the tears of anger that threatened to fall. "The only memory I have of her is reading those books. You've taken everything from me and given me nothing but trouble in return. I never thought I could hate you more than I did when I was paying Hank's debts, but I was wrong." She stared at Helena, but the ghost wouldn't even meet her eyes.

Disgusted, she started her boat and pulled away from the embankment, leaving Helena sitting on top of the bayou. Maryse's life was ruined. She had nothing left, not even the photos of her parents. She felt as if they were being erased from existence, all proof of her and her world being swept away. And even worse, obviously someone wanted her swept away with her memories.

Unless you beat the odds.

The thought ran through her head with a jolt. All of her anger at Helena and the situation with the will, at Hank for running out on her, at her mom for dying too soon, and her dad for following behind her mother with his stubbornness, came together in one instant, and she felt a sudden clarity run through her. There was one way to fix this. One way to make everything right.

Stay alive and keep that damned land.

Her resolution made, she shoved the throttle down on her boat and it leapt out of the water. Whoever had tried to kill her had made a fatal mistake in not getting the job done the first time, because now she was mad.

A mad scientist.

Luc had just pulled away from the dock when the explosion burst into the sky. "What the hell!" He raced down the bayou toward Maryse's cabin. *Stupid, stupid, stupid. You should have followed her more closely.*

He made the last turn and stared in shock. Her home was gone, completely leveled. It looked like something you saw in war footage. He scanned the patch of land for any sign of life, or a body, but couldn't make out a thing. As he zoomed closer to the bank, all hope disappeared. There was simply no way anyone could have survived that blast. No way.

He was reaching for his cell phone when Maryse's boat came around from the back side of the island. He held his breath as he stared at the driver and was relieved and surprised to see Maryse driving the boat. He cut his throttle and yelled at her and she guided her boat over to his. As she drew closer, he could see tiny cuts on her arms and a couple of nicks on her neck.

She came to a stop next to him and he reached over for her arm. "Are you all right? What happened?"

She looked at him, the anger on her face clear as day, but Luc knew that even though she was moving, driving a boat, she had to be in shock. He glanced over at the leveled cabin. No damn wonder. "Maryse," he said, and gently shook her, "are you all right? Are you hurt?"

Maryse blinked and seemed to recover a bit of herself. "What? No, I don't think so. I mean, I don't feel hurt." She gave him a frightened look. "Unless you see something I don't. I'm in shock, right? I might not feel anything."

Luc gave her a quick once-over. "I don't see anything life threatening, although you should definitely be checked out. What happened? Do you know?"

Maryse looked back at her cabin, her face flushed, her jaw tight. "It just exploded. I was pulling up to the dock and it exploded."

She was lying. Luc knew it, but whether it was about something important or something stupid, he could only imagine. "Did you see anyone near the island?"

Maryse shook her head, but Luc could tell she was holding back again.

"There wasn't anyone but me," she said.

Luc flipped open his cell phone and dialed the police.

"The first thing we're going to do is call the police. They need to get someone to look at this. Then we're getting you to a hospital, just to be sure." He held his hand out to Maryse. "Why don't you step over into my boat? I can tow yours back to the office."

Maryse hesitated for a moment, but he was relieved when she took his hand with no argument and stepped over into his boat. She kept looking back at the island—not at the demolished cabin, but scanning the entire area. What in the world was she looking for? Had there been another person there?

Luc got Maryse seated, then secured her boat behind his with a tie line. He was just about to pull away when Maryse yelled.

"Jasper!" Maryse pointed to the island at something moving around a clump of cypress trees. She spun around and looked at Luc. "That's my cat, Jasper. I was afraid he was in the cabin. We have to go get him."

Luc looked over at the small speck of yellow and smiled. "Of course we do." He slowly turned the boat and crept towards the bank. "I'm going slow so I don't spook him," he said. "The poor thing is probably already stressed enough."

Maryse nodded. "Thanks."

It took them a minute to get to the bank, and before he could even assist, Maryse scrambled up the side and called the cat. Luc looked over the embankment in time to see the old tom wrap himself around Maryse's legs and allow her to pick him up. She smiled and kissed the top of his head, then headed back to the boat, passing Luc the cat so she could get in.

Luc reached for the cat, who didn't even protest at being in a stranger's arms. Then again, animals usually had an instinct about when people were trying to help them. He rubbed the cat behind his one ear and passed the animal to

Maryse after she took her seat. "He's a little rough around the edges, huh?"

Maryse nodded. "Yeah. He's definitely a fighter. I think that's why I like him so much."

Luc smiled. "Well, let's get back to the office and drop Jasper off there. Then we can take a trip to the hospital. I want to make sure that head injury from your car wreck wasn't aggravated by being so close to the blast."

Maryse shrugged. "Whatever you think."

Luc looked over at her as he pulled away from the island. She clutched the cat to her chest and stared straight ahead. Her face was drawn, her neck stilled flushed with red. Luc had absolutely no idea what the hell had just happened, but he'd bet his last dollar that Maryse knew something. Something she wasn't about to tell.

And from where Luc stood, that something was going to get her killed.

It took them about forty-five minutes to dock, secure the cat, and make the drive to the hospital. Maryse called Sabine on the way—one, because she knew Sabine and Mildred were bound to hear about her cabin soon and she didn't want them panicking, and two, because she was going to need a place to stay and something to wear if she planned on showering again. She figured Mildred would give her a room at the hotel and Sabine would come up with something temporary for her clothes-wise.

After reassuring her friend that she was unhurt, Maryse flipped her cell phone shut and leaned her head back against the seat, closing her eyes. She was doing her best to hold everything in, but she was still so angry with Helena that she knew Luc was suspicious about what was going on. Like she could tell him even if she wanted to. *Hey, Luc, it's no big deal. I'm just being haunted by my dead mother-in-law who left me a bunch of land full of oil that now apparently people are trying to kill me for.* Yeah, that would work. That was believable.

She held in a sigh as they walked into the emergency room, hoping this was Christopher's day off. The last thing she needed was to be embarrassed on top of depressed and angry. There just wasn't room in her head for another emotion. The admitting nurse took one look at her and motioned her toward the double doors to the side of reception. Maryse asked Luc to wait in the lobby, then followed the nurse down the hall.

Either they weren't busy at all or Maryse looked much worse than she thought. But as they passed a couple of empty rooms, Maryse decided it was the first. Obviously she'd picked a great time to have an emergency. They had passed three empty rooms when the nurse's pager went off. She glanced down at the pager, then shook her head.

"The second room on the left," the nurse said, and pointed down the hall. "If you don't mind taking a seat in there, I'll send the doctor right in."

The nurse muttered something under her breath as she turned, and although it wasn't clear, Maryse could swear she'd said "as soon as I find him." How exactly did one lose a doctor in a hospital? Didn't they have pagers too? She glanced back at the nurse who strode down the hall with obvious purpose and shook her head.

Turning back around, Maryse studied the doors in front of her. Second room on the right or left? Hell, she couldn't remember. Maybe she *did* have a head injury. Oh well, what was the worst that could happen—she opened the wrong door and saw someone naked or something? God knows she'd seen worse, especially lately.

She took a couple of steps forward and pulled open the door on the right. It was immediately obvious that this was not the right room. In fact, it wasn't a room at all—it was a storage closet, but the most interesting thing was it was already occupied.

By Dr. Christopher and a candy-striper.

Christopher apparently had a bit of a sweet tooth, because he'd taken the "candy-striper" title to heart. His mouth was all over the girl, and if the volunteer coordinators saw what was going on under that uniform, Maryse was fairly sure they'd have had heart attacks right on the spot.

They jumped apart as the light flooded in, but it was too late. Maryse had already seen enough. "What the hell are you doing?" she yelled, and took a good look at the rumpled candy-striper, who was grabbing for the thin strip of lace wrapped around her ankle and trying to shove it back up her butt where it belonged. "That girl isn't even eighteen. Are you crazy?"

Christopher jumped up and ran over to her. "Now, Maryse, this isn't what it looks like. I was just helping Emily with her anatomy class, and she didn't want anyone to see. She's a bit shy about presentation."

Maryse stared at him in disbelief and disgust. Why in the world had she thought this guy was a great catch? "Do you think I'm that stupid?" she asked, and Christopher inched toward her, his hands out.

Maryse stepped back. "Don't step one foot closer to me. I'm warning you."

"But, Maryse, honey, I swear I can explain."

Honey? Honey! She glared at Christopher as he made the fatal error of touching her arm. To hell with it. She clenched her hand and punched him as hard as she could in the jaw, causing him to cry out in surprise. Staggering backwards in shock, he fell over a towel rack, knocking Emily, who was still trying to reassemble her clothing, down on the ground in a heap. The sound of material ripping seemed to echo in the tiny closet. Maryse looked down to see the lacy thong now hanging in two pieces around one of Emily's skinny white thighs.

The commotion brought the admitting nurse and two orderlies rushing down the hall where they all screeched to a halt and stared at the spectacle in front of them. "Dr. Warren," the admitting nurse said, her lips pursed in disapproval. "I thought Director Stone was very clear about this the last time. I'm afraid I have no choice but to report you. And I'd start packing my things if I were you." The nurse looked at the candy-striper and frowned. "And shame on you, Emily. When your mother hears what I have to say . . ." She shook her head in obvious disgust and stomped down the hall, apparently in search of the director.

"Now see what you've done?" Christopher accused, struggling to rise from the floor.

Maryse laughed. "What I've done? Have you lost your mind? I wasn't the one in a compromising position with a minor."

Christopher rose from the floor and glowered at Maryse, his face bright red with embarrassment and anger. Emily, now reasonably covered and clutching what was left of her almost nonexistent underwear, scurried past and fled down the hall, probably trying to figure out how to avoid going home until she was sixty.

"Like you weren't seeing other people," Christopher accused. "We've only had one date anyway, and it was horrible. Hardly grounds for a commitment."

"You think I want a commitment with you?" Maryse

stared. "You *have* lost your mind. At least I don't date children. You need serious help, Christopher, and if I were that girl's dad, I'd shoot you." Maryse paused for a moment, a vision of the rumpled Emily flashing through her mind. Why was she familiar?

Then it hit her—a video replay of her meeting with one of Hank's "lenders," who had insisted on receiving payment during his daughter's soccer game. "Oh my God," Maryse said. "You've been fooling around with the underage daughter of the biggest loan shark in Mudbug." Maryse began to laugh. "That nurse was right—you better pack, and right away. If Lou Marcel catches you, there won't even be anything left for the nutria."

Christopher blinked and stared at her, wide-eyed. "Lou Marcel is Emily's father?"

Maryse nodded and gave him a big smile. The orderlies chuckled beside her.

"Oh shit!" The color drained from Christopher's face, and he glanced down both corridors. "I've got to get out of here." With that, he spun around and sprinted down the hall. At the end, he made a sharp turn and slid on the waxed floor of the hall until he had to place one hand down to maintain his balance. The orderlies dashed after him, either wanting to see more of the show or to ensure he didn't leave the hospital before the director got a hold of him.

Maryse stared after them, shaking her head. What the hell had she been thinking? For once, she should have listened to Helena, and that was just wrong on so many levels.

First Hank, then Dr. Deviant. What a track record.

Maryse heard laughter behind her and spun around, afraid she recognized that voice. She did. Helena Henry stood in the hall, her shoulders shaking. Her guffaws would have carried to the next state if anyone could have heard her besides

Maryse. "Oh my God," Helena said as she tried to regain control of herself. "That was the funniest thing I've ever seen. I wish I would have caught it from the beginning."

Maryse glared. "I am not in the mood for you, Helena. I left you back at the cabin for a reason. Why did you follow me here?" Maryse stalked across the hall toward the lobby. She needed the correct room, and apparently a new doctor. "My blood pressure is going to be through the roof when they take it, no thanks to you. I'll end up hospitalized for sure."

Helena looked contrite as she struggled to keep up with Maryse's pace down the hall. "I know you're mad, and I can't say that I blame you, but I had to make sure you were all right. I checked at your office, but when I saw your boat docked and Luc's Jeep gone, I hoped he took you to the hospital."

Maryse stopped short and gave Helena a hard look. "We need to talk, and we will, but not right now. You have a lot to answer for."

Maryse pushed the door to the lobby open and stalked through. Luc jumped up from his chair, looking somewhat surprised. "What's wrong?" he asked.

"Bachelor number two," Helena said and hooted.

Maryse shot her a dirty look and mumbled, "Don't even start." She waved one hand at Luc. "Nothing's wrong. I just need to find out if I'm actually going to see a doctor today."

Luc raised his eyebrows and looked from Maryse to the admitting nurse, who was standing behind the admissions desk frowning at both of them. "I saw that doctor take out of here like he'd been shot," Luc said, and gave Maryse a questioning look.

"Ha!" Helena said. "He hasn't been shot yet." She looked over at Maryse and shook her head. "I still can't believe you went out with him."

Maryse tried to block Helena from her mind and walked over to the nurse. "Can you please find someone else to take a look at me? I really need to get on with my day, and I've had quite enough of this hospital. I'm sure you can appreciate that."

The nurse gave her a curt nod and pointed back to the doors. "Take a seat in room two. The first one on the right. I'll have Dr. Breaux right in. But Ms. Robicheaux, the hospital director will want to speak with you about this situation with Emily."

Maryse sighed. "If he can't make it down before the exam is over, he can reach me at the Mudbug Hotel. Leave a message with Mildred." Maryse turned from the desk and stalked off to room two. She had just perched her hiney on the cold, hard table when Helena entered the room, followed closely by Luc.

Luc sat in a chair in the corner and looked over at Maryse. "So am I getting this right? Those orderlies said you caught that doctor in a storage closet with a loan shark's underage daughter?"

"Yeah," Maryse replied. "That's pretty much it."

Luc whistled. "Boy, I don't give him ten minutes to hide after her dad hears."

"Serves him right."

Luc gave her a curious look. "And you went out with this guy?"

Maryse stared at him. "How in the world did you know that?"

Luc smiled and pointed at Helena. "The ghost said so."

Chapter Eleven

Maryse froze at Luc's words and knew that she had stopped breathing altogether. After a couple of seconds of complete immobility, she cast an anxious glance at Helena, who was standing stock still, staring at Luc in obvious shock.

Maryse realized he was looking straight at Helena. "You can see her?" she managed to squeak out.

Luc nodded. "Plain as day. Absolutely horrid pink suit."

Maryse gasped and struggled to maintain her cool.

Helena stared at him in disbelief. "But how is that possible?" she asked.

Luc shrugged, not the least bit bothered by the situation. "I don't know. Family tradition, I suppose."

Maryse stared. "You hear her, too?"

Luc grimaced. "Unfortunately. Why do you think I looked behind you when you entered the lobby? I heard two voices approaching clear as day, but then you were the only one who came through the door. Helena walked through the wall a couple of seconds later." He looked from Maryse to Helena. "How long has she been hanging out with you?"

"Since the funeral, much to my dismay," Maryse said.

Luc looked at Helena, then back at Maryse and smiled. "No wonder you've been so bitchy. What the hell did you do to earn being haunted by your dead mother-in-law?"

Maryse bristled at his words. "First of all, I didn't *do* anything to make her show up. She just did, and now my life is pure misery. Second of all, I've always been bitchy to rude, pushy people. Helena has nothing to do with that."

"Man, that's bad karma in a way I've never seen before."

Maryse shot him a dirty look, and Luc wisely decided to lead off from that line of conversation. "So the storage closet story?" he asked.

Helena hooted and dissolved in laughter, sinking down the wall and onto the floor in a heap. "I tried to tell her that doctor was a loser and a cad, but would she listen? No way."

"And you would know a cad, right?" Maryse shot back. "Especially since you married one and had the nerve to continue that genetic defect into the next generation. You should have at least done the world a favor and had Hank neutered when he hit puberty. That way we'd be sure the scourge on humanity couldn't continue."

Helena clamped her mouth shut and looked a bit sheepish.

Luc laughed and gave Helena a once over. "So what's with the pink suit?"

"Do you think it was mine?" Helena shouted, an indignant look on her face. "Last I checked, the morgue didn't ask the dead to pick out their wardrobe."

"Maybe it was one of Harold's floozies," Maryse suggested and took a good look at Helena. Something was different. It took her a second to realize that instead of the uncomfortable twenty-year-old pumps she used to wear, Helena's feet were now decked out in a brand new pair of Nike running shoes. Maryse stared at the shoes in amazement. "Helena, how did you change your shoes?"

Helena huffed. "Don't you think if I knew, I would have changed the whole outfit? Damn it, I was walking to the hospital and thinking a pair of running shoes would really come in handy. Next thing I knew, that's what I was wearing. As soon as I figure out how I did it, this pink monstrosity is gone."

Before Maryse could reply, Dr. Breaux entered the room, giving Luc a curious look.

Figuring that was his cue, Luc nodded to the doctor and said to Maryse, "I'll wait for you in the lobby." Then he left the room with Helena trailing behind him, yapping away as only Helena could yap. Maryse let out a sigh of relief. Maybe Helena would start hounding Luc and give her a break.

Thirty minutes later, Dr. Breaux pronounced her fit for anything that didn't encompass fast movement, eye strain, stress, or aggravation. Given her life at the moment, Maryse figured the only way to avoid that was death. Which would apparently fit right in with someone's plan.

At the front desk, she signed the papers for yet another insurance claim and turned to find Luc standing alone in the lobby. She glanced around but didn't see hide nor hair of Helena. She studied Luc for a moment. If he'd figured out a way to get rid of Helena, he might be worth keeping around. The lesser of two evils. Luc motioned to the front door, and she followed him out of the hospital with a clear view of the back end of his Levi's. Definitely the better looking of the two.

Maryse figured Luc would drive her straight to the hotel, but instead he parked in front of Johnny's Bar.

"You need to eat something," he said. "You have to take pain meds and probably haven't eaten today, have you?"

Maryse thought back to the odd phone call from the bank that had started her day. Good God, was that really only *this* morning? If every day was as long as this one, staying alive for another four days was going to age her a hundred years. She was definitely going to have to get a better moisturizer.

Luc was staring at her, and it took Maryse a moment to realize she had worked through everything in her own mind but hadn't answered his question. "Sorry. I had to think about it for a minute, but you're right, I haven't eaten yet today."

Luc gave her a sympathetic nod. "Then let's get some food in you. Besides, you and I have to talk." And after delivering that cryptic phrase, Luc headed into the bar before Maryse could even formulate a question.

They sat at the table in the corner—the private one that Maryse and Sabine preferred. They'd barely gotten seated before Johnny appeared at their table, wiping old grease off his hands with a dirty dishcloth, the worry on his face clear as day.

"Maryse!" He studied the cuts on her head and arms. "Are you all right? I was cleaning the grease traps and heard that blast all the way back in the kitchen. I thought for sure you were a goner until Mildred called and said you were on your way to the hospital." He scanned her again, an anxious look on his face. "So, you're okay? Nothing serious?"

Maryse smiled up at her father's friend. "I'm fine, Johnny. Just a raging headache and some cuts, but nothing life threatening."

Johnny looked a little apprehensive but nodded. "What happened?"

Maryse shook her head. "I have no idea. I was just pulling up to the cabin when it exploded. Good thing I wasn't any closer."

"Jesus, Maryse." Johnny tugged his blue jeans back up around his waist and took in a deep breath. "I saw the fire department head that way. Are they going to investigate?"

Maryse nodded. "Oh, yeah. The fire department, the

police department, and who knows who else. Not that there's much left to look at."

"Doesn't matter," Luc said. "If the fire department suspects foul play, they'll call in specialists. There's very little that gets by an investigator trained for this sort of thing."

Johnny paled a bit and looked at Luc, his eyes wide. "Foul play?" He looked back at Maryse. "I never thought . . . you're sure?"

"The entire place was leveled," Luc said. "What are the chances that's accidental?"

Johnny stared down at Maryse and hesitated a few seconds before speaking. "Maryse, I heard a little about the will reading. Maybe you should take an extended vacation or something. Get the hell out of here until it's safe."

"And when will that be, Johnny? No one has any way of knowing, and I'm not leaving here with this whole inheritance mess hanging over my head." She clamped her mouth shut, not about to reveal the real reason she couldn't leave.

Johnny nodded but didn't look pleased. "Harold was in here raising hell last night about him and Hank being cut out of the will." He frowned. "You know, he'd be just crazy enough to try something like this."

Mayrse nodded. "He's already threatened me, and believe me, that will be the first name I give to the police."

Luc shook his head. "I could be wrong, but I think whoever set that blast knew what they were doing. Someone with experience." He looked up at Johnny. "You got any ex-military in Mudbug?"

Johnny let out a single laugh. "Are you kidding? Hell, practically every man in this town over the age of forty was military. The economy back then didn't offer as many opportunities for young men as it does now."

Luc sighed. "I was afraid of that."

Johnny scrunched his brow in obvious thought. "Harold was military. He's always in here bragging about it."

"What did he do?" Luc asked.

Johnny shrugged. "No way of my knowing for sure, but he's always claimed he was special forces."

"Thanks, I'll look into that." Luc studied Johnny for a moment. "What about you?"

"Me?" Johnny laughed. "Oh, hell, I was a mess cook. Why do you think I opened this place? Toss some food on the grill, pour some beers. Just like being back in the service."

Maryse smiled. "You might need to throw a burger or two on the grill for yourself, Johnny. You've dropped a few pounds."

Johnny looked a bit embarrassed. "Wouldn't hurt me to lose a couple more." He placed a hand on Maryse's shoulder. "You let me know if you need anything. I'll send Jeff over to get your order." Johnny nodded to Luc, then walked back to the kitchen.

"Well," Luc said, "looks like the first thing we need to do is find out exactly what Harold did during his time in the military."

"And how are we going to do that?"

Luc grimaced. "We should probably start with asking Helena."

"Great," Maryse mumbled. She stared out the window for a moment, trying to roll everything that had happened to her in the past couple of days into some kind of sense, but it was so extraordinary that she couldn't even start. Giving it up as futile, she looked back at Luc. "What family tradition?"

"Huh?"

"Back at the hospital, you said you could see Helena because of family tradition. What does that mean?"

"Oh, well, it's simple really. People in my family have been seeing the dead for as many generations as there are stories about it. My great-great grandmother claimed to have seen over sixty ghosts in her lifetime. But then, she lived to be a hundred and five."

Maryse gasped. "Sixty ghosts!" She was completely unable to grasp the idea of seeing, and more importantly *hearing*, sixty Helenas. "How in the world did she live past a hundred with all those ghosts around? I'm ready to kill myself over one."

Luc laughed. "They weren't all around at the same time. Hell, that would give anyone a heart attack. In fact, I think the most she ever had speaking at once was two and they were twins, so I guess it sorta figured."

Maryse shook her head in disbelief. "And none of this bothers you? Because I have to tell you, I'm creeped out every time I see her, even if only for a millisecond."

"Hell yeah, it bothers me," Luc said. "Why do you think I left a small town and hightailed it to the city? There may be more ghosts roaming around, but it's a lot harder for them to figure out you can see them if they're among so many people. I've managed to fly below the radar for ten years. Until now. Damn small towns."

Luc glanced around the room and leaned across the table toward Maryse. "You know someone's trying to kill you."

Maryse was a bit taken aback at the directness. "Wow. I know the explosion couldn't have been an accident, so that's really the only explanation, but when you put it that blunt, it makes it even scarier than before."

Luc nodded. "It's not the first time, either."

Maryse stared at him and narrowed her eyes. "What do you mean?"

"My buddy at the dealership said someone cut your brake lines on your truck. Your wreck was no accident."

"And you're just now telling me about this? Don't you think that was information I needed before now?"

Luc had the decency to look embarrassed. "I'm sorry, Maryse, but I was a bit confused at first since your wreck happened *before* the reading of the will, so it didn't add up. Then after I heard about the whole inheritance thing, I figured Harold or someone else found out ahead of time and took a snipe at you. Cutting brake lines is not exactly a clear-cut route to death. In fact, it's probably not a good route at all."

Maryse slowly nodded, understanding his point. "But an explosion is a whole different story."

"Bet your ass it is," Luc said and narrowed his eyes at Maryse. "So are you going to tell me what you're involved in that's going to get you killed?"

Maryse nodded. "It's got to be the land. There's a clause in the inheritance."

"What clause?"

"The land inheritance has clauses tied to it that have to be fulfilled over the next week in order for the title to pass to me. One of the clauses is that I have to outlive Helena for seven days following her burial."

"Jesus Christ!" Luc stared at her for a moment, then lowered his voice again. "Then Johnny's right—you've got to get out of town for a while. I have family in places no one would ever find you. They can keep you protected for a week, easy."

Maryse shook her head. "I can't leave Mudbug. That's another one of the clauses. If I leave, everything passes to Hank, and he'd lease the land as fast as possible."

"He'd have to find a taker first," Luc said. "Maybe in ten years or so development would be pushing this way, but right now? Even the chemical company couldn't put together an expansion plan quickly. It would take years."

"Yeah, but didn't I tell you? Helena's only just bothered to mention that the preserve is full of oil."

Luc stared. "Good Lord, the woman's practically signed your death warrant."

"I don't think that was her intention, but it's certainly starting to look that way."

Luc looked out the window for a moment, then shook his head and looked back at Maryse. "Well, this problem is way too big to be solved over lunch, but I guess the first thing we need to do is get you somewhere safe. You think the hotel is okay?"

Maryse shrugged. "Heck if I know. Mildred lives there, and the hotel is usually at least half-filled with salesmen and such for the chemical company. I should be okay there, but I hate putting Mildred in the middle of this mess."

"I don't like it either, but you have to stay somewhere that's easy to watch, and the hotel is your best option in Mudbug. Are you going to tell Mildred what's going on?"

"What other choice do I have? My house exploded. She's going to wonder what happened, and Mildred's too sharp for me to pass off some bullshit explanation."

"And what about the Helena returning from the dead part?"

"Oh, no! I don't need Mildred worried about my sanity, too. She doesn't believe in this sort of thing and isn't likely to start regardless of what I say. No, Helena has to remain mine, yours, and Sabine's little secret."

"Sabine?" Luc asked.

"My best friend. She owns the psychic shop in downtown."

Luc's face cleared in understanding. "Ah, psychic, huh? So I guess she has no trouble taking on a haunting."

"Oh, she has plenty of trouble, especially with exactly who's doing the haunting, but she's doing some research to try and help us figure out some things—mainly how Helena can ascend or depart or whatever."

"You might want to put a hold on that."

"Why?"

"I would imagine that Helena knows plenty she still hasn't told you. Not to mention she's a much better choice for eavesdropping on suspects than either of us." Luc sighed. "Unfortunately, until we figure out exactly what's going on here, Helena is worth more to us dead."

The fear on Mildred's face was clear as day when Luc came hauling Maryse into the hotel. The hotel owner ran across the lobby, as only large women can run, and started to gather her up in a hug. Apparently, she remembered Maryse's injuries and placed a hand on her arm instead. "Oh, my God, child, are you all right?"

"I'm fine, Mildred. Just a few cuts and my head's pounding a bit again, but nothing to be concerned with."

Mildred stared at Maryse as if she'd lost her mind, then looked over at Luc, whose expression apparently didn't do anything to convince her to the contrary. She looked back at Maryse. "Nothing to be concerned with? Are you kidding me? That explosion at your cabin carried all the way to downtown. Why, when I heard it was your place, Johnny had to stop me from swiping his boat and heading over there myself. I swear I would have swam if I had to."

Maryse smiled. "I know you would have. I'm surprised Johnny won the fight over his boat."

Mildred flushed a bit. "Well, I couldn't get the damned thing started or I would have gotten away with it. Then I came back into the hotel and was just about to grab my keys and head to the dock when Sabine called and told me to hold tight and prepare a room for you." She gave Maryse a hard look. "What the hell is going on, Maryse?" She looked over at Luc. "And what is he doing taxiing you around?"

"It's sort of a long story. Why don't you put on a pot of coffee, and I'll take a shower. Luc will fill you in on the high points in the meantime."

Mildred pursed her lips, obviously wanting an answer right away but not about to argue the fact that Maryse could obviously use a shower. "Okay," Mildred said finally. "I've got a new caramel blend I can put on and some butter cookies I just baked yesterday. You go on with your shower. Sabine brought some clothes by earlier to tide you over until you can buy some more." She pointed a finger at Luc. "*You* can follow me to the kitchen and start explaining exactly what the hell happened and how you got in the middle of it."

Maryse smiled at the look of dismay on Luc's face. She knew he was probably itching to make phone calls or revisit the blast site or something that proved his cleverness or masculinity. Instead, he was stuck answering to Mildred over caramel coffee and butter cookies.

"Go ahead and tell her everything," Maryse instructed.

Luc nodded and headed through the double doors that Mildred had indicated. The hotel owner pulled back her shoulders and followed him. Maryse took one final look at

Luc's retreating figure and sighed. Like she needed to feel any more attraction to Luc LeJeune. She'd spent the last couple of days trying desperately to ignore the sparks between them, and now here he was, looking out for her and seeing her ghost.

The first time she'd met him, Maryse had thought he was just another playboy with a roving eye, but apparently there was another side to Luc that he obviously didn't let out for just everyone.

He'd shown Maryse that other side, but for the life of her, she had no idea why.

Luc watched the hotel from across the street and saw Maryse close the blinds to her hotel room window. Good. She should stay put for a while, and if she got any foolish ideas about leaving the hotel before he returned, Mildred had promised to handcuff her to the stair railing. She'd even showed him the handcuffs, which had given him a moment of pause.

He looked across the parking lot, half-expecting to see Helena strolling around like she hadn't done anything wrong, but apparently the ghost had decided to lay low for a bit. He shook his head and walked toward his Jeep. He wasn't happy about seeing Helena, but it did explain why Maryse had been acting so strangely. In fact, given everything she had going on, he was somewhat surprised she'd held things together as well as she had.

He took one final look at the hotel, satisfied that Maryse was in capable hands, and pulled his cell phone out of his pocket as he climbed in his Jeep. He'd already had one text message today from his boss, and with everything that had happened, he hadn't had an opportunity to call in without blowing his cover. But he couldn't put off calling the office any longer. Wilson rarely called Luc when he was in the field. If he felt the need to leave a message, something must be up.

He dialed his office and his boss picked up on the first ring.

"Damn it, LeJeune!" Wilson shouted. "Where the hell have you been all day?"

Luc moved the phone a couple of inches from his ear until he was sure the yelling was over. "There was a situation with my suspect."

"Spill it, LeJeune. I don't have all day like you do."

"Someone tried to kill her."

"Are you positive?"

"Her house exploded."

There was a couple of seconds pause, and Luc knew Wilson was rolling this piece of information around in his mind. "Well, I guess that might be hard to construe any other way. So I take it she wasn't in the house?"

"On her way up to it when it blew. We just got back from the hospital."

Wilson groaned. "Do not tell me you're white knighting this woman around to doctor's appointments and to have her hair done. Are you trying to look suspicious? As far as she's concerned, you barely know her, LeJeune. Act like the stranger you're supposed to be before someone makes you."

"I'm not going to hair appointments, and I just happened to be in the vicinity when her cabin exploded so I took her to the emergency room. Any decent person would have done that—stranger or no."

"Maybe, but be careful. Remember, I never wanted you on the assignment in the first place. Your grandparents lived entirely too close to Mudbug for my comfort. There's still the possibility of you being recognized."

"My grandparents moved almost five years ago," Luc argued, "and I haven't been there to visit since I was in high school. They preferred to come to the city to see me."

"Family visiting preferences aside, you better stay low on this one or I'm going to yank you out."

"I understand, but I'm wondering if all this is related to our case. There's no way this was an amateur job. There's not a single piece of that cabin left over two feet long."

Wilson sighed. "Well, keep an eye on her for now, but I have to tell you, it's looking more and more like the informant is that accountant that Agent Duhon is on. I'm expecting a break anytime. And when I get it . . ."

"I understand," Luc said, and closed his phone. His time was running out. As soon as they had the informant, his business with Maryse was over and he would be expected back in New Orleans. And that left Maryse with no one to protect her but a fake psychic, a hotel owner with a pair of fuzzy handcuffs, and a ghost wearing bad polyester.

Luc gave her ten, fifteen minutes tops.

Maryse awoke the next morning with another pounding headache and immediately decided that head injury headaches were much, much worse than the drinking kind. Her poor body had seen more abuse in the last couple of days than it usually did in years. She groaned as she got out of bed and turned a tired eye to the alarm clock on the nightstand. Only six A.M. Habit, she knew, but if ever there was a day she'd have liked to sleep in, this would have been it.

The day before had been long and intense, first Luc filling Mildred in on the basics, with Sabine joining them for most of the conversation. Then Maryse had made her appearance, and it was all she could do to keep Mildred and Sabine from bundling her up and hauling her out of town, regardless of land, oil, inheritance, or anything else. She'd finally convinced them to leave it alone for the night at least, but she could tell that no one was happy going to bed with no plan of action.

She shuffled into the bathroom to survey the damage and groaned. It wasn't a pretty sight and definitely wasn't going to help her "stay in Mudbug" argument. Even Jasper, who was drinking out of the toilet despite a perfectly good bowl of water in the bedroom, paused for a moment and stared.

The bruises on her arms and legs from the truck wreck were purple with that nasty-looking yellow around the edges. The cuts were not deep and wouldn't scar, but they dotted her hands like bright red freckles. Fortunately, in all of this, she'd remembered to protect her face, but the stress and lack of sleep were showing there. The bags under her eyes were so dark they looked like she was ready to play a quarter in the NFL, and to top it all off, they were puffy, probably from all the yelling she did yesterday mixed with the intermittent tears last night.

She looked like a hybrid raccoon strung out on acid.

Although she knew her appearance should be the least of her concerns at the moment, Maryse also knew that unless she managed to pull off a semblance of control, she'd never convince Mildred and Sabine she should stay in Mudbug. Or if she did, they'd never want her to leave the hotel, and that just wasn't an option since it put Mildred at risk.

And then there was Luc.

A whole other problem and definitely an enigma. She knew he was more than a little troubled, especially with Helena in the mix, but if he had any thoughts or opinions on the situation, he'd held them in last night, instead choosing to listen for a change. Which made Maryse more than a little nervous. What was going on in that head of his? His revelation about seeing Helena had thrown her for a loop but also made her feel closer to him, something she'd definitely been trying to avoid.

Realizing she wasn't going to solve all her problems or get a decent cup of coffee standing in front of the bathroom mirror, she shrugged off the T-shirt Mildred had loaned her to sleep in and made a quick pass through the shower. Sabine, in her infinite wisdom, had started off Maryse's replacement wardrobe with loose-fitting sweats and T-shirts from Wal-Mart.

Given the bruises and the overall soreness, Maryse was happy with Sabine's choices. The sweats were a light, thin fabric and wouldn't be hot at all, and they were much less restrictive than the jeans Maryse usually wore. Probably wouldn't stand up very well to a day in the bayou, but at the moment, it appeared her days in the bayou were coming to a screeching halt. She fluffed her damp hair, pulled on her tennis shoes, then headed to Mildred's office, hoping the woman had taken mercy on her and picked up some donuts.

Mildred was in her office, but she wasn't alone. Sabine sat across the desk from her, and surprisingly enough, Luc occupied the other chair. Conversation ceased the moment Maryse entered the room, and she immediately knew that the three had been plotting some way to "take care" of her. She looked from face to face, but no one met her gaze. It seemed that the floor was far more interesting.

"It's a little early for a booster club meeting, isn't it?" Maryse asked. "And don't even bother making excuses. Sabine hasn't been out of bed before eight o'clock since high school."

Apparently, they hadn't prepared for her to wake so early, and no one had a ready excuse for their treason. Mildred cast a guilty look at Sabine, and Sabine and Luc stared at the wall past Mildred's shoulder. Maryse raised her eyebrows and stared at them one at a time, waiting for a response. "Cat got your tongues?" she finally asked.

"Now, Maryse," Mildred said, obviously going to take a shot at the peacemaker role. "We're just worried about you is all. This whole situation has gotten out of hand. And don't tell me you can handle it yourself. It's just too big for one person."

Maryse turned her back to them and poured a cup of coffee, making note that the coffeepot was the old one that Mildred had claimed was broken. Not that it surprised her.

She stalled for another couple of seconds, not yet ready reply. The truth was Mildred was right. This situation *was* too big for her to handle alone. But the last thing she wanted to do was involve people she cared about in her mess—people she considered family. Which left only Luc, and Maryse was too scared to have the sexy zoologist that close too her. She didn't need her attraction to him confusing things even more.

She stirred some sugar in her coffee and turned back to them with a sigh, easing herself into a chair next to Mildred's desk. "Look, I appreciate what y'all are trying to do, really, I do. But don't you see that I can't risk anyone else being involved? I've already lost too much. I can't afford to lose anything else. Surely you understand that."

They all looked at her for a moment, but no one said a word. Finally, Sabine blurted out, "I've lost a lot, too. You're the only family I have left, Maryse. Don't ask me to leave you alone, or you're going to piss me off." Sabine stared defiantly at Maryse, and Maryse knew it was hopeless. This was one of those areas where she and Sabine were cut from the same cloth.

Hurt one, you hurt the other.

And Maryse was forced to admit that if the situation were reversed, it would take her own death to peel her off protecting her friend. She shook her head at the impossibility of the situation, not having a clue how to proceed. "Well, did you geniuses come up with any way to get me out of this?"

They all shook their heads. Finally, Luc cleared his throat and spoke, his voice barely disguising his anger. "This entire situation is ridiculous. What the hell was that woman thinking? It's no wonder everyone hated her."

"Got that one right," Mildred agreed, and gave Luc a nod.

Maryse sighed. "I don't know what Helena was thinking." *Even though I talk to her on a semi-regular basis.* "Probably she just thought that the land would remain in the care of the state. And as long as I owned it, Mudbug wouldn't become one big oil field."

Mildred wasn't convinced. "Helena or her attorney should have known that worthless son and husband of hers wouldn't let you keep something so valuable."

Maryse stared at the wall for a moment, casting her mind back to the will reading. "I got the impression that all the 'rules' of the inheritance weren't exactly in the forefront of Wheeler's mind. He even said he needed to review everything again before we talked because it had been so long since he'd read everything over. Probably Helena forgot too, since she inherited everything as a child."

Luc shook his head. "Well, Helena should have reread the rules before she handed you a death sentence."

"There's nothing that can be done about this clause?" Mildred asked. "Can't you just give the land back?"

Maryse shrugged. "I honestly don't know. I've never asked."

Mildred looked at the others and gave them a nod. "Then

I say your first order of business is getting in touch with that attorney of Helena's and finding out what your options are. He's got to be able to do something to protect you."

"Maybe," Maryse said. It was a thought, anyway, and better than anything Maryse had come up with so far. "I'll call him as soon as his office opens."

Sabine nodded to Mildred, then looked over at Maryse. "And what do you plan on doing today? We don't think you should be alone. One of us should be with you at all times, and we don't think you should be in the bayou at all."

Maryse stared at them. "You've got to be kidding me. You can't spend your entire day following me around. Mildred, you have a hotel to run. Sabine, you have a business, and Luc . . ." What the hell *did* Luc do exactly? "Luc has to do whatever it is he does for the state. Besides, I'd like to know what any of you could have done to protect me from that explosion. More likely, you'd have been hurt as much or more than I was."

"I can stick with you," Luc said. "I have a ton of vacation accrued. Long overdue, as a matter of fact. I can take a couple of days until the attorney can figure something else out."

Maryse stared at Luc in disbelief. "You actually want me to spend every waking hour of my day with you? Take you everywhere I go? We don't get along all that great in the few minutes a day we're in contact at the office. How the heck do you think we can manage an entire day?"

Luc shrugged. "I get along just fine. You're the one with the problem."

Maryse felt her pulse quicken. Luc was right. She was the one with the problem. The main problem being that even a small amount of time around Luc LeJeune led to thoughts that she had no business thinking. How in the world was she supposed to manage an entire day? "I am not going clothes shopping with him," Maryse said finally, "and that's my first order of business for today."

"Oh, c'mon, Maryse," Sabine pleaded. "What's the big deal? It's not like he's going to follow you into the dressing room."

Luc perked up a bit and smiled, and Maryse felt a flush start at the base of her neck and slowly creep up her face. She shot him a dirty look that should have cut him to his knees, but it only made him smile more. "I am not selecting undergarments with a man."

Sabine laughed. "You don't even wear underwear, Maryse."

"I do on Sundays," Maryse grumbled, feeling her independence slipping away even as she made her futile arguments.

"It's only Friday," Luc said, and grinned. "You've still got time to change your mind."

Chapter Twelve

Shopping with Luc wasn't quite as bad as Maryse had originally imagined and probably not near as sexual as Luc had
hoped. But given her slightly rough condition and the fact
that her job didn't exactly involve tailored dresswear, Maryse
saw absolutely no reason to shop for anything cute or nice at
the moment. Even if she was back in the bayou sometime
soon, alligators and nutria didn't appreciate fashion.

So a trip to Wal-Mart was as much shopping as Luc was
going to see.

Maryse walked right into the women's athletic section
and pulled shorts, sweats, and T-shirts off the racks and
shoved them into the cart she'd conned Luc into pushing.
That was it. No tube tops, no spandex, no sexy lingerie—
no dressing rooms. Then it was off to find some sports bras.

Luc stared wistfully at the rows of lacy, multi-colored underwear and reached up to finger a pair in girly pink. Maryse
hid a grin. He was barking up the wrong tree with her. Not
only was underwear purely optional, but Luc LeJeune was
the last person she wanted getting a view of anything she
might wear in that area. There were some temptations you
just avoided altogether.

Apparently deciding Maryse wasn't going to contemplate anything even remotely sexy, Luc gave up and yanked
out his cell phone. Maryse ignored him and continued
looking over her selection of activewear. She had just

narrowed her choice down to two different crossed-back sports bras when Luc snapped the phone shut and gave her a curious look.

"There was a message on the office phone from someone named Aaron. He said that the mice cruised through the trial and he was moving on but he's going to need more of the sample before he can go any further after that. What does that mean? What is he testing?"

Maryse tried to appear completely normal, even though she wanted to jump and shout, head injury not withstanding. "It's nothing," she said, and waved a hand in dismissal. *Nothing but a successful Trial 3, which you've never made it through before now.* "Just some different stuff I'm trying out—you know, herbal remedies and such."

Luc narrowed his eyes. "What kind of remedies?"

Maryse turned away from him and concentrated on the bras. "Nothing that would interest you. Although two weeks ago, I found a natural cure for gas." She looked back at him with a broad smile.

Luc shook his head and shot her a disbelieving look, but thankfully he dropped the subject and took up position at the edge of the department where he could scan the magazines. *A successful Trial 3.* It was all she could do to keep from dancing in the aisles. She was close to the answer, she could just feel it. And for now, at least, that thrill totally overrode all the bad things going on.

Maryse picked a couple of sports bras from the rack and tossed them in the basket, then pushed her cart down the aisle, whistling as she went. She was just about to leave the section altogether when the pink, lacy underwear that Luc had been studying earlier caught her eye. She glanced down the aisle at Luc, who had a magazine open and was concentrating intently on whatever he was reading. Looking back

at the underwear, she bit her lip, knowing that even looking at the underwear was trouble. Buying them was even
worse. It was the equivalent of purchasing a ticket to the
"Sleep With Luc" concert.

But then there was that whole death thing to consider,
and that was the clincher.

If she died today, the last man she would have slept with
was Hank. Hell, the *only* man she'd slept with was Hank,
and on so many levels, that was just wrong. She glanced
over at Luc once more. Before she could change her mind,
she snatched the underwear off the rack, tugged them off
the hanger, yanked off the tag, and stuffed them in her
pocket. No way was she letting Luc see her buy those panties. That was just asking for it. At least this way, she was
still in control. Unless of course, she was arrested for
shoplifting before she could get through checkout and use
the underwear tag to pay for her secret bounty.

She tried to act normal as she walked to the end of the
aisle and called out to Luc. "I'm going to head over to check-
out. Take your time. I'll meet you at the end of the register."

Luc nodded, and she could feel his gaze on her as she entered the only available check-out line, which was a mere
six feet away from the magazine stand. She began placing
her items on the belt, and when she finished, stepped close
to the register, slipping the underwear tag to the clerk. "I
liked these so much, I decided to wear them," she said, her
voice low.

The clerk stared at her for a moment, obviously trying to
decide if she was a loon or a thief. Loon must have won out,
because the clerk took the tag from her, scanned it, and
tossed it in the bag with her bras. "That will be one hundred eight dollars and thirty-two cents." She gave Maryse a
shrewd look. "Unless you're wearing anything else."

Maryse shook her head and swiped her debit card, certain her face was beet red. She looked over at Luc, who plopped the magazine back on the shelf and turned toward the check-out lane. Catching her eye, he smiled and walked over to her.

"Ready?" he asked.

Maryse felt a slow burn in her center as she stared at the smiling Luc. Her hand moved involuntarily to her pocket and closed around the lacy underwear. "You have no idea," she said.

"Then let's do it."

Oh God. Maryse felt her knees weaken. There was no way out, she was certain. If someone didn't kill her first, she was going to sleep with Luc LeJeune.

As they exited Wal-Mart, Luc scanned the parking lot for possible threats but finally decided that the only threat to Maryse at the moment was him. He glanced over at her and held in a sigh. It simply made no sense at all. Maryse was so unlike the women he normally went for. His past conquests had all been girly and clingy and had the helpless woman routine down pat, whether helpless or not. They were fluff, eye candy . . . the kind of woman who made you look like a stud at the company Christmas party but not the kind you'd ever introduce to your family.

Especially not his family. Women like his mother and grandmother did not suffer weakness or fools.

Maryse, with her fierce and sometimes frustrating independence, was a breath of fresh air. And the fact that she didn't fall at his feet and overload him with compliments only made him more interested rather than less. He glanced down at the shopping bags he carried and shook his head. Her wardrobe definitely needed work, but for whatever reason, the faded jeans and rubber boots she'd worn into the bayou had never been a turnoff. In fact, it was exactly the opposite, which was uncharted territory for him.

He'd been with women who'd worn their stiletto heels to bed, and he had to admit, it was a huge turn-on. But on the occasion when his guard slipped and he allowed himself the luxury of that one-second vision of Maryse in his bed, damned if she wasn't completely nude except for those rubber boots. He felt his pulse quicken every time that picture flashed through his mind and knew that he would have to be very careful with Maryse Robicheaux.

Women who caused high blood pressure by wearing rubber boots were not to be taken lightly. If he made a genuine move in that direction, he knew there would be no going back. Maryse Robicheaux was no good-time girl or one-night stand. Maryse Robicheaux was the kind of woman who inspired men to make long-term plans.

They climbed into Luc's Jeep, packages in tow, and Luc pulled out of the parking space. As he exited the parking lot, Maryse pulled out her cell phone and punched in a number. Luc felt his pulse quicken for a moment, wondering who she was calling, but relaxed when she asked to speak to the attorney, Wheeler.

Clutching the steering wheel, he stared down the highway. What the hell was wrong with him? He was acting like a jealous husband, worried that his wife might be talking to another man. He needed to get a grip and get a grip fast. He wasn't going to be any help to Maryse if he spent all his time mentally undressing her rather than protecting her.

As Maryse finished her conversation and snapped the phone shut, he erased the rubber boot scene from his mind and looked over at her. "Wheeler meeting you this afternoon?" he asked.

Maryse nodded. "Yeah. I'm pretty sure he thinks I'm losing my mind with the questions I asked, but I didn't want to get into everything over the phone."

"Probably best to spring a house exploding on him in person," Luc agreed.

"He's meeting me at the café at two, hopefully with answers to all the questions that I asked." She sighed. "You know, somehow having this discussion over a cup of coffee and blueberry pancakes just seems wrong."

"Probably more of a shot of rot-gut whiskey sort of moment."

"Or battery acid," she said, and frowned.

Luc studied her for a moment, the questions she'd asked Wheeler rolling through his mind. "Are you really thinking about signing the land over to Hank?"

Maryse shook her head. "No. But if everyone thought that I could, and had, that would take the pressure off of me if the whole point of this mess was someone thinking Hank was going to inherit in the first place."

Luc studied Maryse for a moment, then frowned. She'd processed things quicker than he thought she would, so the thoughts rolling through her mind must be overwhelming. "You realize what you're saying?" he asked, just to be sure they were on the same page. "You think someone wanted that land so bad that they killed Helena Henry thinking Hank would inherit and make a deal. And when you inherited instead, they shifted to killing you."

He paused for a moment, carefully deciding on his next words. "It would take someone very desperate to attempt that in the first place. And it would take someone who knew enough about the land, and you and Helena, to know the score."

"I know what I'm saying," Maryse said, and stared out the

car window. "Someone I know, possibly someone I consider a friend, is trying to kill me."

Maryse's two o'clock meeting with Wheeler started off a bit rocky. First off, both Luc and Sabine insisted on attending. Apparently they had decided that if Maryse couldn't come up with a better idea for protecting herself, they were going to wring one out of the attorney. Wheeler entered the café, took one look at Maryse, and gasped.

"Oh, my word," he said as he slid onto the chair across from her. "What happened to you?"

"A couple of things you should be aware of," Maryse said, and told him about the truck wreck and the explosion at her cabin.

Wheeler looked at Maryse, then over at Sabine and Luc, apparently hoping this was all a joke and they were the hidden-camera crew. When no one said a word, Wheeler looked back at Maryse, cleared his throat, and finally said, "Are you implying that someone is trying to remove you from the inheritance line?"

"Jesus, Wheeler," Maryse said, her exasperation with the situation overcoming any subtlety she might have otherwise had. "Where did you learn to talk that way?" She supposed his highbrow, cultured existence didn't allow him to say or think of such sordid things as murder, but damn it, they had no time to pussyfoot around reality. "I'm saying someone is trying to kill me. Are you with me now?"

Wheeler paled and used his table napkin to wipe his brow. "You're sure?" he asked, but as soon as the words left his mouth, he shook his head and looked contrite. "I'm sorry. Of course you're sure or you wouldn't be here talking to me. I guess it's just so startling because I can't imagine anyone running the risk of an arrest for something that may be worth considerable money someday but isn't really worth all that much right now."

"If only that were true, Wheeler," Maryse said, "but your client neglected to inform you of the billions of dollars in oil that are in the marsh. Seems she neglected to tell everyone that little bit of information, but apparently someone out there knows."

Wheeler stared at her for a moment, then drained half his glass of water. "Billions? I can see where that might be a problem. So what can I do?"

"I need to know what my options are. That's why I gave you that list of questions to research earlier."

Wheeler nodded and pulled a tablet from his briefcase. "I have all the answers here. Where would you like to start?"

Maryse took a deep breath and looked over at Luc, who nodded. "Can I give the land back to the estate?" Maryse asked.

Sabine stared at Maryse in shock. "If the land goes back to the estate, won't Hank inherit? I'm not saying you shouldn't do it, Maryse, but I thought you were dead set against that idea."

Maryse put one hand up. "I'm not saying that's what I want to do, but I need to know all my options and how they would work."

Maryse looked expectantly at Wheeler, but he shook his head. "I couldn't find any provision that would allow you to forgo your inheritance."

"Except being dead, of course," Luc threw in, his expression dark.

Wheeler paled and tugged at his tie. "Well, yes, of course there is that."

Maryse shook her head. "That's the kind of option I was looking to avoid." She drummed her fingers on the table and thought about her next move. "And the will you're drawing up for me won't be legal until the week has passed, right?"

Wheeler nodded. "That's correct. The land isn't yours to give until after the probationary period has passed. The only way you could create a document legally leaving the land to another party before the week was up is if there were no other direct heirs in line to inherit, but since there's Hank . . ."

Sabine straightened in her chair and glared at Wheeler, her normal good manners shot to hell. "This is bullshit! You're telling me she's inherited this land whether it gets her killed or not, and she has no choice but to sit around and wait for someone to fire the shot?"

Wheeler blotted his forehead with the napkin again. "I'm afraid that's the long and short of it, and I am truly sorry. I never would have let Helena put you in this position if I'd had any idea it would come to this. I just never imagined . . ." the attorney trailed off, obviously not even able to put what he couldn't imagine into words.

Maryse sank back into her seat and considered the information. "So you're telling me there's no way to back out of this except to take a short ride in a long hearse. And if something happens to me, you have no choice but to pass the land to Hank, a direct heir, who will most certainly lease it to the oil companies before my body's even cold. There's no option to preserve this marsh other than me remaining alive for another three days?"

Wheeler gave her an apologetic look. "You could kill Hank."

Sabine glared at him. "Do *not* give her any ideas."

Maryse patted her friend on the arm. "Don't worry, Sabine. As satisfying as that may sound, particularly at this moment, I'd still have to find him first." She leaned in closer to Wheeler and scanned the café, just to make sure no one could overhear. "Okay, Wheeler, so we agree there's no legal way for me to get out of this inheritance except dying, which sorta isn't a good option for me, so what if we drew up a fake document that said I was giving up all rights to the land inheritance and shifting the title to Hank?"

Wheeler stared at her in obvious confusion. "But such a document wouldn't be legally binding. That's what we just discussed."

Maryse nodded. "I know that, and you know that, but would anyone else?"

Wheeler's face cleared in understanding. "Normally, I would never be party to such an act, and I'm not real clear on the legality of my drawing up such a document, even just for talk, but given the situation, I agree that this might be the only way to buy you the time you need."

"Then let's do it," Maryse said. "Who knows. I might get really lucky and bring Hank out of hiding long enough to serve him divorce papers. I'd really like a divorce before I die and not the other way around."

Wheeler cleared his throat and looked at her, obviously uncomfortable. "Of course, this plan will only work if whoever is after you intended Hank to inherit in the first place."

Maryse nodded and stared down at the table. She'd already rolled that one around in her mind, but really, what other choice did they have? Surely whoever murdered Helena thought Hank would inherit. If even Wheeler had to look up the complete restrictions of the land inheritance, could anyone else possibly know all the mundane details?

Then there was the other thought, the thought still nagging at her from her earlier conversation with Luc. Maybe whoever wanted her dead hadn't planned on Hank making it through the week either. What if by pretending to shift the inheritance to Hank, she made him the next target?

"How long would it take you to draw up the fakes?" Maryse asked.

"I can probably have something by this afternoon," Wheeler said, "and there's nothing stopping me from notifying all concerned parties now about the documents in the works if I knew where to find them. That would buy you some safety. I'll give you my home number in case you locate Harold over the weekend."

"I don't think locating Harold will be a huge problem, and I'd bet anything he's in touch with Hank," Maryse said. "I'll tell Mildred to spread the word during her manicure at the beauty shop, and the whole town of Mudbug will know within a couple of hours." Maryse said. "So if you have the fake ready this afternoon, then the fraud just has to hold for three days."

"That's correct," Wheeler replied.

Maryse bit her lip. "Do it. I'll track down Harold so you can let him know." Maryse took a deep breath and stared out the café window, trying to assuage her guilt by thinking of everything rationally.

After all, if she was wrong about everything, Hank would probably only have to worry about staying alive for twenty-four hours or so. Way better odds than her three and a half days.

Luc insisted on taking Maryse back to the hotel after the meeting with Wheeler and Sabine seconded the motion, leaving her with no choice but to comply. Not that it mattered. She was sore and tired, and a nap probably wouldn't be the worst thing that could come out of the day, especially since she had a loosely formed plan rolling around her mind. A plan that involved a nightly escapade.

Maryse protested when Luc insisted on accompanying her to her room, but he refused to let her inside without checking the room first. Not wanting to waste valuable energy on an argument that she was going to lose anyway, she waved him inside. A minute later, he popped back in the hall and declared everything clear.

Which would have been accurate if Helena hadn't walked through the wall from the room next door, sending Jasper scurrying under the bed.

"Oh, no," Luc said, and pointed a finger at Helena. "You have caused quite enough trouble already. Maryse needs to rest, no thanks to you, and you need to start working on how to fix this mess you made instead of just popping through walls and aggravating people."

Helena looked a bit repentant, but it passed so quickly that if you hadn't been looking closely, you would have missed it. "I *am* here trying to fix this mess. Do you think I meant for any of this to happen? I might have been a bitch . . . might still be . . . but I never wanted to get anyone killed. And I certainly didn't want to roam the earth in cheap polyester."

Maryse waved a hand at Helena. "Don't you two start. There's no use getting your feathers all ruffled—or your polyester. Besides, I have something you might find interesting."

Luc narrowed his eyes at her, wondering what she had up her sleeve and why she hadn't mentioned it before now. Helena looked expectant, like an eight-year-old opening birthday presents. "What is it?" Helena asked.

Maryse reached into her pocket and pulled out a small ring of keys. "Christopher dropped these when he was scrambling in the storage closet. I figure one of them ought to open the door to medical records, right?" She dangled the keys in the air, jiggling them in front of Helena.

Helena's eyes widened, and she smiled. "Holy shit! Jackpot."

"Wait a minute." Luc cut in. "You're not thinking of breaking into the hospital, are you? That is just plain foolish."

Maryse turned to face him. "Oh yeah, and what would be less foolish? Letting Helena walk the Earth every day annoying the ever-living hell out of me until we find her murderer? Or maybe we should just let him get me first, then I can be stuck in limbo with her." She narrowed her eyes at him. "Of course, you'd be able to see and hear us both, right?"

Luc's jaw twitched at Maryse's words, and Maryse could tell she'd struck a nerve. "So can I ask exactly what you think you can gain by reading medical records?" he asked.

Maryse nodded. "I'm hoping that if I can figure out what someone put in the brandy snifter that killed Helena, it might tell us who did it, or at least narrow down the list of who I need to avoid for the next three and a half days. There can't be that many people in this town who know poisons *and* explosives."

Luc crossed his arms in front of him, silent for a moment and clearly not convinced. "Do you have any idea what could happen to you if you get caught? I don't even want to know what kind of charges you'd be up on. Medical information has gotten to be such a big deal lately that the authorities could probably find a way to make it a federal case if they wanted."

"Doesn't matter," Maryse said. "It would be a hell of a lot harder to kill me if I was locked up in a jail cell somewhere, right? So what's the downside?"

Luc placed his hand on her arm and squeezed. "You are *not* safer in jail. That I know for sure. Anyone in jail, including the guards, can be paid to get to you."

Maryse shrugged and pulled her arm away from his grasp. "So what do you suggest? That I sit around Mudbug and wait to die? Maybe I should spend every day standing in the middle of Main Street just to make it easier on everyone. At least that way, Mildred and Sabine would have a body to bury and would be less likely to be caught in the crossfire."

Luc crossed his arms in front of him again. "You put things in motion with Wheeler to cover you."

"Yeah, but can you guarantee that whoever is behind this will be fooled? They seem to know a lot about the inheritance rules. What if they don't buy the fake?"

"What fake?" Helena asked. "What have you done with Wheeler?"

Maryse looked over at Helena. "I asked him to draw up a fake document to transfer the land to Hank. I was hoping it might throw the bad guys off my trail long enough for the title to pass."

Helena stared at her for a moment. "Hmm. That's not bad, really."

"It's not a bad idea," Maryse agreed, "but it's hardly foolproof. Whoever is behind this was making their moves before the will reading ever happened, so there's always the chance they'll know the transfer document isn't legal."

Luc started to argue but apparently didn't have a good enough comeback. "Hell, I guess I don't like you taking chances, but you're right—sitting still isn't going to solve this problem either, no matter how much I hate admitting it."

"It has to be done, Luc," Maryse said, "and probably a lot of other things that border on illegal and go beyond unethical. But I'm simply out of options and running out of time.

Whoever is after me has made it very clear what he's willing to do to get what he wants, and I'm not going to depend on a legal document to keep him from completing what he's already begun."

"She's right," Helena said. "I'm dead proof of it. This land has caused a mess of trouble that I swear I didn't even consider. I guess I really was beyond my prime if I didn't see this coming." She sank down onto the bed with a sigh. "All I was trying to do was avoid leaving the land to Hank. I couldn't trust him to do the right thing—with the land, or with the cash he'd get from making a deal with the oil companies."

Luc frowned at Helena. "I know you think you were doing some great service for this town, but I have to ask—what made you so certain that Maryse wouldn't sell out? How could you possibly know that she wouldn't be swayed by billions of dollars?"

He looked over at Maryse. "In fact, why the hell *aren't* you swayed by that much money? Jesus, you could afford to relocate the entire town if what Helena says about the oil is true. So why bother to keep this place as is?"

Helena looked over at Maryse, but when she never answered, Helena turned to Luc and said, "Maryse won't give up this land until she finds the cure for cancer that native woman made for her father. She knows it's out there, and she won't allow one single sprig of green to be cleared out, paved, or removed from that marsh until she's found her magic mixture."

Maryse spun around and stared at Helena. "How did you know?"

Helena shrugged. "I give a lot of money to the university you're using for the tests. It wasn't hard to find out from them what kind of tests you were running."

Maryse let this information sink in without replying.

"Cancer?" Luc said and looked a bit surprised. "Is that what you're doing in that lab?"

Maryse glared at Helena for letting out her secret and finally nodded. "Yes, but the subject is private and not open for discussion. Not now, not ever." She nodded toward the door. "Now, if you two could please leave me alone. I've got to plan a breaking and entering, and I'm probably going to need some rest."

Luc nodded and pointed a finger at Helena. "*You* are to meet me in the parking lot. I have some questions about your worthless husband and his military service."

"Okey dokey," Helena said, and flashed Maryse a grin. "I'll be back tonight." She waved goodbye and dashed through the wall, looking more excited than Maryse thought the situation warranted.

Luc walked over to stand directly in front of Maryse. "If you're going to go through with this crazy plan, at least let me drive you. You might need backup, or to leave in a hurry."

Maryse was surprised at his change in tune, but then she saw the compassion and admiration in his eyes. He got it. Maryse could tell. It probably hadn't taken more than a phone call to his grandparents to find out how Maryse's parents had died, and she knew with certainty that Luc understood why her research was so important, without her even saying a word.

"Okay, you can drive," she said, "but no more trying to talk me out of it."

Luc shook his head and stepped so close to her that she could feel the heat coming off his body. Her breath caught in her throat, and the overwhelming desire to have Luc LeJeune touch her crashed through every nerve ending in her body. When he placed his hand on her cheek and lowered his lips to hers, she felt her knees go weak.

His lips gently pressed hers, and she was surprised by the tenderness in his kiss. Then he ran his tongue across her lips, and the room began to spin. Her mouth parted, and she groaned as he wrapped his arms around her and deepened the kiss. His tongue swirled with hers in an erotic dance, and he pressed his hips into hers, his body lean and hard in all the right places.

She was just about to do something foolish, like rip off his clothes, or her own, when he ended the kiss, brushing his lips once more across hers. He released her and stepped back with a smile. "Just in case things go wrong," he whispered. "I didn't want to live with never having kissed you again." He ran one finger down her cheek, then walked out of the room.

Maryse shut the door and leaned back against it, not sure whether to head straight to a cold shower or fling herself out the window.

In case things go wrong.

Bastard. He'd just given her more to lose.

Chapter Thirteen

It was close to midnight when Maryse, Luc, and Helena pulled into the hospital parking lot in Maryse's rental. There were only a few cars parked in front of the administrative building, which was a good sign. That meant staff was light and could probably be worked around. Plus, Maryse had the added advantage of the invisible scout, Helena. It took a little convincing, but Luc had finally agreed to remain in the car, ready to start the engine and haul ass at a moment's notice, not to mention keep an eye on the outside just in case a sudden influx of staff should appear.

Maryse looked at the building once more, took a deep breath, and stepped out into the dim light of the parking lot. Helena stepped through the back door of the car and Maryse did a double take. "You changed clothes. But what in the world are you wearing?"

Helena looked like a Michael Jackson video combined with a Saturday morning streetwalker. The cat suit was solid black from neck to feet and had leopard patches across the boobs and each cheek of her butt, which amounted to a whole lotta leopard. Not to mention Maryse couldn't help but think there should be a legal weight limit on who got to wear spandex. Lumps abounded in all directions, mostly in places that lumps weren't supposed to be, and to top it off, she wore a black nylon mask that completely covered her head with only her eyes left showing.

"You like it?" Helena asked. "I thought I'd surprise you with my new ability. This is my covert operation outfit. Kind of a combination of James Bond and Catwoman."

Maryse frowned. That wasn't exactly the combination she'd come up with. "You can't run around wearing that, Helena."

"Why not?" The ghost put her hands on her hips and glared. "It's not like anyone else can see me, so I can hardly attract attention."

Unable to hold it in any longer, Maryse started to laugh, then clamped her hand over her mouth to muffle the noise. Luc stepped out of the car to see what the holdup was and his expression, a mixture of horror and confusion, was enough to put Maryse in tears.

"That is not necessary," Helena huffed.

Maryse peeked over at the ghost and saw she'd changed into black slacks, a black turtleneck, and black loafers. Thank God. There was simply no way Maryse could have followed that large leopard butt through the hospital without losing it.

Helena glared. "Now that I'm dressed as boring as you, can we get on with this?"

Maryse got control of herself and nodded. Luc took one final look at Helena and climbed back into the car, shaking his head. Maryse glanced around the parking lot, ensuring no one had witnessed her lapse in self-control, and was relieved to find the parking lot still clear. She gave Helena one final look, just to make sure she hadn't thrown in anything on the sly, like buttless slacks or a tear-off top with pasties, then started creeping toward the hospital.

"You know, it would have done us a lot more good if you'd learned how to touch things instead of change clothes. Then you could have gotten the file yourself," Maryse whispered as they snuck down the side of the building toward the employee entrance. "And I do not dress boring."

"Sure you do," Helena said. "I saw two decent outfits the whole time I've been hanging around and only one pair of spiffy shoes. According to the *Fashion Today* show I caught when I was hanging out at the beauty shop, you should be wearing those spiky heels everywhere, even to bed."

Maryse shook her head. "Do you really think I can tromp through the marsh in a pair of stilettos? The state would check me into the nearest mental institution if they caught me in something that stupid. Not to mention that outrunning an alligator might be a little difficult with those spiked heels in bayou mud."

Helena shrugged. "Okay, so maybe you can't wear them all the time, but you could when you're not working. If I could balance on the damned things, I'd wear them myself. I saw a real spiffy pair with a titanium heel advertised last night. You ought to get those. Very sexy."

Maryse stopped at the employee entrance and stared at Helena. "And just who do I need to look sexy for? My eligible doctor turned out to be a closet pedophile, literally on the closet part. Besides, I'm still married to your son, the disappearing idiot. *And* someone is trying to kill me. Lots of men would have a problem with all that, you know."

Helena gave her a smug smile. "Doesn't look like it bothers Luc."

Maryse stiffened. "Luc and I are friends. Sorta. That's it."

"Hmmpf. Didn't look like friends the way he kissed you back at the hotel. I could feel the heat off you two from twenty feet away."

Damn. She'd thought Helena was long gone before Luc

had kissed her senseless. Maryse pulled the keys from her pocket and turned to the door. "You imagined it."

"Keep telling yourself that. You might start to believe it, but no one else is going to."

Maryse found the right key and eased open the side door designated for employees. "I am not listening to you, Helena," she hissed. "I have enough on my plate right now, and God knows, a man has never been the answer to my problems. They've usually been the cause. After all, I wouldn't be saddled with you if I hadn't married Hank."

Helena didn't look convinced but finally gave up her argument and followed Maryse down a dim hallway to the main corridor. "Where's the records room?" Maryse asked as they crept down the hallway.

"We turn left at the end of the main hall, and it's the last room on the left." Helena looked behind her, then ahead toward the corridor. "You know, this is sort of ironic. Walking down this hallway has the look of one of those near-death experiences you always hear about. Long white hallway, light at the end."

Maryse smiled wryly. "Did you see anything like this when you died?"

Helena frowned. "No. Not a thing. When I woke in that casket, I thought someone was playing a horribly cruel joke. It never occurred to me that I was dead, even after I yelled at everyone in the church and they didn't respond. Well, except you. But you passed out, so that wasn't exactly a help."

Maryse considered for a moment what kind of shock that must have been. "So what did you do after that?"

"I walked downtown, hoping someone would see me, say something to me, but everyone passed right by as if I wasn't there. I stopped in front of that big plate-glass window at the café and stood there, trying to see my reflection in the glass, but all that showed was the pickup truck behind me." She sighed. "It took me an hour to walk to your place. I cried the whole way. Not much else to do."

Maryse took a minute to absorb this and couldn't help but feel bad. What a nightmare. She couldn't possibly imagine how awful it must have been, but Maryse was certain of one thing—an hour of crying wouldn't have been enough for her. She'd probably still be wailing.

"Well," Maryse said finally, "let's get this over with and maybe we can see about getting you on to where you belong."

Helena nodded and stepped out into the lighted corridor. "It looks clear, but let me check at the end to make sure, then I'll yell for you. No use you sticking your head out or anything. You should be able to hear me yell from the end of the hall."

"That shouldn't be a problem," Maryse agreed. She could probably hear Helena yelling from the next building.

Helena disappeared around the corner, and Maryse leaned against the wall and waited for the yell to come. Her hands were sweating like mad between her anxiety over what she was about to do and the latex gloves that Luc had insisted she wear. It was a minute or so later when she heard Helena yell.

"All's clear!"

Maryse took a deep breath, stepped around the corner, and set off down the hall. Helena stood at the end of the hall next to a door with the words *Medical Records* stenciled on it in clear black letters. Maryse flipped to the first key on the ring, making sure she held the others tight to avoid any noise, and tried it in the latch.

No luck.

Maryse looked over at Helena, and Helena nodded, assuring her the hallway was still clear. She flipped to the second key and slipped it in the lock.

Bingo. They were in.

Maryse nodded to Helena and eased the door open. There was a loud squeak as she pushed, and she stopped for a moment, listening to see if anyone was coming to investigate. Helena checked both hallways and shook her head, so Maryse pushed the door open the remainder of the way and crept inside.

The room was pitch black, and she fumbled around for a moment, trying to find something solid to hold on to. Instead, she ran face first into a bookcase. "Damn it. That hurt." She rubbed her nose and grimaced, not even wanting to think about yet another bruise on her already battered body.

"Why don't you make more noise?" Helena asked. "I don't think everyone heard you."

"Don't give me any shit, Helena. Not all of us can walk through furniture."

"Then turn on your flashlight."

"I don't want anyone to see."

"Including yourself? Oh hell, I'll go back out into the hall and stand guard. Then will you turn on some damned light and stop running into everything imaginable?"

"Yes," Maryse hissed. "Just leave."

Maryse waited a minute in the inky darkness until she heard Helena call out to light things up. She pulled the small flashlight from her pocket and directed it at the bookshelf in front of her. The label at the top read "Current." Probably not the place she needed to look. She crept carefully down the row of bookcases, using her flashlight to scan the labels, and watched carefully for a change. *Current, Current, Current. Where the heck is Past?*

She turned the corner at the end of the row and shined her flashlight at the top of the next row of bookcases. "Dead Records," it read in large letters. *Dead Records?* Wasn't that a bit politically incorrect for a hospital? Maryse shook her head and ran her light across the folders jam packed on the shelves until she came to the H's.

"Find anything?" Helena's voice sounded next to her, and it was all Maryse could do not to scream. She glared at the ghost, but wasn't sure how effective it was because she wasn't positive Helena could see in the dark either. "Are you trying to ruin this? And why aren't you outside?"

"I saw the light go out and came to investigate, but it was just because you moved around to this side of the bookcases. You can't see the light now through the door."

Maryse swung her light toward the sound of Helena's voice and lit her up, standing right in front of the next set of shelves. "Yeah, well, that's great, but I can't see through you, so would you move over to the side a bit so I can read these files?"

Helena complied, and Maryse scanned the first row of files. *Harris, Hartman, Hector . . . aha . . . Henry!* Maryse ran her flashlight over the row of files until she reached Helena then stopped the light on the shiny label on the side. "Got it," she said, and reached for the file.

Helena reached at the same time and her hand passed right through Maryse's, sending a chill straight through her body. "Cut it out. You know I hate that cold, and besides, you haven't figured out how to pick up things anyway."

Helena yanked her hand back in a huff. "I keep practicing. I figured, of all things, I'd be desperate enough to want that file that I'd be able to touch it." She sighed. "Guess not."

"Now is not the time for you to practice ghost games," Maryse hissed. She yanked the file from the shelf, dropped quickly to the floor, and opened it, directing her flashlight onto the papers inside. The coroner's report was right on top, listing the death as *natural causes*. She scanned the page and found out that when Helena had been brought in, the attending physician was a ·doctor from New Orleans who had been filling in for Dr. Breaux, who was out of town that weekend for a medical convention.

But the attending physician had gotten in touch with Dr. Breaux right away and was given all the particulars of Helena's asthma problems and her subsequent failure to take his advice seriously. That was it. That statement alone had sealed Helena's fate as far as an autopsy was concerned, and without any other evidence to support foul play, Helena Henry had been buried without an argument.

But she'd come back to correct the mistake.

"What does it say?" Helena asked, hunching over Maryse and trying to make out the tiny print.

"It says you're dead," Maryse replied, trying to brush her off so she could make out the medications at the bottom of the page. "I really need a copy of all this, but I don't want to risk running the copy machine." Maryse rose from the floor and carried the file over to an available desk in the corner. Helena trailed behind her.

"I'm going to write down the names of these medications and a couple of notes," Maryse said, and grabbed a pad of paper and a pen off the desktop. "Anything you were taking on a regular basis would change your reaction to certain poisons. I need to narrow down the options as much as possible if we're going to get anywhere."

Helena nodded, and Maryse began to makes notes from

Helena's file. She finished quickly, snapped the file shut, and was just about to suggest they get the hell out of there when a familiar name caught her eye.

She shined her flashlight at a file on top of the desk and drew in a breath. *Sabine LaVeche*. Why would Sabine's file be out on this desk? She hadn't been sick that Maryse was aware of. Not even a cold.

"What's wrong?" Helena asked. "Why aren't you leaving?"

Maryse pointed to the file, and Helena stared. "You shouldn't look at it. I know how you feel about Sabine, but it's her place to tell you if something's wrong."

Maryse glared at Helena, angry that she'd clued right in on her current ethical problem. "Oh, yeah. And just when do you think she should have taken the time to tell me about any crisis in her life—after my truck wreck or after my cabin exploded? Maybe she doesn't want to cause me any more worry than I've already got."

"Exactly. All the more reason not to look at it now."

Maryse looked back at the file and tapped her fingers on the desk. Surely Sabine would tell her if it was something serious, right? Even if things were a little weird right now. But there was that niggling doubt in the back of her mind. What if she didn't? What if something was seriously wrong and Sabine didn't want to tell her at all? In fact, if it wasn't serious, why hadn't she mentioned anything?

Maryse sucked in a breath as the one thing that Sabine would withhold from her came to the forefront of her mind. She grabbed the file up from the desk, yanked the cover open, and stared at the contents. Holding in a cry, she stared at the pristine white paper with those horrible words that confirmed her worse fear.

Sabine was being tested for cancer.

* * *

Maryse ignored the icy fear in her stomach and tried to slam down the cover on the file before Helena could see the horrible word on the test sheets. But she wasn't fast enough. Helena sucked in a breath and looked at her, her eyes wide.

"Oh my God," Helena said finally, her voice barely a whisper. "I thought maybe an unexpected pregnancy or some other nonsense that your generation is usually up to. I never thought for a minute . . ."

Maryse opened the file again and began to scan every page. The pages were all crisp, clean, and neat—so passive resting there, totally belying the information they contained.

"Are the results there?" Helena asked.

Maryse finished looking through the file and closed it. "No, only the request for the tests. But that wasn't the first one. There have been four others, all over the last three years."

Helena gave her a shrewd look. "But the others turned out okay, right? That's probably why Sabine never told you anything. She probably figured this one would be the same as the others."

Maryse looked over at Helena, her mind racing with the awful thought of a life without her best friend. "But what if she's wrong? What if this time is the one? More than once a year is an awful lot of times to think someone might have cancer. Doctors don't usually jump to that conclusion. And why now, right when I feel like I'm so close to discovering the secret and can't even get into the bayou to work?" She gave Helena a determined look. "This changes everything. My life isn't the only one at stake anymore."

Helena gave her a solemn look. "I promise, Maryse, I will do everything within my power to see that this turns out all right for everyone."

Maryse nodded, not even wanting to think about Helena's meager power. If only she could make Helena visible to the bad guys, maybe she could distract them with her wild wardrobe changes.

Maryse sighed. The earnest look on Helena's face let her know right away that she was sincere in her promise, if not entirely adequate to do the job, and Maryse didn't have the heart to point out her shortcomings. Not at that moment, anyway. "Let's get out of here," Maryse said. "We've already pushed our luck far enough."

Maryse had just replaced Helena's file when she heard a jangle of keys outside the record's room door. "Holy shit," she hissed, and Helena stared at her in alarm. "Don't just stand there," Maryse said, waving her arms at Helena. "Figure out a way to stop them from coming in here."

"How?" Helena's eyes were wide with fright.

"I don't know," Maryse said, and dove under the desk. "But you need to come up with something in a hurry."

Maryse peered through a narrow crack in one side of the desk, watching Helena hustle toward the door just as it swung open and someone entered. A second later, the lights came on and Maryse squinted, trying to focus in the bright glare. As her eyes adjusted, Maryse made out a nurse walking across the room toward the desk.

Helena vainly tried to knock items over in her path and finally resorted to jumping in front of her, but the nurse passed right through her continuing on her task. And it looked like that task was taking her, straight to Maryse's hiding place. When the nurse was a foot or so from the desk, Helena really turned up the volume. Only problem was, no one could hear her but Maryse.

Wailing like a banshee, Helena pummeled the nurse with invisible fists and feet that never connected with their mark. Oh, but she'd managed another costume change and was now wearing long, bright purple boxing shorts with a neon green muscle shirt and swinging at the nurse with a pair of black boxing gloves. Apparently, something had gone wrong in the change, however, and instead of the new Nikes, she was back in the old pink pumps.

Maryse shook her head and almost hoped she'd get caught. Jail had to be better than this. Just as she thought the nurse would swing around the desk and discover her hiding spot, the woman turned and walked down a row of the shelves. Maryse let out a breath and sucked it back in again until the nurse returned from the row and made her way back out of the room, securing the door behind her.

"Are you still breathing?" Helena leaned down to look underneath the desk.

"I'm not sure," Maryse said as she crawled out from her hiding spot. "Ask me again in a minute." Maryse brushed some dust off her pants legs and looked back at Helena, who was still wearing the boxing outfit. "What's up with the shoes?"

Helena threw up her gloves in exasperation. "Hell if I know. I hope this isn't going to happen often. I'd hate to see a mixed combination of everything I've worn since my death each time I try to change clothes."

"Well, at least take off those gloves. You look ridiculous."

Helena glared, then focused on her hands, a wrinkle of concentration forming across her forehead.

Nothing.

She relaxed for a moment, took a deep breath and focused again.

Nothing.

Maryse groaned. "Forget it. You can figure it out later. Let's just get the hell out of here before the nurse comes back."

Helena stomped through the wall of the record's room, then stuck her head back inside. "It's clear. We can make a run for it."

Maryse nodded. "Good." She eased open the door and stepped into the hall, locking the door behind her. She had just started down the hallway toward the employee exit when Helena yelled, "She's coming back. Run!"

Run? How was she supposed to do that without making any noise? She yanked off her shoes and ran as fast as possible down the hall, slipping her way across the cold, hard tile. She could hear the clacking of heels behind her and knew Helena wasn't far behind. She rounded the corner to the employee exit and stopped for a moment to peer back around, using a medical cart that was positioned at the corner to hide her face.

Helena was huffing down the hall as fast as her heels would allow, which wasn't exactly setting speed records compared to the nurse about twenty feet behind her wearing those white tennis-looking shoes that they all wear. Maryse spun away from the corner and dashed toward the employee exit. Helena could fend for herself. It wasn't like anyone could see her anyway.

Maryse had just unlocked the exit door and was about to edge through when Helena rounded the corner and hit the medical cart, sending all of the contents flying down the hall. Maryse let the door close with a bang and ran across the parking lot, waving her sneakers like an idiot and hoping like hell Luc was paying attention.

Apparently, he was on high alert, because the car started immediately, then raced across the parking lot, headlights off. He screeched to a stop beside her and she jumped in and yelled, "Let's go!"

Luc tore out of the parking lot without question, and Maryse turned around, kneeling over the front seat, her eyes fixed on the employee exit door. Sure enough, the nurse burst out of it as soon as they hit the parking lot exit. Helena came barreling behind the nurse and knocked her clear to the ground as she ran out the door.

"What about Helena?" Luc asked, watching the fiasco in the rearview mirror.

"We'll wait for her at the gas station down the road. There's no way I'm taking a chance on getting caught here. After all, no one can see her."

Maryse turned around and slid down into the passenger seat. "We can stop at the Texaco at the end of the street. I need a cold beer anyway."

Luc frowned. "You shouldn't drink while you're taking pain medication."

Maryse waved a hand in the air in dismissal. "I'm not taking those pills, and besides, there's not a painkiller strong enough to cover what I've been through tonight."

Luc looked in the rearview mirror once more. "That bad, huh?"

Maryse slumped in her seat, her entire body aching from all the running. "I don't think a beer is going to cover it, either."

Luc smiled. "Jack Daniels with a shot of cyanide?"

"Only if you make it a double."

Maryse had downed one beer and was seriously contemplating a second when Helena rounded the corner at the gas station. She was still wearing the gloves and apparently hadn't had any success in the shoes department, either. The only switch was her top, which had reverted back to the polyester suit jacket, but it was layered on top of the neon green muscle shirt. Put together with the purple shorts, it was a nightmare of monumental proportions.

Luc took one look at her and spit his soda on the ground, his face contorted in agony, and Maryse knew he'd taken as much soda up the nose as he'd put onto the pavement.

"What the heck happened?" Luc finally managed.

"Apparently, Helena is having a bit of a wardrobe malfunction," Maryse replied. "Don't even ask how she got that way. She can't tell you." Maryse turned to Helena and glared. "And why did you have to pick running out of the hospital as the time to figure out how to touch things? Are you trying to get us caught?"

"Do you think I was trying to turn that damned cart over? If I wanted for it to happen, it never would have. Then that nurse with an ass as wide as a barn had to get in front of me on my way out the door and it happened again. But can I get these things off?" She shook the gloves again. "No, that would be far too convenient."

The throbbing in Maryse's head began to amplify. "Let's just get back to the hotel," she told Luc. "I have some research to do on Mildred's computer."

Safely back at the hotel, Luc tried to insist that Maryse go straight to bed. Maryse had worked to hide the fact that her head was killing her, but she figured it showed on her face plain as day. Luc finally convinced her to take half of a pain pill, and after fifteen minutes or so, she started to feel a bit more human.

Normally, she would have thought that anyone taking Vicodin after drinking beer probably wasn't in the best condition to research the chemical makeup of prescriptions drugs, but Maryse didn't feel the least bit out of it. Maybe all the stress had worn off any chance of a buzz. It figured.

The only good side effect was that the issues with her head had completely distracted her from her carnal thoughts of Luc.

She glanced over at his perfectly formed butt, tightly clad in faded jeans.

Well, almost completely.

She tore her gaze away from the Adonis of asses and plopped down into Mildred's office chair. Then she pointed at the door. "I can't work with you two underfoot."

Luc frowned but didn't say a word. After checking every window in the office and securing the latches—again—he perched outside the door and sent Helena outside to patrol the perimeter of the hotel. She didn't look particularly pleased with her assignment, especially as she was still wearing the pumps, but couldn't exactly argue since Luc strolling around the hotel at two A.M. would have looked a bit suspicious.

When her self-imposed bodyguards left the room, Maryse logged onto the Internet and began her research. She started with the chemical makeup of the medications Helena was taking and did a quick map of the areas of the body affected by them. Then she did a search of agents that would cause a respiratory collapse in spite of the medications taken, but without causing so much of an attack that it brought on suspicion. Last was the really fun part—figuring out how someone could have gotten their hands on one of those agents. It took a little over two hours to complete her work, and she had narrowed it down to a liquid contained in nuclear reactors and two different plants, one of which grew across almost every square inch of the preserve.

Which narrowed her suspects down to everyone in Mudbug. Again.

Chapter Fourteen

Morning came far too soon for Maryse, and she groaned as she pressed the buzzer on the alarm. She forced herself to a sitting position and looked at Jasper, who was curled up at the foot of the bed, giving her a hard stare. She reached over to rub his head. "I know you don't like being cooped up here, Jasper, but I swear it's only temporary and it's for your own good." She sighed and rose from the bed, hoping a shower would help her clear her mind and focus on the day ahead.

The shower refreshed her far more than she'd thought possible, and Maryse decided that staying alive for another day probably had a great effect on her mood. She dumped one of her Wal-Mart bags out on the bed and pulled a pair of gray yoga pants and a pink T-shirt out of the pile. The pink and white sports bra would do nicely, so she pulled that on first. She was just putting her first leg in the yoga pants when she saw the pink panties peeking out of the pocket of her sweats.

Damn. She'd forgotten about those undies. She bit her lower lip and stared at the tiny bit of string and lace. *It's not Sunday.* She tore her gaze away from the sexy panties and stuck her other foot in the yoga pants. *But they match.* She looked at the undies again. *You have no business dividing your attention right now.* She closed her eyes, trying to block the pink lace from her mind. *What if someone kills you and you're not wearing underwear? They'll talk about you forever.*

That did it.

Before she could change her mind, she stepped out of the yoga pants and grabbed the panties. The barely-there scrap of fabric clung to her curves, revealing more than they covered. The shade of pink was perfect against both the tanned and non-tanned parts of her body, and since a lot of both was showing, that was a good thing. Maryse turned to face the mirror and was surprised at the woman that looked back at her. She was almost . . . well . . . sexy.

She lifted one hand to her hair and fluffed her bangs a little. Okay, so she needed a cut, and a few highlights wouldn't hurt, and the combination of too much stress and not enough sleep had left bags under her eyes that her tinted sunscreen wouldn't put a dent in, but the rest of her wasn't all that bad. Which surprised her. How long had it been since she'd taken a real interest in her looks— months, years? She couldn't even remember.

And now Luc LeJuene had her longing for highlights and a better brand of makeup. Like she didn't have more important things to worry about. But even the thought of sudden death didn't stop her from pulling out the sunscreen, teasing her bangs just a bit to get that fluff she wanted, and positioning her breasts in the sports bra for the best display possible. By God, if she was going to croak, at least she was going to look good in the coffin.

With all her vacillating over underwear and makeup and eye bags, she was twenty minutes late for the morning meeting and still racking her brains trying to come up with assignments. Her goal was to make everyone feel useful while cleverly keeping them from harm's way without them figuring out what she was doing. A bit of a challenge to say the least.

"Good morning, everyone," Maryse said, and tried to sound cheery as she entered Mildred's office. She poured a cup of coffee and glanced around at the sober group. Luc still looked as frustrated as he had the night before when she'd delivered the bad news about the plant used to kill Helena. Sabine and Mildred both wore grim expressions, and she figured Luc had spent the last twenty minutes filling them in on the hospital escapades and subsequent lack of information they'd gained.

"Try and look a little more festive, people," Maryse said. "As far as I'm concerned, every day I can stay alive is cause for celebration."

They looked a bit guilty, and Maryse could feel some of the tension lift.

"Sorry, Maryse," Sabine said. "You're right. We should approach this with a positive attitude."

Like you approached your testing? Maryse wanted so badly to ask her friend that question, but now was definitely not the time. She looked closely at Sabine but couldn't find a single item different than it had been for years. Her skin looked fine, her hair was as thick and lustrous as ever, and although she seemed a bit less perky than usual, it was not quite seven-thirty in the morning and a good two hours before she usually awoke.

Maryse was just about to start in with her plans for the day when Helena entered the room through an exterior wall. Maryse did a double take. The gloves were gone, thank God, and so was the boxing/pink suit outfit. It was replaced, however, with blue jeans, the Nikes, and a T-shirt that read "I See Dead People."

Maryse tried to contain herself over the T-shirt but made

the mistake of looking over at Luc, who had his face buried in his coffee mug, obviously straining not to laugh. She shot Helena a frown and cleared her throat to begin the meeting. "I suppose Luc filled you in on last night's hospital raid?"

Sabine and Mildred nodded, not saying a word, but Maryse noticed that Mildred's lips were pursed. Oh, boy. Maryse knew that as soon as Mildred got her alone, she was in for it. And since Mildred didn't know about Helena's rising from the dead, it was going to be hard to convince the hotel owner that last night was a necessary risk.

Maryse held in a sigh. It seemed that at almost every turn, she was pissing people off. Except Helena, who spent all of her time pissing *Maryse* off. "Okay," Maryse said finally, "so you know that we're back at square one with trying to figure out who might be trying to kill me. I have assignments for everyone so that we can cover more ground."

Maryse looked around the group, waiting for dissenters, but no one said a word. "Mildred, I need you to check in with your friends at the beauty parlor and find out where Harold's living and what he's been up to. I need to give Wheeler a way to reach him, and his cell phone's been disconnected."

Mildred nodded. "I think I know some people to get in touch with about that."

"Good. Luc, I need you to contact your uncle with the state and see if he can get a line on any of the oil companies who've shown serious interest in the Mudbug preserve. I know a corporation is a lot of ground to cover, but if we know who's interested, we might be able to find out who's been talking to them about the land."

Luc looked thoughtful for a moment, then said, "I'll call him as soon as the office opens this morning. He should have some ideas."

"Good. Were you able to find out anything about Harold's military service yesterday?"

Luc glanced at Helena again and frowned. "My sources seem to think we're on the wrong track there. Regardless of what Harold bragged about in Johnny's, they don't think there's any way the man had the skills for anything beyond cleaning toilets—and that's a direct quote."

"Got that shit right," Helena said. "Not that he actually ever cleaned a toilet."

Maryse shook her head and sighed, careful not to even glance in Helena's direction. "I'm inclined to agree with your source. So we'll leave that one alone for now unless more information comes to surface."

"What can I do?" Sabine asked.

Maryse glanced around at the group, not knowing at all how her next statement would go over with them. Finally, she looked back at Sabine. "I need you to make a trip to New Orleans and talk to Raissa."

Sabine gasped and her mouth formed a small o. But the reaction was only temporary. Apparently, her memory of Helena following Maryse around kicked in and the request no longer sounded strange.

Mildred cleared her throat and gave Maryse the ole lifted eyebrows look, and Maryse knew she wasn't buying one word of it. Given that Mildred didn't know about Helena, Maryse figured the hotel owner thought she was assigning Sabine something trivial to get her out of town and to safety, and she wasn't entirely wrong. But there was also the flipside. Now that Maryse had been forced into believing in the "spirit world," she figured she'd tap all sources. Raissa had made some interesting revelations in the past—all of which turned out to be true. Maybe she could do it again.

At this point, Maryse would take any edge she could get.

"What are you going to do?" Sabine asked.

"First, I'm going to check with the police and see if they have any information on my cabin exploding, and then I've got a couple of things to check at the office," Maryse replied. "Luc can drive me, so you don't have to worry about that." She looked over at Luc for confirmation. "That okay by you?"

Luc nodded, casting a sideways glance at Helena. "Fine by me."

"Okay, then, it's settled, and everyone knows the plan."

Mildred started to speak when the bells at the hotel entrance jangled. She jumped up from her desk and hustled out front to deal with her customers. Sabine waited until Mildred had closed the office door behind her before giving Maryse a shrewd look. "Helena's here, isn't she?"

"Oh, yeah. Sitting right next to you on the couch, as a matter of fact. How did you know?"

Sabine looked at the space on the couch next her, then back at Maryse. "You got that look on your face."

"What look?"

"Well, for lack of a nicer description, a look like you had really bad gas. Then Luc almost spit up his coffee, and I knew he could see her, too." She turned to look at Luc. "You *can* see her, can't you?"

"Every bit of her," Luc agreed, "which is sometimes very unfortunate." He gave Maryse a grin.

"I don't have to take this grief," Helena said.

"Yes, you do," Maryse said, and translated the conversation for Sabine.

Sabine shook her head in dismay. "This is so unfair. Why do you two get to see her and I can't? All those séances and midnight cemetery ceremonies trying to call my parents, and nothing. I've spent my entire life studying the paranormal to get the answers I need about my family, and I'm the only one in the room who can't see a ghost."

Luc shrugged. "It's not really all it's cracked up to be, Sabine. And believe me, you should be grateful you can't see and mostly *hear* Helena. She's no Casper."

Sabine tried to continue her pout but couldn't stop the giggle that finally erupted from her. "I guess you're right. Helena certainly isn't my first choice of the dead person I'd like to speak to."

Helena crossed her arms in front of her and glared. "You people should have more important things to do than rag on me. Why don't you get on with them?"

Maryse narrowed her eyes at Helena and smiled. "Funny you should bring up everything that needs to be done, because something I need done involves you directly. I just couldn't say anything in front of Mildred."

Helena gave her a wary look. "Okay, so what am I supposed to do?"

"Find Hank."

There was one beat of silence before everyone started in on her at once.

"I don't like it," Luc began.

Sabine jumped at the same time. "For Christ's sake, Maryse, what if he's the one trying to kill you?"

"Calm down, people. I didn't say *I* was going to confront Hank. I just want to know what he's up to. It's the only way to figure out whether he *is* the one trying to kill me. Do you think I just want to wait around waiting for it?"

Helena pursed her lips. "All of this is irrelevant because I have absolutely no idea where Hank is. I checked that pad of paper at my house. It was a motel room on the outskirts of town, but he's not there anymore. I checked."

"If we play this right," Maryse said, "we may be able to get him to come to us."

"How's that?" Helena asked.

"I'd bet my boat that Harold's still talking to Hank. As soon as Mildred finds out where Harold is staying, you can sit tight with him until he talks to Hank or leads you to where he is."

"Absolutely not," Helena said, and shook her head. "I am not spending my day watching over that man and whatever whore he's taken up with. No way."

Maryse leaned over, her face just inches from Helena's. "You'll do it all right."

"Or what?"

Maryse pointed at Sabine. "Or she'll start the proceedings for an exorcism."

Helena looked back and forth between Maryse and Sabine, not entirely convinced Maryse was serious but afraid of the alternative. And since Helena knew as much about ghosts as Maryse, even though she *was* one, she had no way of knowing whether or not an exorcism would do something harmful to her.

Which is what Maryse was counting on to keep her in line.

"You'd do that?" Helena asked, looking at Sabine and Maryse made the translation.

Sabine gave the couch a solemn nod. "In a heartbeat."

"Well," Helena said, and huffed. "Fine lot you are, ganging up on a defenseless ghost."

Luc snorted. "You're about as defenseless as a rattlesnake, Helena."

Sabine smiled and rose from her seat. "Means to an end, Helena. I'm going to get out of here. I need to put a closed sign on the shop and head to New Orleans to catch Raissa before she gets too busy." She leaned over to give Maryse a hug, then gave Luc a stern look. "Don't let anything happen to her."

Luc raised one hand as if giving his oath. "I promise."

As Sabine left the office, Helena turned to Maryse. "So what am I supposed to do until Mildred finds Harold—plot ways to kill him, write my memoirs, bikini wax . . . ?"

Maryse grimaced. "Sit tight at the hotel and keep a watch for anyone who might attempt to blow it up. When Mildred gets the info, Luc and I will pick you up and take you wherever." She looked over at Luc, who nodded in agreement.

"Stay at the hotel?" Helena pouted. "This has got to be one of the most boring places on Earth."

Maryse grinned. "There's a whole group of traveling salesmen on the second floor. I bet they're on the pay-per-view movie log."

"Yuck," Helena said as she rose from the couch and disappeared through the wall.

Luc raised his eyebrows, and Maryse smiled. "Old joke."

Luc shook his head and put one arm around her shoulder, giving a light squeeze. "Let's go take care of things at the office."

Maryse nodded and started toward the door, not wanting to think about how nice Luc's arm felt draped across her shoulder. Not wanting to remember how her hair raised on her arm when he'd kissed her the night before. But that thin strip of lace beneath her yoga pants gave her away. She may be fooling Luc for now, but she wasn't fooling herself.

It took a five-minute phone call to confirm that the local cops didn't know any more now than they did the day before. Then Maryse and Luc headed out for the office. When they pulled into the office parking lot, Maryse was momentarily surprised to see cameras mounted on each corner of the building. She looked over at Luc who hurried to explain. "I had a buddy of mine who does security put up a couple of things. Just in case."

Maryse absorbed this for a moment, not sure how to feel about her every move being watched or recorded, but she couldn't argue with the advantage the cameras provided. "Thanks," she said, even though the thought of starring in her own movie made her more than a little self-conscious. "I really appreciate this, Luc." She squeezed his arm and pulled out her keys, wondering why Luc had gone to so much trouble for someone he barely knew.

After all, he was just another low-paid governmental scientist. He could study rat droppings in any set of mud and water across the state of Louisiana. There was no reason for him to stay here, especially with the danger that was very, very real.

Unless his reasons are personal.

She shook that thought off and unlocked the door. Luc insisted on entering first and did a quick inspection of all the rooms. When he was satisfied everything was clear, Maryse took a seat at her desk and checked phone messages. The first three were from Aaron, and he sounded excited. The fourth trial had worked and the mice hadn't gotten sick yet—something most cancer treatments couldn't offer at all.

Ecstatic, Maryse made a hasty call to Aaron, explaining that she was temporarily staying at the Mudbug hotel, just in case he needed to reach her after hours and couldn't get her on her cell. Aaron asked what was up with the hotel, but Maryse figured her house exploding would be information overload, so she played it off as repair work being done. She didn't want Aaron's focus to be on anything but the trials. After getting a few more details on the tests, she hung up the phone, jumped up from her desk, and danced a jig.

Luc looked over at her and smiled, her excitement obviously infectious. "Good news, I take it?"

"The best! Aaron said the mice came through the fourth trial with flying colors and haven't even had to take a sick day."

Luc frowned, and she felt her spirits drop a bit. What could possibly be wrong with that news? "What's the matter?" she asked.

"What?" Luc's eyes took on focus, and he appeared to jerk himself back into the present. "No, nothing's the matter. In fact, that's great news."

"Then what was the frown for?"

He gave her a direct look and asked, "Is this Aaron another Christopher?"

It took Maryse a second to figure out what he was trying to ask in an indirect way. Then she let out a laugh. "No way. Aaron's been in a relationship with the same person for eight years now."

Luc narrowed his eyes at her. "That doesn't make a difference to some people."

"With a man."

Luc blinked once and looked a bit startled. "Oh, well I guess that does make a difference." He gave her a curious look. "What exactly are you using for the test, and where did you find it?"

Maryse shook her head and gave him a smile. "If you're really nice, one day I might show it all to you, but for now, I'd like to keep it on the down-low. At least until I know I'm really onto something." *And I can find it again.*

"Oh, I can be nice."

He smiled and stepped directly in front of her, his body

so close she could feel the heat radiating off him. The hair on her arms immediately stood on end, and her heart beat so loudly, she was certain he could hear it. This time, Maryse knew there was no way in hell she was holding herself back. She had the underwear to prove it.

He lifted one hand and gently touched the side of her face. "But research is not exactly what I'm really interested in seeing at the moment," he said.

Before she could reply, or protest, or breathe, he lowered his lips to hers. Even though he'd kissed her twice before, she was still unprepared for her body's instant response as his lips connected with hers. Every inch of her skin tingled.

She moved closer to him as the kiss deepened, aligning her body with his. She pressed her hips into him. He stiffened immediately, and she reached around and placed her hands on the butt that she'd been longing to squeeze for days. Luc's hands dropped to cup her breasts.

He stroked the sensitive nipples through her shirt as his tongue mingled with hers, first slow and sexy, then increasing in intensity. Maryse could feel the warmth of his hand and groaned as his fingers stroked her engorged nipples and wished there wasn't so much fabric between them. She was just about to tear off her own clothes, then launch for Luc's when he slid his hands down to her waist and pulled her T-shirt and sports bra over her head.

Her breasts stood at full attention as the cool air of the room blew over them, but Luc immediately set to warming them back up, cupping her breast in his hand, stroking the nipple with his thumb, while trailing kisses down her neck. When he put his lips on her other breast she felt her knees weaken. Luc paused for a moment and gave her a sexy smile, knowing with certainty what he was doing to her untrained flesh.

"Don't stop," she whispered. "I want you to touch every square inch of me."

Luc laughed and lifted her onto the desk. "Oh, I have absolutely no intention of stopping. I was only repositioning you for what I had in mind next." He lowered his head to her breast again and took it in his mouth, swirling his tongue around and around until she thought she would beg for more. As his mouth worked its magic, he reached down and slid her yoga pants off and let them fall into a heap on the floor. His hand went back to her waist, but when he came to the lacy underwear, he paused. He pulled back ever so slightly and looked down at the thin strip of pink that barely covered her. He placed one finger inside the fabric at her hip and started to slide it toward her center. "My God, Maryse. Do you have any idea what you do to me?"

Maryse sucked in a breath as his hand moved slowly downward to the place she desperately wanted it to be. "I was hoping you'd show me," she said.

Luc lowered his head to her neck once more and trailed kisses all the way down to her breasts, all while slowly inching his finger toward her core, building a sweet anticipation that she thought might send her over the edge before they got any further. Maryse bit her lip to keep from encouraging him to hurry. Finally, he rubbed his finger across her sensitive nub, and pleasure flashed through her, making her groan.

He stroked her slowly, gently, as his mouth continued its assault on her breasts, and just when she thought she was going to lose it, he stopped and started trailing kisses down her stomach as he worked the bit of lace off her body. As he inched closer and closer to her throbbing sex, she eased back until she was lying on the desk, certain that any moment she would melt into a puddle on the floor.

When his warm tongue made contact with her, it felt like a jolt of electricity burning from her center and spiking through the top of her head. Her vision blurred, and the room moved in waves. Up and down, he continued his assault, then switched to a gentle swirl. Maryse wished like hell she had something to grip . . . comforter, bedsheets . . . anything. Luc increased his speed, and her legs began to quiver, her breathing stopped altogether, and she clutched his hair in both her hands. Then the orgasm hit her like an atomic bomb, and she cried out as wave after wave of intense pleasure rushed over her body.

Her hips began to buck and thrash around, but Luc held them in place, obviously not yet done with her. He slowed his pace, and Maryse panted, trying to get her breath back, and before she knew it, the heat at her center was building again. Just when she thought he would send her over the edge again, Luc stopped his assault and rose up. It was only then that Maryse realized he'd pushed down his jeans and she could see every perfect square inch of him.

Luc rolled on a condom, gathered her in his arms, then kissed her deeply. Holding her face in his hands, he entered her. She gasped as he filled her and gently bit the soft flesh of his neck. Luc groaned and increased his stroke both in speed and length. She dug her nails into his back, clinging to him like a drowning woman, as he entered her over and over, each stroke better than the last, until she felt the fire building to an inferno.

"Oh God, Luc," she started, then couldn't continue.

Luc held her tighter and drove deeper. As her body clutched around him, they moved together again and again until she climaxed, pushing him over the edge with her.

They clung to each other for a while, neither of them wanting to move. Then Luc moved back enough to lower his lips to her again. "You are the most incredible woman," he whispered and kissed her again.

Maryse smiled as he finished the kiss. "I'd have to say that incredible thing works both ways. I don't think I can move my legs."

Luc laughed and drew her close to him again. "Then I guess we'll just have to stay here until you can."

Maryse lay her head on his shoulder and tried to concentrate on breathing. She was beginning to think she might actually recover when the alarm went off, shrieking with a high-pitched whine. Maryse jumped off the desk in a panic, scanning out the windows for movement, and certain that any minute, she was going to have a heart attack. But hey, at least it removed the necessity of finding something to say during that uncomfortable period following post-coital recovery.

Luc yanked on his pants, ran to his desk, and pulled a 9mm out of his top drawer. "Get down and stay down," he ordered, then left the office through the back door.

Maryse sank down onto the floor and slid around behind the desk, dragging her clothes with her as she went. She wiggled around on the cold, hard tile to pull on her yoga pants and T-shirt, then peeked around the desk and snagged her tennis shoes. These days she never knew when running might be called for.

Ready for action, she peeked over the top of the desk looking for a weapon, but the two best options were a stapler and a letter opener. Both required a proximity to the killer that she wasn't really interested in achieving, but unless she wanted to scotch tape the killer's hands together and mark the event on the calendar, the stapler and letter opener were her best options. She grabbed the two items and slid back down behind the desk.

She listened intently for any sound of Luc, but the alarm was so loud it drowned out everything. What had tripped it? And more importantly, what did they have planned for her?

And what was Luc doing toting around a gun, especially something like a 9mm?

Sure, most people that worked on the bayou carried some form of protection. Maryse had a 12-gauge and the pistol with the rubber bullets, but a 9mm? There wasn't anything in the bayou requiring that kind of rapid fire to stop. Even an alligator would back off a gunshot in a heartbeat.

Her mind flashed back to Luc's actions when the alarm went off—the way he crept down the hall, pressed flat against the wall. And when he'd left out the back door, it had been weapon first, just like in the movies. Except she got the feeling Luc wasn't imitating a movie when he'd left. It appeared to be a natural reaction from someone who had been through that same routine over and over again. Which made no sense at all for a zoologist.

But made all the sense in the world for a cop.

Chapter Fifteen

It was probably only five minutes before Maryse heard the back door creak open, but it felt like hours. She peered between the cracks of the desk and tried to see who had entered the office. She clutched her weapons and made the hasty decision that if the bad guy found her hiding place, she would stab him in the crotch with the letter opener, then staple his eyes. It was the best she could come up with.

When she heard Luc's voice yelling from down the hall, she let out a huge sigh of relief. She crawled out from under the desk and had just achieved a standing position when Luc ran into the office.

"Are you all right?" he asked and did a hurried check of the room, gun still firmly gripped in his right hand.

"Was anyone out there?"

Luc frowned. "No. But they could have gotten away before I made it outside."

Maryse nodded. "So what do you think happened?"

"I'm not sure, but I'm going to find out." He pulled out his cell phone and pushed in a number.

Whoever was on the other end of the call must have been sitting with the phone already at hand because Luc spoke as soon as he finished dialing. "Did you get anything?" he asked.

Maryse stared at him for a moment. She'd assumed he

was calling the police, but that question didn't sound like anything you'd start with when calling 911.

Luc was quiet for a couple of seconds, then clenched his jaw. "I see," he said, and flipped the phone shut.

"Who was that?" Maryse asked, almost afraid to know the answer.

Luc picked his gun up off the desk and shoved it in the waistband of his jeans, then strode to the front office window and peered between the blinds. "We've got to get out of here," he said, ignoring her question.

"Why? Who did you call? What did they say? What's going on, Luc?"

"Later," Luc said, and opened the storage closet. On the top shelf sat computer and a monitor, flashing alternating pictures of each side of the outside of the office. Luc pulled a flash drive from the CPU and slid it into his jeans pocket.

Maryse stared at him in disbelief. "You had that recording? And couldn't someone just steal the flash drive?"

"Wouldn't do any good. There's a satellite on the roof. It's sending a feed to my buddy in New Orleans. That's who I called. The flash drive only covers part of the building."

Satellite feed? Monitored footage by remote in New Orleans? Maryse's head started to spin. Something was very, very wrong here. That was an awful lot of energy and time, not to mention the cost, to spend on a woman Luc hadn't even known the week before. "Luc, has someone broken in here before?"

Luc barely glanced at her and nodded, then looked out the window again. "The back door was unlocked the day after your truck wreck. I thought maybe you'd just forgotten to lock it, but then I clearly remembered checking it the night before. After your cabin blew up, I figured it couldn't be a coincidence."

Maryse blinked, trying to absorb everything, but it was like trying to take in *The Godfather* trilogy in a single sitting. "So what exactly did your buddy in New Orleans see when the alarm went off?"

Luc turned to face her, his expression grim, his jaw set in a hard line. "The suspect was behind the office. He was wearing a backpack and holding what looked like a spool of wire."

"And he probably wasn't hiking." Maryse studied Luc's face, certain there was more he wasn't telling her—like maybe why a zoologist was using words like "suspect."

Luc shook his head. "Not likely. He was probably about to rig another device like the one used on your cabin. Regardless, we need to get out of here and stay out until the week is over. This place is too remote. Not nearly enough escape routes."

Maryse narrowed her gaze and stared Luc straight in the eyes. "And exactly how many escape options does a zoologist need?"

Luc's expression went completely blank, and he looked away. "There's something we need to talk about," he finally said, "but it needs to wait. It wouldn't take much to launch a fire bomb in here."

Fire bomb? Launch? Hell, her stapler wasn't going to cover that one at all. "Fine. We're leaving now, but as soon as we're out of the parking lot, you're going to start talking."

Luc nodded and pulled the 9mm from his waistband. "Wait here a minute." He opened the front door and peered out with the gun clutched up near his shoulders, ready to take aim and fire. Then he edged out the door. A couple of seconds passed before he stuck his head back in and motioned her beside him.

Given that Maryse was certain she wasn't going to like whatever Luc was about to tell her in the car, the last place she wanted to be was close to him, but it was a better than running with her stapler. Barely. She slipped outside and waited while he locked the door, then crept behind him, practically glued to his hip. Luc was on high alert, scanning all directions for a sign of movement.

Or bomb setters.

Maryse tried to maintain her cool, but with every step she grew more and more anxious to get away from this isolated stretch of bayou. This was all Helena's fault—her and her damned money. If this is what you got for mingling with "society," when it was all over, Maryse was burying herself deep, deep in the bayou where only the mosquitoes could find her.

They were almost to the car when a nutria scurried out of the underbrush directly in front of them. Before her mind could even register the small, beaverlike creature, Maryse dropped the stapler and hauled ass to the car, beating Luc's strides by a mile. She grabbed the door handle and yanked, thankful she didn't have long nails to break, jumped inside, and scrunched down as far as possible on the floorboard. Luc jumped in a second later, started the car, and tore out of the parking lot like they were on fire.

Which lately could be a real possibility.

When the rattle from the floorboard went away, Maryse knew they'd reached the highway. She inched up from her fetal position and onto the seat, albeit somewhat slouched, but at least in a semi-sitting position.

"You all right?" Luc asked, the concern evident in his voice.

"Oh, just peachy. I'm getting so used to people trying to bump me off that tomorrow I probably won't even run. In fact, I was just thinking I ought to wear my best dress every day to save the undertaker the time later on."

Luc gave her a small smile. "You're doing great, Maryse. Most people wouldn't have made it this long without having a nervous breakdown."

Maryse glared. "And what makes you think I haven't? Do I seem remotely normal to you?"

"You're completely out of your element. You've had a ton of physical and mental stress put on you in a very short time—not withstanding your new paranormal abilities."

A gross understatement. "Yeah, out of my element. Sorta like a zoologist toting a nine like a character from *Law & Order?*"

A light flush crept up Luc's face, and Maryse knew she was in for some very bad information. Luc stared out the windshield a few seconds before speaking. "I got involved with you because it was my job."

"And that job is . . . and let's just stop pretending the answer is zoology."

"I'm a special agent for the DEQ."

Maryse straightened up in her seat. This was definitely not the answer she'd expected. "You're kidding me."

Luc pulled his ID out of his pocket and passed it to Maryse. Son of a bitch. Special Agent Luc LeJeune. Maryse's hands dropped into her lap seemingly of their own volition, like the badge was too heavy. "What in the world would the DEQ want with me? I'm the most boring person on Earth—or used to be anyway. What could I possibly be doing so wrong that it would bring a state investigation down on me?"

Luc shook his head. "It's not you. At least it didn't start out being you."

"What the hell are you talking about?" Maryse felt beads of sweat begin to form on her brow, frustration and confusion overwhelming her.

"The agency got a tip that a chemical company was dumping waste into the bayou. The informant claimed to be a resident of Mudbug, and on the surface, the information seemed to check out. Then the intel stopped—no more letters, no phone calls, and all attempts to locate this person failed. I was sent down here to find the informant and verify his claims. We're under a bit of pressure from the EPA."

"Oh my God! Is it toxic? Where is it?"

"We don't even know for sure that the dumping is going on, much less what the waste is or where it is. There's no reason to get excited just yet. If the dumping is going on, the site could be anywhere in the surrounding area, not necessarily in Mudbug."

Maryse took a minute to process this information. "So you think someone is dumping toxic waste into the bayou somewhere, and you're undercover to find the guy who tipped you off. Then why are you hooked up with me?"

Luc stared out the window again. "At first it was business. Then it got personal. I thought you'd figured that out."

Personal? As in he liked her so he was trying to protect her? And business—what business? She wasn't in any danger when Luc first arrived. "So you came down here to locate a mole and instead, you end up seeing ghosts and playing protector for me. Does that cover it?"

Luc nodded. "I guess so. I care about you, Maryse, and you don't have the training or ability to deal with something like this. I was afraid something bad would happen if I didn't help—am still afraid."

He cared about her? He *was* spending an awful lot of time putting himself in danger. But the fact remained that he didn't care enough to tell her the truth. Not until he was left with no other choice. "And what does your agency think of your extra-curricular activities?"

Luc frowned. "They're not happy. They think I've drawn too much attention to myself and they're afraid it will blow my cover."

Maryse narrowed her eyes, certain that something in his story didn't ring true—not exactly. How was Luc supposed to discover the informant when he'd been shut up in an office with her? "But you're still here."

"I couldn't leave you this way."

Bullshit. "Why not? You could lie to me this way." Then a thought came to mind—a memory of Luc trying to read her notebook that day in her lab. "You thought I was the informant."

"That was one possibility, yes."

"And the other possibility?"

Luc looked out the window down the highway, a slight flush creeping up his neck. Maryse stared at him for a moment, then it hit her. "Oh, my God. You thought I was covering for the chemical company. Somehow hiding the evidence of the pollution."

Luc jerked his head around to look at her. "No, I never thought that, even when the agency suggested it. I looked into your research because I thought you'd come across the source. I didn't know what you were working on until Helena let the cat out of the bag." He sighed. "I'm sorry, Maryse. I didn't want to lie to you, but I couldn't tell you the truth. Don't you understand that?"

Maryse looked directly in his eyes. "All I understand is that every man I've been with has used me in one form or fashion, and you've turned out to be no different."

He put one hand on her arm, but she brushed it off. "Don't even bother. In fact, you can drop me off at the hotel and return to your high security office in the bayou. I won't be needing your services any longer, *Agent* LeJeune."

Maryse didn't say a word as Luc drove the rest of the way back to the hotel, and Luc was obviously smart enough to know he wasn't going to talk his way out of this one. But the longer she sat in silence, the angrier she became. What the hell had she been thinking? Not only had she allowed herself to be used by another lying asshole, she'd actually welcomed him with open arms—and legs. What was it about her that she couldn't find an honest man to save her life?

Which was sort of an ironic question since apparently a *dishonest* man had done just that.

She stared out the window and held in the tears that threatened to fall. Damn it. Why did she always have to cry when she was mad? Just when she'd thought her life couldn't get more screwed up than it already was, she had to go add insult to injury by sleeping with Luc.

And even worse—she'd enjoyed it.

No more men, she vowed, as Luc swung the car onto Main Street. Society might as well give her a wimple and start calling her "sister."

They pulled into the hotel parking lot, and before Luc brought the car to a complete stop, Maryse jumped out, slamming the door behind her, and stalked into the hotel. She could hear the car idling behind her but forced herself to look straight ahead and never hesitate in her stride.

When she reached the door to the hotel, she heard the engine rev as the car screeched out of the parking lot. She glanced down the street as she stepped into the hotel and saw the car round the corner to the highway.

Probably going to see his "buddy" in New Orleans. Another DEQ agent, she had to assume at this point. Maybe they were going to review the tapes and see if Luc recognized the man outside the office. And then a terrible, horrible thought hit her. Her eyes blurred, and she walked headfirst into the corner of the door.

Video tape! Satellite feed!

And she'd been having sex with Luc right there on the desk in the middle of the office.

Sex on her desk wasn't exactly the way she'd always pictured herself on film. No, for her first foray onto camera, she'd had something a bit more dignified in mind, and something requiring a lot more clothes. Something like accepting the Nobel Prize for Medicine.

Her one foolish dream.

"Something wrong with you?" Mildred asked as she entered the hotel office, completely cutting into her thoughts of a royal romp.

Maryse frowned. A shorter list would probably be what *wasn't* wrong. "Nothing more than the usual." *And a video-taped orgasm with a lying DEQ agent.*

Mildred stared, not looking in the least bit convinced. Time for a distraction.

"Any luck locating Harold?" Maryse asked.

"Yep. Sara Belle down at the salon says she's almost positive she saw Harold unloading a suitcase at that fleabag motel on the outskirts of town."

Maryse groaned and slapped her forehead. "Helena left him that motel. Why didn't I think of that?" And even more, why didn't Helena think of that? Did she have to do all the work here?

Mildred narrowed her eyes at Maryse. "You're not thinking of tailing Harold, are you? 'Cause I don't have enough savings to post bail for murder. I don't want you anywhere near Hank Henry unless the police are involved. With guns. And Mace. Lots of Mace. And maybe one of those electric rods that makes you stupid senseless when it touches you."

"A stun gun," Maryse provided, although it was pointless information. Hank was already stupid senseless. Being jolted with fifty thousand or so volts of electricity might even make for an improvement. And if not, it would certainly make for a good show. "I'm not going to tail Harold," Maryse assured her. "I'll have someone else do it. Someone less conspicuous than me."

Mildred nodded. "Good. Probably needs to be Luc then. You know I love Sabine, but she's not exactly the sharpest tool in the box. You don't have to know where you came from to decide where you're going. If only she'd get her head out of the damned clouds and down her on Earth, that girl could probably make a lot of herself."

"Sabine's fine, and lately, she's backed off a lot on the whole parental search thing." Maryse waved a hand in dismissal. "I know you think the whole paranormal thing is complete bunk, but at least she's making money. There are probably worse things."

Mildred stared at her for a moment. "I think the whole paranormal thing is bunk? Last time I checked, you weren't exactly jumping on that bandwagon either. Did you hit your head too hard in one of those mishaps of yours?"

Oops. Momentary lapse of consciousness. And definitely all Luc's fault. She gave Mildred a sheepish smile. "Of course, I don't buy into that stuff. I've just given up trying to convince Sabine otherwise. As long as her business is successful, I guess I just decided who cares."

Mildred narrowed her eyes, and Maryse knew the hotel owner suspected something was up. Something Maryse wasn't telling her. In ten billion years she'd never come up with the ghost of Helena Henry, so Maryse figured she was in the clear as long as she didn't spout off something stupid again.

"Well, why don't you try to rest," Mildred said finally. "I'll be right here if you need me." She pointed to the front of the hotel. "And no standing in front of the plate-glass window."

Maryse nodded and left the office. There was no way possible she could rest. Between ghosts, attempted murder, and videotaped sex, she was about to have that nervous breakdown she'd been putting off. And avoiding Mildred until she had control of her racing emotions probably wasn't a bad idea. If she stayed in the office with Mildred's hawk eye on her, she knew she'd end up confessing her sins of the flesh. And she wasn't ready to discuss her romp with Luc the Liar, especially given her track record with questionable men.

She snuck in a call to Sabine but got her voice mail. She left her a brief message with instructions to come directly to the hotel when she got back from visiting Raissa, then closed her phone, shoved it in her pocket, and sighed. Finally deciding she couldn't stand around in the hallway until Sabine showed up, she grabbed a bottle of Pledge and a rag from the storage closet and began to polish the spindles on the stairwell. She finished that chore in about thirty minutes, and then Sabine walked in, saving her from doing something really strange, like vacuuming the lobby. Sabine stared at her for a moment, then sniffed the air. Since the entire stairwell smelled lemony fresh, there was really no hiding what she'd been up to.

Sabine raised one eyebrow. "You want to tell me why you're avoiding Mildred?"

Maryse glared. "I thought you weren't psychic."

Sabine laughed. "It doesn't take a genius to see that something's wrong if the woman who hates cleaning more than root canals starts breaking out the Pledge on a building that's not even hers."

Maryse shrugged. "I'm stressed."

"Bullshit. You drink when you're stressed. You clean when you're avoiding."

"Well, Mildred hasn't figured it out, so I guess it doesn't matter."

Sabine shook her head. "Mildred knows damned good and well why you're cleaning. She also knows that you won't breathe a word to her about whatever secret you're keeping until there's no other choice."

"Got that right," Maryse mumbled.

"She also knows that you'll tell me if it's important, and I'll tell her."

Maryse stared at her so-called best friend in dismay. "Is this what the two of you do when I'm not around? Plot ways to analyze my life and then share things I've told you in confidence?"

Sabine had the good sense to look guilty. "It's not like that. It's just that Mildred and I both worry about you, and you don't make it easy on people by secluding yourself so much on the bayou. I've seen you more since Helena died than I have in the past six months."

Maryse sank onto the stairs. "You know you're welcome at my place anytime, or at least you were when I had a place. And Mildred too. I know I didn't come to town often, but it just wasn't necessary. I had everything there that I needed."

Sabine sat beside her on the stairwell and gave her a sad smile. "But don't you see, Maryse? You didn't have every- thing you needed. You're losing sight of people, how they operate, what motivates them. If you were more social, you would have seen Christopher coming a mile away." She paused for a moment, then took a breath before continu- ing. "And I hope this doesn't make you mad, but I don't have to be psychic to see what's going on between you and Luc. Right now, I'd bet anything that's what drove you to dusting."

Maryse felt her back tense at the mention of Luc's name. Was she really that easy to read? "Are you saying I have to become the life of the party or I'm always going to get screwed? If so, then I'm in trouble. I just don't have what it takes to conquer the world."

"Raissa's worried about you. She has the feeling that you're overlooking something important because it's too close to you. She's going to do another reading tonight and call me." Sabine placed her hand on Maryse's and squeezed. "You don't have to conquer the world, Maryse, but you can't hide from it either."

She wasn't hiding, Maryse wanted to yell. But somehow the words hung in her throat. She wasn't hiding. Was she? Her laboratory work was the most important thing in her life, and it required an enormous amount of time, but surely no one was going to blame her for spending her time in the lab.

But as soon as that thought crossed her mind, she got flashes of long Saturdays where she'd finished up every- thing at the lab by noon and spent the rest of the day reading medical journals or cruising the bayou looking for hybrid plants that she might not have used for testing before. If she wasn't working on her research, then she was tearing apart her kitchen to put in shelves or some other household chore that wasn't really necessary. She hadn't even picked up a novel or turned on the television in longer than she could remember.

Was her motivation to find a cure really as selfless as she'd thought? Or had the strain of watching her father waste away provided her with a convenient excuse to lock herself away from life?

"Maryse." Sabine gently shook her arm. "Are you all right? I wasn't trying to hurt your feelings."

"I know," Maryse said. Sabine hadn't hurt her feelings, but she'd unknowingly unlocked a floodgate that made it frighteningly clear that Maryse had been living away from the world far too long.

Chapter Sixteen

Before Maryse could mull over her newfound revelation and figure out what the hell it meant for her future—if there was one—Helena walked through the hotel wall and ruined the entire moment.

"Helena's here," Sabine said.

Maryse stared at Sabine.

"It's that look on your face . . . remember, like you have gas," Sabine explained.

Helena shot Sabine a dirty look, then asked, "Did Mildred find Harold?"

"Yeah," Maryse said, "he's at that motel where you left him. Are you ready to do this?"

Helena sighed. "I'm as ready as I'll ever be to see Harold again, or Hank, for that matter. But I guess I sorta owe you given that this whole mess is my fault."

A bit of an understatement.

"Okay," Maryse said. "I'll check out with Mildred and tell her Sabine and I are going to the store to pick up some stuff I forgot yesterday." She turned to Sabine. "That's assuming, of course, that you'll drive, since Luc sorta left in my car."

Sabine wrinkled her brow, obviously wanting to delve into the topic of Luc but not wanting to do it now. "Sure, as long as you're not carrying any kind of weapon in case we run into Hank. I don't have enough money for bail."

Maryse sighed. "Now you're starting to sound like Mildred."

There was a bit of a scuffle in the parking lot while Sabine and Helena argued, with Maryse as the translator, over who would ride shotgun. Sabine thought Maryse should ride shotgun and Helena thought she deserved the seat as she would be doing all the legwork once they got there.

Maryse looked at Helena and pointed to the backseat. "You can't sit in the front, Helena. Sabine is not going to drive around town with me in the back like she's chauffeuring. The key to investigating is to avoid attention, not attract it."

Maryse guessed the image of two adults and a ghost in a car flitted through Helena's mind, because she got into the back seat and stopped grumbling. Sabine made the drive to the Lower Mudbug Motel in under twenty minutes and parked across the street in a lot for an all-night diner. Maryse scanned the seedy area with a critical eye and hoped they wouldn't get jacked for Sabine's 1992 Nissan Sentra while sitting there, but the only other choices were an X-rated video store or a tattoo parlor.

Helena frowned when Maryse pointed to the motel, but she didn't say a word as she left the car and walked through the lobby into the dilapidated old building. She returned a couple of minutes later to report that the asshole was indeed inside with one of his floozies, and not even the same one he'd left in the car at the reading of the will. Maryse's mind flickered for a moment onto exactly what kind of woman, much less two, took up with someone like Harold Henry, but she didn't have the time to ponder it now and probably didn't have the requisite intelligence, or lack thereof, to understand it all.

Their mark established, she pulled out her cell phone

and gave Wheeler a call, instructing him to give her five minutes, then make the call to Harold at the motel. She closed the phone and looked at Helena. "You're on. Maybe this time you'll get lucky and Harold will be naked."

Helena glared at her, got out of the car, and stomped all the way to the motel and through the wall. Sabine shook her head and looked over at Maryse. "You know, you really shouldn't bait her that way. It just frustrates you more."

"I know, but the woman is impossible. I'm fairly certain that if it turns out either Hank or Harold killed her, a Mudbug jury would not only let them off, but probably give them a medal."

Sabine smiled. "I know what you're saying, I really do, but I'm starting to think that maybe Helena isn't all that bad. After all, she made sure the town was protected by giving you the land, and she used the money you paid her to pay down your debts."

"Which, now that you mention it," Maryse interrupted, "she still hasn't really explained."

"And she gave all that stuff to an orphanage," Sabine continued, ignoring her outburst. "I guess I'm starting to wonder if there wasn't a purpose behind Helena being a bitch all these years."

Maryse stared out the windshield at the Lower Mudbug Motel. "Well, if there was, I'm not getting it."

It seemed to take forever for Helena to return, but it couldn't have been more than ten minutes before Maryse saw her leap from the second floor and hit the ground with one of those military rolls. She was wearing green camouflage and looked like a rolling bush except for the black smudges glistening under her eyes, which made her resemble a linebacker given her rather dense frame. When her body finally lost all momentum, Helena lay completely still, sprawled on the weedy lawn of the cheap motel, and for a moment, Maryse wondered if it was possible to die twice.

A few seconds later, Harold came hurrying out of the hotel entrance. Maryse and Sabine ducked down in the car, trying to peer over the dashboard. Helena burst into the backseat seconds later, still huffing and puffing from her Rambo acrobatics.

"Where's he going in such a hurry?" Maryse asked Helena.

"He called Hank as soon as he got off the phone with Wheeler," Helena replied. "He's going to meet him now."

Maryse repeated the information to Sabine, who had already started the car and was inching toward the parking lot exit as Harold left the motel in a late model, rust-covered sedan. "Hang back a little," Maryse instructed. "I don't want him to see us."

"I'm trying," Sabine said as she pressed down on the accelerator, "but he's driving like an idiot."

"He is an idiot," Helena said.

"Hell," Maryse said as she peered over the dashboard and watched as Harold pushed the upper limits of the rusty sedan. "We should have had Helena ride with Harold."

Sabine's hands were clenched on the steering wheel as she inched her car faster down the highway. Maryse was pretty sure her friend had almost reached her limit of speed and fear when suddenly Harold's car jerked over to the side of the road and disappeared into the brush. Sabine cut her speed and eased onto the shoulder, then slowly pulled up to the spot where they'd last seen Harold.

A rutted trail overgrown with grass and weeds led into the bayou. Maryse cursed under her breath. "We can't follow him down there. He'd see us coming for sure, and we have no idea what we'd be running into."

"We don't have to follow him," Helena said. "I know where he's going."

Maryse yanked around in her seat to look at Helena. "Where?"

"My family had a camp off this trail," Helena said. "Harold told me years ago that it had fallen in such disrepair that it wasn't habitable."

"And you never checked?"

Helena looked at Maryse as if she'd lost her mind. "Tromp around in the bayou? No thanks. Not all of us have your higher aspirations, Maryse. And I damned sure don't cotton to running into snakes or alligators or even bugs."

"The only snake down that trail is Harold," Maryse shot back, "and probably Hank."

Helena shrugged. "Probably. Harold only started staying at the motel a couple of years ago, so he was taking his bit of snatch somewhere before that. Most likely it was the camp, but I never thought of it."

Just like Helena to forget something important. Maryse pointed to the trail. "Well, now's your chance to get caught up on things happening behind your back."

Helena crossed her arms in front of her and shook her head. "Absolutely not. I am not wading into the marsh."

Maryse threw her hands in the air. "What do you think is going to happen to you? You're already dead!"

Helena glared. "You don't have to keep reminding me of that, you know. It's rude."

"Maybe it's hard to take you seriously when your face looks like a linebacker for the Saints."

"Well, crap," Helena grumbled and waved her hands in front of her face like a magician. If she pulled a rabbit out of her ear, Maryse swore she was going to kill her.

"What about this?" Helena asked a couple of seconds later. "Is the black gone?"

Maryse took one look at Helena, then closed her eyes and counted to ten. The black was gone, but she had managed to replace it with a vibrant, traffic-stopping orange. "Yeah, it's gone, and just in case it's deer season, you've got that covered too."

"Well, it will just have to stay that way," Helena said as she drifted through the car door and tromped off into the marsh.

As soon as she was gone, Maryse repeated the conversation to Sabine. "So now we just have to decide what to do next," Maryse said.

Sabine shook her head. "No, we don't. You're going to call your attorney and have Hank served. That's it."

Maryse cast a wistful glance down the trail. Oh, but for the chance to throttle the life out of Hank Henry. "But don't you think—"

Sabine cut her off with a hand. "No, I don't think, and you don't either. You promised."

Maryse turned in her seat and looked Sabine straight in the eyes. "Just like we promised to never keep secrets from each other?"

Sabine averted her eyes. "I don't know what you're talking about."

Maryse wanted to be angry with her friend for keeping something so important from her, but her fear was so evident that Maryse's heart broke in two. She clasped her hand gently over Sabine's. "I know about the tests."

Luc leaned over Brian and studied the monitor, then banged one fist on the desk, unable to hold in his frustration any longer. "Damn it! There's no clear shot of his face."

Brian looked up at him and let out a breath. "I tried everything, Luc. I know what you were hoping for, but this guy just didn't give us the right view. Man, I'm sorry."

Luc scanned the blurry image one last time and clapped Brian on the shoulder. "It's not your fault. This guy knew what he was doing."

Brian nodded. "Yeah, with the collar on that jacket turned up, the sunglasses, and his cap pulled down so low, one might think he was trying not to be recognized."

"One might," Luc agreed. "So what were you able to get?"

Brian pulled a sheet of paper off the printer and handed it to Luc. "I figured you'd want a copy of the analysis, but basically, this is what we have: the guy is about six feet tall, large frame, and looks like he was built at some time but his body's lost its tone. His body movement puts him roughly in the fifty to sixty age range, assuming no debilitating injuries on a younger man, and he's white. That's about all I can give you."

Luc sighed. "Great—an old, flabby, white male. You've just described half of the men in Mudbug."

"I know it's not much, but this along with the info you got on the explosion at the cabin makes me think you were right on your military assumption. Whoever this is, they had rigged explosives before, and based on the switches, they're either former military or learned from someone who was."

Luc nodded. "Once again, half the men in Mudbug. And what about the petroleum company info I called you about on the way here?"

Brian nodded and pulled up another file on his computer. "I cross-referenced all the companies licensed to drill in Louisiana with current operating locations. I figured companies with a base already established near the area would be the most likely to know about the land and want to acquire it."

"Good thinking." Luc leaned toward the monitor and studied the page as it opened. "Three companies, huh? You think it's good information?"

"I think it's as close as we're getting to start. But don't ask me what you're supposed to do with the info from here."

"I have an idea about that," Luc said.

Brian groaned. "Man, I hate it when you get ideas."

"Don't worry. This one is easy and completely legal."

"Well, that's a change. Lay it on me."

"I need to know if any residents of Mudbug own a significant amount of stock in any of the companies. I can't imagine a board of directors would vote to bump someone off in the hopes that they can acquire some oil-filled land. There's plenty of it to be had in Louisiana and other people willing to lease. So it's got to be someone outside the company but with a vested interest in the company's success."

"Already ahead of you." Brian clicked to open a spreadsheet and pointed to a list of names. "These are the eight Mudbug residents who own stock in any of the three petroleum companies. Most have small investments. Nothing worth acting crazy for sure. But this one . . ." Brian pointed to a name on the spreadsheet. "He has a 5 percent share and a brother on the board of directors."

Luc read the name. "Thomas Breaux." He looked at Brian. "The doctor? Shit. That would explain everything."

"How do you figure?"

"We have to figure that Maryse wasn't the first target. Her mother-in-law had to be first, and Breaux was her doctor. If anyone would know how to bump off Helena Henry and get her buried without an autopsy, it would be her doctor."

"I don't suppose I have to tell you how he paid for medical school, right?"

"The military. Jesus, Brian," Luc said, and shook his head. "How do I get myself mixed up in this shit?"

Brian looked up at him and cocked his head to the side. "You know, I would say it's the white-knight syndrome—that whole damsel-in-distress thing, but this time it's different."

Luc shoved his hands in his pockets and avoided his buddy's gaze. "I don't know what you're talking about. This is hardly the first woman I've helped out of a tough spot."

"Yeah, but it's the first one you've fallen for." Brian smiled. "Unbelievable, LeJeune. I never thought I'd see the day. This botanist must be something else to have you so wound up."

Disappearing husband, exploding cabin, killer inheritance, a dead mother-in-law who hadn't quite left this world, and let's not forget trying to save the world from one of the worst diseases known to man. "Yes, she's something else all right," Luc agreed.

Brian grinned and opened his mouth, probably to rib Luc some more, but the door to the lab flew open and the boss strode in. "Damn it, LeJeune," he ranted. "You don't check your messages, you don't return calls, and now you're standing in the office and haven't checked in with me. I yanked you off the Mudbug assignment yesterday. Why weren't you in the office this morning?"

Luc looked at Wilson but didn't meet the other man's eyes. "I have a couple of things I need to wrap up down there."

"The hell you do! We've got our informant."

Shit. "Who is it?"

"That accountant that Duhon was following. Seems the

profit margin increased a little too much for his taste, and he decided he was James Bond or something. Fucker isn't five foot two and scared of his own shadow, but he went poking his nose into things and found all the big shot's secret files. Then he made the phone call to the DEQ, got scared they'd kill him or something, and has been trying to find a new job ever since. Dumbass."

"Sounds like it," Luc said, stalling until he could figure out some reason to convince Wilson to let him stay in Mudbug another couple of days.

"Anyway, I need you to work with our scared shitless Sherlock and the other agents to gather enough evidence to prosecute. We have enough information to pin down the dumping sites, so your days of dallying with that botanist are over."

"There's some other things I'm looking into. Just a couple of days, boss, that's all I need."

"No way, LeJeune. You better be in this office at ten tomorrow morning for debriefing. Otherwise, don't bother coming in at all." Wilson spun around and strode out of the office, slamming the door behind him.

Brian whistled. "I haven't seen him this worked up since the Superbowl."

Luc nodded. "Football can be very emotional." He stared out the window for a moment, then looked back at Brian, the vaguest notion of an idea forming in his mind. "Hey, have you started mapping out the spots that informant said the dumping occurred?"

"Yeah, we've drawn samples from three so far."

"Can you get me the info on the exact locations and the results of your testing?"

"Not a problem. I'll e-mail everything as soon as I scan it all in."

"Okay," Luc said. "Do me another favor. E-mail me the phone number of the lab guy here who researched Maryse's work."

Brian narrowed his eyes. "I'll do it, but, dude, you are gonna be in some serious shit if you don't let this botanist thing go."

Luc stared at the shadowy figure on the monitor. "I can't. Not just yet."

Sabine stared at Maryse in shock. "How did you find out? Everything was supposed to be confidential."

"Your file was on the medical records desk when Helena and I broke into the hospital," Maryse said. "I'm sorry, Sabine, but I had to look. You understand, right?"

Sabine sniffed and rubbed her nose with her free hand. "I guess so. I probably would have done the same thing. But, Maryse, you have to know that everything is going to be fine. This one is no different than the others. I'm sure of it."

More than anything in the world, Maryse wanted to believe Sabine, wanted the faith of her friend's conviction, but the scientist in her knew the reality. And the girl who'd lost both her mother and father to the same disease was scared to death. "How can you be sure? Maybe you need to see a specialist. I know a doctor in New Orleans."

Sabine shook her head. "I'm nowhere near needing a specialist now or in the future. I've asked Raissa about this. She thinks I'm going to be fine."

"She thinks?" Maryse squeezed Sabine's hand. "That's just not good enough, Sabine. Please, please promise me that as soon as this is over, you'll let me take you to New Orleans and see that doctor I know. For me."

The tears that had been hanging on the rim of Sabine's

eyelids finally spilled over, and she nodded. "Okay. I promise." She leaned over and clutched Maryse in a hug. "If you promise to be around to take me, I'll promise to go."

Maryse sniffled and tried in vain to hold back her own tears. "That sounds fair."

"Who died?" Helena's voice cut into their moment. "Oh wait, that would be me." The ghost grinned.

Maryse frowned at Helena and instructed Sabine to drive. "We don't want Harold catching us parked on the side of the road or we're busted."

Sabine edged off the shoulder and onto the highway, then made a quick U-turn and stomped on the accelerator. Maryse waited until they were out of sight of the trail, then turned in her seat to face Helena. "Well, are you going to fill me in?"

"Hank was there," Helena said, and frowned.

"And?"

"And what? The moron was there with his even more moronic father."

Maryse counted to five. "What did they say, Helena?"

Helena sighed. "Harold yelled at Hank for being so useless that I didn't leave him the land. Hank said it wasn't his fault and he didn't know anything about my will before the reading, which is true."

Maryse stared at Helena, but the ghost wouldn't meet her gaze. "What are you not telling me?"

Helena looked at Maryse, her sadness evident in her expression. "Harold said Hank wouldn't have to worry because it looked like he'd scared you into giving up the land."

"So it *was* Harold who tried to kill me." Maryse slumped back in her seat, not sure whether to be happy the mystery was solved or alarmed that Harold still walked the streets.

God forbid he caught on to the fake land transfer before the week was up.

"I guess it must have been Harold," Helena said finally, "but I still can't believe it. Luc said those explosives were rigged by a professional. Harold was military, but I married the man, and I can tell you for certain, no one would ever let him work with explosives. Hell, he couldn't even grill chicken without burning himself, and the television remote—forget it."

"But according to Mildred, Harold was always bragging at Johnny's about his special forces tour," Maryse argued.

Helena shook her head. "I never went to Johnny's so I can't say, but if Mildred says so, then I guess it's so. All I know is Harold used to tell me after he came home from a bender that it was amazing how the world 'evened things out' over time."

Maryse stared at Helena. "What the heck is that supposed to mean?"

Helena shrugged. "I don't know, but I always took it as some remark about his military service."

"What's going on?" Sabine asked.

Maryse felt instantly guilty. "I'm sorry, Sabine. I keep forgetting you can't hear her." She filled in the blanks of her conversation with Helena.

"I don't like it," Sabine said when she finished.

"Maybe Harold had help from someone else. After all, if he's in cahoots with the oil companies, couldn't he find someone to pay for that kind of service—especially with the amount of money on the line?"

"It's possible," Sabine said, "but somehow it just doesn't feel right. Maybe we've been looking in the wrong place. Maybe it isn't Harold at all."

Maryse yanked her cell phone from her pocket and

pressed in the speed dial for her attorney. "But what else is there?"

Thirty minutes later, a new stun gun in hand, Maryse took one look at Mildred's hotel, knowing she should probably go inside. As Sabine had pointed out before, they couldn't be certain Harold was the one gunning for Maryse, and it was much smarter for her to lie as low as possible until they were certain no one else had a hidden agenda. But the very thought of closing herself up in that tiny room, or even worse, sitting in Mildred's office and enduring the older woman's scrutiny, made her feel claustrophobic. And what difference did it really make in the big scheme of things? She could be inside in an interior room, hidden in a closet, and covered in Kevlar with a stun gun pointed at the door, and a bomb would still kill her.

"Maryse Robicheaux," Mildred's voice broke into her thoughts. "Get your skinny butt into this hotel." Mildred stood in the doorway of the hotel, hands on her hips and a disapproving look on her face. "Why don't you just stand in the middle of the street wearing a target on your back next time?"

As Maryse stepped onto the sidewalk, she heard the zing of something small and fast passing right by her head, then a crack of glass. She took the remaining two steps to the plate-glass window on the front of the hotel and looked eye level at a tiny hole that had pierced clean through the glass. A hole the size of a bullet.

Maryse jumped back from the window in horror as a second shot hit the brick building just above her head. In the split second she was trying to decide which way to run, someone slammed into her, half-shoving, half-carrying her into the entrance of the hotel. They landed on the hardwood floor of the hotel foyer, and Maryse struggled with the weight of the person on top of her, pummeling the attacker as much as she could given the restraint. She screamed for Mildred to call the police, when the weight lifted and she was yanked to her feet.

"Hank!" Maryse stared at him in disbelief. "What the hell are you doing?"

Her wayward husband grimaced and touched a growing red spot on his shirt, just below the chest. "I'm getting shot and beat to a pulp, that's what."

"Holy shit! We have to get you to the hospital."

Before she could move, Hank grabbed her arm. "Are you stupid? Someone is shooting at you."

Maryse's jaw dropped, and she stared at her husband, then laughed. Hank calling her stupid was a real eye-opener.

"Don't worry about it," Mildred said. "I've already called 911." She shot Hank a dirty look. "And the coroner, just in case I get lucky." She motioned them to the office. "Get off my rug before you bleed on it," she said, then stalked into her office and began yanking first-aid supplies out of a storage cabinet.

Maryse had to hand it to her—for someone who had professed the burning desire to saw Hank Henry's balls off with a dull butter knife, Mildred showed a remarkable amount of restraint and concern. Grabbing a clean towel from the cabinet, she instructed Hank to lie on the couch. Kneeling beside him, she gently pulled his shirt away from his chest. Hank moaned in agony. Mildred placed the towel against his side to soak up the excess blood, then lifted it to assess the damage.

Maryse leaned over, almost afraid to look when Mildred sighed with obvious relief. "It's only a surface wound," Maryse said.

"Only?" Hank stared at them in disbelief. "Well, it hurts like death."

Mildred folded the towel over to a clean side and pressed it back against the wound. "It's going to hurt," she said. "That's a tender part of the body, and it bleeds a lot."

"Try to calm down," Maryse instructed. "Deep breaths. It will help slow the blood flow."

Hank looked up at her, still not convinced he wasn't going to die right there on the couch, but he nodded and took a couple of deep breaths. A minute later, the paramedics and the cops came storming into the hotel. The paramedics carted Hank off to the hospital, one officer riding along, and the rest of the Mudbug police department took a stance in Mildred's office and began firing questions like a semi-automatic weapon.

When they were done, Maryse ran some water in the sink and placed the stained towel in there to soak. She didn't know why. The towel was most certainly ruined, but the activity kept her from thinking about Hank and about how she felt finally coming face to face with him. She thought she'd hate him. She thought the sight of him would either disgust her to the point of illness or madden her to the point of homicide.

And then he'd gone and taken a bullet that was meant for her.

Shit.

Chapter Seventeen

It was almost two hours later before one of the cops could provide Maryse with an armed escort to the hospital. Mildred had voted against it, but Sabine, who had run into the hotel shortly after the police, understood why she needed to go. Or maybe not why, exactly, but just that it was something Maryse had to do. Besides, a bullet wound and restraint in a hospital bed might be the only way she could have a face to face with Hank Henry.

As Maryse walked down the hospital corridor toward Hank's room, she wondered for the millionth time what she was going to say. She'd had two years to rehearse this moment, and now that it was here, she couldn't think of a damn thing to say to the man who'd saved her life.

Her husband.

That last thought stopped her dead in her tracks. She leaned against the wall outside Hank's door and caught her breath. What in the world could convey the range of emotions that Hank brought out in her? She didn't think words existed to describe what she felt, even if she was certain of what that was.

She had just built the courage to enter the room when Helena stepped into the hall and put one finger to her lips. "Not now," she whispered, and Maryse wondered what possibly could have made Helena Henry go quiet. She motioned to Maryse's pocket where she kept her cell phone. "Does that thing have a recorder?"

Maryse pulled her cell phone from her pocket and nodded.

"Then turn it on. We might be able to use this."

Maryse had no idea what Helena was up to, but she pressed a button and hoped it was the record. Otherwise, she'd just taken a picture of her own crotch. She leaned in closer to the door, and placed her phone as close as she could to the opening.

And that's when she was able to make out Harold's voice. A very unhappy Harold.

"What the hell were you thinking?" Harold raged. "You could have been killed and that damned land would have reverted back to that worthless piece of ass you married!"

Maryse clenched her jaw. Harold Henry had the nerve to call her worthless?

"Maryse is not worthless," Hank said.

Maryse frowned. Now Hank was defending her? Things were definitely weird.

"Besides," Hank continued, "that attorney said she drew up papers to transfer the land, right?"

"Oh, yeah," Harold said. "As long as she stays of that mindset for the next couple of days, there's no problem at all. But it's not like her death would exactly be a bad thing. At least then we'd know she couldn't change her mind."

"You're the one who tried to kill her," Hank accused.

"I already told you I didn't shoot at anyone." Harold's voice grew louder. "I would never risk shooting someone in broad daylight, and why the hell would I shoot you?"

"Well, someone shot at her," Hank argued. "I have the proof under these bandages."

"Which is why you should damned well stay away from

that slut. I don't know what kind of crap she's into that has people shooting at her, and I really don't give a damn, but you need to stay away from her. I put my ass on the line over that piece of marsh, and I will not see it fall into the hands of some pseudo-hippy scientist."

"How exactly did you put your ass on the line?" Hank asked.

"Stop pretending you don't know," Harold said. "Left to nature, Helena would have outlived me by a good fifty years just to spite me."

There was complete silence for a moment. Then Hank said, "Are you telling me you killed my mother?" His voice registered his disbelief, and once again, Maryse wondered just how dumb Hank really was. She glanced over at Helena, but the ghost stood stock still, her expression completely blank.

"You killed my mother?" Hank repeated.

"Oh, good God, Hank. Grow up." The disgust was evident in Harold's voice. "Your mother was a royal pain in both our asses. She thrived off being hateful, and no one is sorry to see her go, least of all me. So I slipped some rat poison into her coffee, so what?"

Maryse frowned. Helena had said she'd died after drinking brandy, not coffee.

"What the hell is wrong with you?" Harold continued to complain. "The woman cast you out of her life years ago. Why would you give a shit what I did?"

"She didn't cast me out," Hank said. "She paid me to leave. She's been paying me to stay gone. A monthly transfer to a bank account in New Orleans."

Maryse's jaw dropped, and she stared at Helena.

"Uh-oh," Helena said, and bolted through an exterior wall, making following her an impossibility.

Coward. But Maryse would deal with Helena later. Right

now, she needed all the damaging evidence she could get on Harold.

"What do you mean she paid you to stay away?" Harold asked.

"She said I wasn't going to ruin Maryse's life, and as long as I kept out of town and didn't contact her, she'd keep making the payments."

"Well, why didn't you divorce her before you left, or in absentia, or something?"

"I'm no attorney. I figured Maryse could get a divorce even if I was gone. I had no idea we were still married. Mom said to leave right then and never contact Maryse or anyone else in Mudbug again. And I kept that promise until I saw Mom's obituary and called you."

"Moron! It never occurred to you that if Helena kept you married to Maryse, she intended even then to leave that land to her? There is no way you're my son. You're too stupid for words."

"I think this conversation is over," Hank said. "Get out of my room."

"Oh, this is far from over," Harold threatened.

"Yes, it is. The land will transfer to me in a couple of days. I'll lease it out and give you a cut of the money, but you have to get out of my sight. I would never have been part of any of this. And if anything happens to Maryse, I will disappear and leave you with nothing."

"I've already told you I had nothing to do with shooting at that tramp," Harold raged.

"And her cabin exploding," Hank pointed out. "Rumor has it the device was military issue, and we all know who was special forces."

"Oh, for Christ's sake, I lied. I was a mess cook. I've never even shot a gun after basic training. Are you happy now?"

"If Maryse is alive in two days, I will be. Are we clear?"

Maryse looked for a place to hide. Either Harold was going to stomp out of the hospital and figure out how to shoot a gun again or throttle Hank right there in his hospital bed. Either way, she didn't want to get caught eavesdropping in the hallway.

There was an empty room across the hall, so Maryse slipped inside, leaving the door cracked a tiny bit so that she could see Hank's room. A couple of seconds later, Harold stormed out of the room, his face beet red.

Unbelievable. Hank Henry had finally grown a set of balls. If she didn't have it on tape, she wouldn't believe it herself. She waited until Harold had rounded the corner before easing out into the hall and slipping into Hank's room. He looked up in surprise as she entered. Then a guilty look crossed his face.

"You heard everything, didn't you?" he asked.

"Yeah."

He sighed and stared at the ceiling. "I'm really sorry, Maryse. Sorry for everything. Me being a shitty husband and leaving you high and dry. My dad causing you all this trouble, and my mom putting you in this position to begin with. If I hadn't married you, none of this would be happening."

Maryse felt her heart begin to pound in her chest. She wanted to yell at him or maybe throw something large and heavy, but as she studied his face, she realized that for the first time since she'd known him, Hank Henry was actually being sincere. Before she could think better of it, she crossed the room and sat on the edge of his bed.

"Why did you marry me, Hank? Was it all some big joke or some ploy to make your mother think you'd grown up? And why me? I'd never done anything to you."

Hank shook his head, his expression sad. "I never meant to hurt you, and I swear I didn't marry you because of Mom. I married you because you are the best person I've ever known." His gaze locked on hers. "I figured if I was going to change for anyone, it would be you."

Maryse bit her lower lip, not sure what to say. Hank Henry respected her? That was news. But in the back of her mind lurked the question that had burned inside of her for two long years. "Did you love me?" Maryse finally asked.

Hank nodded. "I loved you as much as I could love anyone. I'm just not sure I understand what love really is, or if I'll ever be able to do it right." He took her hand and squeezed. "You deserved better than me, Maryse. So much better."

"Then why didn't you contact me? You left me hanging for two years, Hank. Your mom's money aside, you could have at least called or wrote a letter or something."

"You're right, and I'm sorry. It was a shitty thing to do, and I'm ashamed of it." Hank dropped his gaze. "When I first left, Mom arranged for me to be in rehab. She hoped I'd get straight and make my marriage to you work. But I wasn't ready to change, so it was a futile effort."

Hank looked back at Maryse, unmistakable regret in his eyes. "I was selfish, and I was immature. I convinced myself that you were better off without me, and that wasn't exactly a lie. So I took the easy way out and disappeared. Hell, I didn't know you wouldn't be able to divorce me. Mom never said anything, and I guess now we know why."

Hank reached over and took Maryse's hand in his. "I am so sorry for everything, Maryse. Can you ever forgive me?"

Maryse sniffed, trying to keep her unbidden tears at bay.

"Hey," Hank said. "You're going to be fine. You know that. And I don't want that damned land, okay? This whole mess makes me sick."

"What about Harold?"

Hank's jaw set in a hard line. "My murdering father will get his eventually." He gave her an apologetic look. "But I'm afraid I can't sit around and wait on it. I don't think I'd come out too good with the cops. Dad will make sure everyone believes I was in on it from the beginning."

Maryse shook her head and held up her phone. "That's not a problem. I have the entire conversation recorded."

Hank looked stunned for a moment. Then his face broke out in a broad smile. "You're really something. Holy shit, that's something." He laughed, then clutched his side and groaned.

Maryse handed him a cup of water and watched him grimace as he took a sip. "You have to be tired," she said, realizing his injury hurt more than he was letting on. "I should get out of here and let you rest. And don't worry about a thing. I'll turn this over to the police and everything will be fine. You'll see."

Hank gave her a sad smile. "Thanks, Maryse, for everything."

Maryse removed her hand from Hank's and eased out of the room as Hank's eyes closed. When she reached the hall, the dam burst, and the tears she'd been holding in for two long years came pouring out. Tears of sadness and joy and relief, all at the same time.

Hank had actually cared about her, and that made her feel so much better about herself and her marriage. But more importantly, she had realized that her marrying Hank hadn't been the stupid action of a grieving daughter. The truth was she'd loved Hank then. She just didn't love him now.

But admitting that at one time her feelings had been true and real had allowed her to let it all go.

* * *

Luc was in the hospital lobby arguing with the nurse behind the desk and growing more aggravated by the moment. "I need you to listen to me! The police said they brought her here—check again. Maryse Robicheaux. Do you need me to spell it?"

The frustrated nurse stood and put her hands on her hips. "Look, Mr. LeJeune. I've lived here all my life, and I know how to spell Robicheaux. No one by that name has been checked in today. Someone is mistaken."

Luc held his tongue and stalked away from the desk. Maryse was somewhere in this hospital, possibly under the care of his primary suspect, and no one could tell him a thing. He yanked his cell phone from his pocket, determined not to leave the hospital until he had seen Maryse with his own eyes. Hell, maybe even checked her pulse. He had just pressed in the number for the Mudbug police when Maryse walked into the hospital lobby, a dazed expression on her face.

It was all Luc could do to stop himself from grabbing her in an embrace and never ever letting her go, but based on their last conversation, he figured that wouldn't be a good idea. Instead, he settled for squeezing her arm. "Are you all right? The police said someone had been shot and they'd taken you to the hospital. I thought . . ."

Maryse came out of her stupor and shook her head. "No, I'm fine. It was Hank who got shot."

"Hank? Are you kidding me? How?"

"He pushed me out of the way and took a bullet in the process." Maryse looked at him. "He saved my life."

Luc felt his heart drop. He should have been the one to save Maryse—be her hero. "Then there are miracles in this world," he said, trying to sound normal. "How bad is he hurt?"

"It's only a surface wound. Hurts like the dickens, and he was bleeding like a stuck hog, but he's going to be all right."

"Good, that's good," Luc said, trying to sound like he meant it. "And you? Are you all right?"

Maryse nodded. "I'm going to be just fine."

Luc wondered a bit at the way she'd phrased her words but was too afraid of the answer to ask. Maryse and Hank had obviously come to some sort of common ground, and Hank *was* still her husband. "Can I take you back to the hotel?"

Maryse pointed to the hospital entrance just as a police cruiser pulled up. "I have an armed escort. Mildred and Sabine insisted."

"Good," Luc said, and nodded, hoping his disappointment didn't show.

"So," Maryse said, and smiled, "I guess I'll see you around."

Luc heard the unspoken question in her voice, but he heard the uncertainty behind it, too, and he knew that if Maryse and Hank were reconsidering their relationship, the last thing she needed was another complication in her life. "Actually, my assignment here is over. I'm supposed to report back to New Orleans tomorrow."

"Oh."

Her smile dropped, and Luc mentally cursed himself for being the bastard Maryse had accused him of being.

Maryse shrugged. "Well, then, thanks for everything, and good luck." She walked out of the hospital entrance without so much as a backward glance, climbed into the waiting police cruiser, and rode away.

Out of Luc's life. Back to her own.

It was long after midnight before Maryse finished explaining her cell phone recording to the police and returned to the hotel. She struggled to keep her emotions under control as she talked to Mildred and Sabine, assuring them that the police were handling everything with the recording, that she was fine, Hank was fine, and she was suffering no lingering effects from almost dying—again. She begged off any further conversation, claiming exhaustion. She managed to make it to her room and into the shower before the tears started to fall.

Tears for her marriage that never really was and a promising relationship that was never going to be. What was it about her that she only attracted men with ulterior motives and no staying ability?

By the time she'd finished her shower and her crying jag, the exhaustion she had claimed earlier was no longer merely an excuse. But as she stepped out of the bathroom, a very contrite Helena Henry was perched on the edge of her bed. Maryse held in a sigh, knowing that it was high time she and Helena had that heart to heart Helena had kept promising her. Maryse just didn't have a clue where she was supposed to get the energy to do it.

"How did it go with the police?" Helena asked.

Maryse pulled some clothes out of the chest of drawers and began to dress. "If you're so interested, why didn't you stick around? Afraid I might figure out a way to strangle you?"

Helena stared at the floor, a guilty expression on her face. "I know what I did was wrong, but I swear, I never imagined any of this happening. I had my reasons, and at the time I thought they were good ones."

Maryse turned her hands palm up. "Then I think it's high time I hear them. Everything, Helena. No more secrets."

Helena raised her gaze back to Maryse and nodded. "You deserve the truth. You deserve a lot more than that, actually, but before I tell you everything, you have to know that

I never, ever intended to put you in any danger. Quite the opposite, actually."

"Okay. Then go ahead. Let me have it."

Helena took a deep breath and gazed around the room, as if deciding where to begin. "I guess I'll start with your mother," she said finally.

Maryse stood straight up and stared at Helena. Her mother had been the last thing in the world she'd expected Helena to talk about. "My mother?"

Helena smiled. "Your mother was the kindest, gentlest person I've ever met. She volunteered at the orphanage, teaching the older kids math and reading stories and playing games with the younger ones. They all loved her very much, and she was so great with them."

Maryse sank onto the edge of the bed next to Helena. "I never knew she volunteered there. No one ever told me."

Helena gave her a sad smile. "She quit before you were born. In fact, she quit right after finding out she was pregnant with you. She'd seen so much sadness, so much heartache in those children that she wanted to make sure her own never suffered a moment's pain, never shed a tear thinking her parents didn't love her."

Maryse nodded, the lump in her throat making speech impossible.

"The doctors had told her she wouldn't be able to carry a child to term," Helena continued, "so you were a real miracle for her."

Maryse felt the tears well up again. "I wish I could remember," she said, the sadness of her loss sweeping over her.

"I do, too," Helena said, her voice barely a whisper. "When your mom was first diagnosed, she thought she'd beat it. But she got worse and worse and knew things weren't going to get any better. Before she passed, your mother asked me to make sure you were taken care of. She knew your dad was a good man, but she was afraid he might not be able to see to all the things you would need."

Maryse stared at her. "My mother asked *you* to look after me? Did she know you at all?"

Helena laughed. "I know it's hard to believe, especially from where you sit, but your mother . . . well, your mother knew the real me. So the first year or so, I did my best to see that you had the woman's input you needed, although your dad did nothing to make it easy on me. We never much got along, even though I always respected him, and I know for a fact that he loved you more than anything."

"And after the first year?"

Helena waved one hand in dismissal. "Oh well, then your dad started seeing Mildred, and I could tell straight off how much she loved you. Almost as if you were her own. So I bowed out, knowing you were in great hands."

Maryse stared at Helena, certain the woman was leaving something out of her story—again. "And you had nothing to do with me after that?"

"Well, not directly," Helena hedged. She waited for a couple of seconds, obviously hoping Maryse was going to go off on another subject, but finally realized that wasn't going to happen. "Fine. I left you to your dad and Mildred until it was time for college. Then I saw to it that you got the education your mother would have wanted you to have."

Maryse's eyes widened in surprise. "You were the source of my scholarships? Good God, Helena, that must have cost you a fortune."

Helena shrugged. "I had more than enough money, and besides, you were a damned good investment."

Maryse took a deep breath and tried to absorb everything Helena had said, finding it hard to wrap her mind around her mother and Helena Henry plotting over her care and nurturing. "So what the hell happened with Hank? I'm pretty sure my mom wouldn't have approved of that arrangement at all. In fact, she's probably turned over a time or two since then."

Helena looked embarrassed. "I didn't find out about you and Hank until it was too late. I tried to get him to have the marriage annulled, but he was hell bent on keeping you." She shook her head. "I knew my son would never do right by you, so I decided to do both of us a favor and send him packing."

"He told me you sent him to rehab."

"Yeah. Well, the people you paid for Hank's debts weren't exactly the only people looking for him. I knew if he stuck around that not only would he be in danger until I could sort the whole thing out, but you would be too."

Maryse considered this for a moment. "I didn't know."

"I know that, and I got it all handled in a couple of months' time. I guess I figured rehab was the last place that sort would go looking for a guy like Hank. And I was hoping he'd straighten out . . . grow up and become a good man and a good husband. I was just fooling myself. Hank is just like his father."

Maryse shook her head, remembering her conversation with Hank. "He's not just like him, Helena. There's some good in Hank. It's just buried under that bullshit front. He didn't know what Harold did, and he's upset about it."

Helena looked at her, a hopeful expression on her face, and in that instant, Maryse realized that regardless of his transgressions, Helena Henry loved her son.

"You really think so?" Helena asked.

Maryse nodded. "And if I ever get my phone back from the police, you can hear it yourself."

"Well, that's something," Helena said. "I guess I didn't give him enough credit, then or now. Maybe you two could have made it work. Now, I don't know. All I knew then was that I'd promised my good friend that I'd make sure her daughter was taken care of, and I didn't see that happening as long as Hank was around."

"I get that, Helena, in a demented, completely screwed up sort of way. But why in the world didn't you arrange for us to divorce? Why keep me hanging all these years?"

Helena sighed. "Because of the land. After Hank left, I had that survey done and found out about the oil, and I always suspected Harold was digging through my safe. That missing letter proves it. I knew if I left the land to Hank that Mudbug would become one big refinery and the town would cease to exist. This was my home. I couldn't let that happen, so I used you, and for that I am sorry."

"And the bills? Why make me pay Hank's debt, then turn around and pay off *my* debt?"

Helena looked down at the floor. "I was worried that you might not be a good choice either, and if that was the case, then I might as well produce Hank and let you two divorce. I didn't really know what kind of adult you'd turned out to be, and marrying Hank wasn't exactly points in your favor."

"So you were testing my character? Is that your ridiculous defense?"

Helena shrugged. "I guess so, and putting it that way does kinda point out how stupid and cruel it was. I figured that out when you made the payments without fail or complaint. That's why I started using the money to pay off your debt. I was too proud to just tell you to stop."

Maryse stared at Helena and shook her head. "Unbelievable."

She looked at Maryse, her eyes pleading for her to understand. "This whole mess is about that damned land. I thought I was saving the town and giving you a great asset at the same time. I swear, Maryse, if I'd had any indication from you that you had started a new relationship or that being married to Hank was preventing you from doing something you wanted, I would have taken care of it . . . regardless of what happened with the land."

"But I just disappeared to my cabin in the marsh and stayed quiet all these years."

Helena nodded. "I didn't figure still being married to Hank made a difference to the way you were living. It never occurred to me that still be married might keep you from trying to have a life again. I've stolen two years from you, Maryse, and there's nothing I can do to fix it now. You have no idea how sorry I am. For everything."

Maryse rose from the bed. "I believe you're sorry, Helena, but what you did was wrong."

"Can you ever forgive me?"

"I forgive you, but I'm not happy with you. I hope you can understand that."

Helena nodded and rose from the bed. "I'm not happy with me, either." She gave Maryse a sad smile and walked through the bedroom wall into the hallway.

Maryse lay on the bed and hugged one of the bed pillows. She had enough to think about for the next ten years.

It was well after two A.M. when Maryse heard Helena's voice right beside her bed. Jasper took off like a shot, and Maryse opened one eye and looked at the agitated ghost, then the alarm clock. "It's the middle of the night, Helena. Go away."

"Ssssshhhhh." Helena put a finger to her lips. "There's someone outside your window. You've got to get out of here."

Maryse bolted upright and stared at the window, trying to make out anything in the inky darkness. A second later, she heard the faint sound of scraping outside, which couldn't possibly be good since her room was on the second floor. She rolled out of bed and onto the floor, then crawled over to the door and eased it open. The squeak of the hinges seemed to blast through the night air, and as Maryse slipped into the hall, she heard glass breaking behind her.

"Run!" Helena shouted, and Maryse stumbled to her feet, dashed down the hall, and then took the stairs two at a time. When she hit the landing on the first floor, she panicked for a moment, not having a single idea which way to go. The only options were out of the hotel or toward Mildred's room, essentially putting the other woman in danger. The pounding of footsteps on the stairs prompted her into action, and she pushed open the back door to the hotel and ran outside.

The shriek of the hotel alarm made her heart stop beating for a moment as she realized she'd just alerted the killer to her exact location. But as she ran down the alley, she realized that it might work to her advantage if the cops responded to the alarm before the killer found her. She felt the sting of glass under her bare feet but didn't care as she dashed around the corner of the hotel, praying that the gate was open. She came to a stop in front of the ten-foot iron gate, securely fastened by a padlock and chain. Shit! Frantic, she scanned the fence for a way over and, finding none, switched to looking for a place to hide but also came up with nothing.

Police sirens screamed in the distance, and she felt her hopes rise. She only had to hold out for another minute or so. Just sixty more seconds and help should arrive. Surely the killer would bail when the police arrived. But as she

• heard the hotel door slam, she knew she didn't have even twenty seconds before she would be looking at the killer face to face. She backed up a couple of steps, then ran toward the fence and leaped as high as possible, clutching desperately at the top rail.

Adjusting her grip, she pulled herself up the fence, her arms straining with the effort, and for a moment, she didn't think she was going to make it. Then a bullet whizzed by her head and struck the building to the side of her and a burst of adrenaline hit her, propelling her over the fence and onto the other side. She landed, slamming into the concrete with such force she was afraid she'd broken something in the process. As she jumped to her feet, a second bullet grazed her shoulder and hit the Dumpster in front of her. Realizing there was no possible way to exit the alley without leaving herself wide open, Maryse dove behind the Dumpster and curled into a ball, hoping like hell the police arrived before the killer got through the gate.

She heard the blast of a bullet hitting metal, then the rattling of a chain and felt her heart drop. She shut her eyes and prayed harder than she'd ever prayed before. Nothing but a miracle was going to save her now. Seconds later she heard his breathing clear as day and knew he was standing right in front of her. She clenched her eyes harder, her life racing before her in Technicolor, and wondered what she had done so wrong in life for it to end this way.

Chapter Eighteen

"I never wanted things to go this way, Maryse," the killer said.

Maryse's eyes popped open, and she raised her head in disbelief. "Johnny?" she said as she stared at her father's best friend. "But why?"

Johnny shook his head.

"If I'm going to die, shouldn't I at least know why?"

"Because you had to go poking your nose in where it didn't belong. Why couldn't you leave things alone?"

Maryse's mind raced with questions but not a single answer. "I don't know what you're talking about. What did I do?"

Johnny sneered. "Don't play stupid with me. I know all about those tubes you send to New Orleans for testing. You knew the chemical company was dumping waste in the bayou, and you figured that's what killed your dad, so you were going to get even. All that crap about trying to find a cure for cancer. You weren't looking for a cure—you were looking for the cause."

Maryse's head began to spin. "You're telling me you knew the chemical company was dumping toxic waste in the bayou? You knew that's what killed my dad and you never said a word?" She stared at the man in front of her. "I thought you were his friend."

"I was his friend, and I watched him waste away from

that disease, and all I could think was that's not going to happen to me. No way."

A wave of nausea washed over Maryse. The thinning hair, the weight loss. She'd thought it was diet or age, but she couldn't have been more wrong. "You have cancer."

Johnny nodded. "And no insurance. As long as I keep the chemical company's secret safe, they'll keep paying for my treatments."

"But other people could die because you haven't told."

"I was going to report them as soon as I was in remission, but then you had to get in the way, and I couldn't afford to have them busted just yet. I've got another year, at least, of chemo to go." He leveled the gun straight at Maryse's head. "I'm sorry it has to be this way, Maryse. Sorrier than you'll ever know. But I promise you won't feel a thing. Not after the first few seconds, anyway."

Maryse felt her blood run cold as she watched Johnny's finger whiten on the trigger. This was it. The end of the line. An entire life devoted to one cause and her work left unfinished. What had been the point? She clenched her eyes shut and waited for the shot to enter her body, waited for her life to fade away, and when the shot came, she almost passed out from fear.

It wasn't until she heard Luc shouting that she opened her eyes. Johnny lay splayed in front of her, his vacant eyes staring up at the night sky, a single bullet hole through his temple. Luc crouched in front of her and pulled her up from the ground, his eyes searching every square inch of her body.

"Am I dead?" Maryse asked.

Luc let out a strangled cry. "No!"

Maryse started to cry, and Luc pulled her close to him, wrapping his arms around her and kissing her forehead. "I wasn't sure," she said between sobs. "I mean, with you being able to see dead people. I just wasn't sure."

Luc let out a single laugh and held her even tighter. "I didn't even think about that." He pulled back a little and placed his hands on each side of her face. "You are very much alive, Maryse Robicheaux, and you're going to stay that way to a ripe old age."

Maryse rested her head on Luc's chest and relaxed as his arms tightened around her. For that moment, she would choose to believe him.

It seemed Maryse had barely gotten her breath before the backup arrived in the form of cops, an ambulance, and the coroner. She felt the thrill of victory pass through her as she realized the morgue could just as easily have been there for her if not for Luc's shooting accuracy. She still didn't know how he'd found her, or why he was even looking, but at the moment, she didn't care.

The paramedics whisked her off to the ambulance to assess the damage, and Luc joined a group of cops over to one side, probably giving his statement of the events. One paramedic was bandaging her shoulder while another tended to her cut feet when Mildred came rushing up. The hotel owner took one look at Maryse sitting in the ambulance and Johnny lying dead in the alley and began to sway.

She sucked in air like a drowning woman, and a paramedic shoved an oxygen mask over her face until her breathing became regular again. Maryse waited until she had taken a few normal breaths before explaining what had happened, leaving out, of course, the part that Helena had played in everything. Which brought Maryse up short. Where was Helena, anyway?

Mildred listened to Maryse's story, her eyes growing

wider and wider with each sentence until finally she'd finished her tale of horror. Mildred gasped as Maryse finished, and the paramedic hovered, oxygen mask in hand. She waved one hand in dismissal and told Maryse her own version of the night's events.

She'd jumped up as soon as the alarm sounded and ran straight to Maryse's room. When she found the door standing wide open, the window broken, and the empty bed, she'd run back downstairs to call the police, expecting the worst but hoping for the best. Maryse kept waiting for Mildred to blast her for running out of the hotel rather than to her for help but was relieved when it seemed that her substitute mother was going to let it go. Or was reserving it for a later date when she needed a good guilt trip to use.

Family was a wonderful thing.

Since Maryse's injuries were minor, the paramedics released her to Mildred, and they headed back to the hotel with instructions from the police to await questioning within the next thirty minutes. Maryse looked around for Luc, anxious to speak to him, to fill in the missing pieces of the story, but she didn't see him anywhere.

Disappointed, she followed Mildred into the hotel lobby, wondering why Luc had left so abruptly. In the alley, it had seemed like he'd really cared. Was that all just part of his job? She was just about to march outside and insist on seeing him when Sabine burst through the doorway in a panic.

As soon as she locked her gaze on Maryse, she ran across the lobby and grabbed her in a hug. "I'm fine," Maryse said as Sabine squeezed harder. "Okay, well maybe now I have a broken rib, but other than that, I'm fine."

Sabine released Maryse and brushed the tears from her face. "Don't you dare joke about this, Maryse Robicheaux. I could have lost you." She hugged her again, and Maryse felt the tears well up in her eyes once more.

"It's all over now," Maryse said through her tears. "It's all over."

Sabine released her once more and gave her a smile as Mildred hustled into the room with a glass of water and some aspirin. "You sit right down on that couch," Mildred directed, "and I don't want one bit of lip. All these goings on, it's a damned wonder you haven't had a heart attack—or given me one. You're going to relax for a minute if I have to sit on you."

Maryse grinned at Sabine, not caring in the least that Mildred was being bossy and pushy. Being bossy was simply her way of assuming control of the situation, her way of finding relief. Maryse relaxed on the couch and propped her sore feet on the coffee table, then took the water and aspirin from Mildred and downed them both.

The hotel door opened, and Luc walked in with a man he introduced as Agent Stephens. Maryse worried for a moment that this man might have seen her in fewer clothes and a much more compromising position, but she wasn't about to go there now.

"More agents," Maryse finally asked. "Is something wrong?"

Agent Stephens smiled. "Not at all, Ms. Robicheaux. And please, call me Brian. Everything is actually great."

Maryse looked from Brian to Luc, hoping for confirmation and an explanation. "Really?"

Luc nodded. "The local police picked up Harold at the motel where he was staying. He's in a small dingy cell, and he won't be leaving for a long time. We're betting the DA goes for the death penalty."

Maryse shook her head. "He can't."

Luc looked confused. "Harold confessed to murdering his wife. That rates the death penalty in Louisiana."

"Except that Harold didn't kill Helena."

All movement in the hotel ceased, and everyone stared at Maryse.

"How can you know that?" Sabine asked.

"Simple," Maryse said. "Harold said he slipped rat poison in her coffee, but Helena's medical file didn't indicate any of the symptoms from rat poisoning at all. He may have tried to kill her—and me—but he didn't succeed in either case."

"Shit!" Luc said. "Not exactly the outcome I was looking for."

Maryse nodded. "I understand, but Harold's confession should be enough to get a court order to exhume Helena's body, right? With a proper autopsy, looking specifically for foul play, we might get some answers."

Luc looked over at Brian, who nodded. "Should be easy enough for the local DA to get," Brian said.

"And what about Hank?" Maryse asked. "Did the police get a statement from him?"

Brian glanced over at Luc, clearly unsure how to answer. Luc looked at Maryse and shook his head. "Hank's gone. His hospital bed was empty when the locals went to question him, and the nurse confirmed he never checked out through proper channels."

"Gone?" Maryse tried to hide her disappointment. Why had Hank left? At this point, he couldn't be found guilty of anything except being stupid, and that wasn't a crime or half the people she'd ever met would be in jail.

Luc handed her an envelope. "He left this in the room."

She took the envelope and opened it, pulling the papers from inside. It was a signed divorce decree. No note. Only

Hank's signature, putting an end to the marriage that never really was. She supposed he figured it was the least he could do for her. Maryse passed the papers to Mildred, who gave an exalted cry and waved them in the air at Sabine, who cheered.

Brian Stephens smiled. "Well, I guess if you guys don't need anything else from me, I need to report back to New Orleans and fill them in on this latest angle in our case against the chemical company. Luc can explain the rest." He gave everyone a wave and exited the room.

Maryse looked over at Luc. "The rest of what? I mean, I guess with the killer being Johnny—" Maryse choked a bit and had to clear her throat before continuing. "He said it was all because of the illegal dumping, so I guess that's relevant to your case, right? But I still don't understand why he thought I was getting evidence against the chemical company."

Luc looked at her and sighed. "I think I do."

Maryse stared at him in surprise. "How can you know?"

"I can't know for sure, but I have a damn good idea what happened. One of those plants you sent for testing was selected from a contaminated area. When the head honchos at the chemical company realized that you pulled a plant from contaminated water and shipped it off to a lab in New Orleans, they assumed you were on to them and put pressure on Johnny to fix the situation."

Luc stared down at his feet for a moment. "I'm really sorry, Maryse, that it was Johnny. I know you thought he was your friend. If it makes you feel any better, I don't think he was in his right mind any longer. The desperation that goes along with a terminal illness can break people. Obviously he wasn't strong enough to do the right thing."

Maryse sniffled. "I know. I keep trying to tell myself it

wasn't personal, and it certainly wasn't about my dad, but it's hard, you know? I mean, Johnny claimed this dumping is what gave my dad cancer in the first place, and he never spoke up. What kind of man does that?"

Mildred stepped over to Maryse and put one hand on her shoulder. "No *man* does that, honey. When it comes down to it, there's just no excuse good enough, and we're all going to have to live with that."

Maryse shook her head. "I guess that explains Harold's comments about the irony of life. He wasn't special forces—Johnny was. Harold was the mess cook."

Luc nodded. "I'm sure you're right."

Maryse took a deep breath. "Then I guess it's just a matter of going through my notes to find the contaminated area. I documented every location that I got plants from. It has to be one of the more recent ones or they wouldn't have panicked, right?"

Luc stared her straight in the eyes but didn't respond, and his hesitation made her nervous. "What?" Maryse asked. "What are you not telling me?"

"We've already found the contaminated area," Luc said.

"But how?"

"The agency found the informant, and he gave us some of the dumping spots. I sorta broke into your lab and copied your notebook back when I first got here. Then things got weird with your inheritance and everything else, and for awhile I totally missed the clues that were right in front of me. But when I started thinking about everything, it made sense. The illegal dumping, your cancer tests, and the recent success that Aaron reported . . . well, I checked your notes and compared it to the information we'd gotten through our informant."

Maryse didn't know whether to be happy that the contaminated area was already identified and could be cleaned up, scared to death that she'd been hanging out in it, or mad at Luc for stealing her data. And despite all that information, she still couldn't help feeling that there was something missing from his explanation. Before she could question what, Luc sat on the couch next to her and took her hand in his.

"I hate to be the one to tell you this, Maryse, but your trials were a sort of false positive."

Maryse stared at him. "What do you mean?"

"You didn't discover a plant that cured cancer. What you discovered was a plant loaded with radiation from the illegal dumping."

Maryse's head began to spin. It couldn't be true. She was right there, right on the verge of the solution. "No," she whispered.

Luc looked at her with sad eyes and squeezed her hand. "I'm sorry, Maryse. So very sorry."

Maryse stared at him, unable to think, unable to breath. Blooming Flower had never had a magical cure. She'd simply given her dad the radiation treatment he'd refused, courtesy of a contaminated plant. Maryse's entire career, her whole adult life, had been a farce. There was no cure, at least not one in Mudbug Bayou, and she was no closer to saving lives that she had been before her advanced degrees and thousands of hours of extra work. And even worse, she'd unknowingly endangered everyone else in the process of trying to find a cure that didn't even exist.

She rose from the couch, unable to face the people in the lobby, her friends, her family who had unconditionally believed in her. Believed the lie. "If you guys don't mind," she said, "I'd like to be alone for a while." She hurried out of the lobby without waiting for a response, not wanting to see the disappointment, the pity, that would probably line every face in the room. All she wanted was to lock herself away in her room until the disappointment was gone.

And the fear.

All this time, Maryse had thought she was right on the verge of success. It's the only reason she hadn't launched into panic over Sabine's test. She thought she'd be able to help her friend if things turned out for the worse.

But it had all been a lie.

Maryse stared at the ceiling in the hotel room . . . but it hadn't changed, not once in the last two hours of her looking at the same spot the painters had missed next to the fan. She sat up in bed, feeling claustrophobic and restless. She needed to get out of the hotel, away from the town and the people and out into her bayou where she felt at home. Where things made sense. But the only way out of the hotel was down the stairs and through the lobby, since setting off the alarm with the back door probably wouldn't be a good idea given the situation.

She got out of bed and opened the window, hoping for a breeze or something to make her feel less like a caged animal, and noticed the drain pipe just outside the ledge to her room. She leaned further out the window and reached one hand over to test the strength of the pipe when Helena's voice boomed next to her.

"What the hell are you doing? Don't tell me you were gonna jump. After all we've been through, you want to end it now? And from the second floor? You'd probably only break your foot."

Maryse slid back inside the window and stared at Helena before sinking onto the bed in a huff. "I was *not* going to jump. And where were you? I kept expecting to see you around, and then finally I wondered if everything had finally, well, you know . . ."

"Made me disappear," Helena finished. "Afraid not." She sat on the bed and frowned. "I just figured you had enough to deal with without me hanging around the room and only you and Luc seeing me, so I sat behind the front desk and took it all in."

"Then you heard everything?"

Helena nodded. "I heard everything." She gave Maryse a shrewd look. "And I know what you're thinking."

Maryse shook her head. "You couldn't possibly."

"You're thinking everything you've done in life was a waste because the cure wasn't real and the only relationship you had wasn't exactly a success." She stared at Maryse for a moment, but Maryse wasn't about to give her the satisfaction of knowing she was right.

"The worst part is," Helena continued, "there's a grain of truth to all of that."

Maryse sat bolt upright on the bed and glared at Helena. "You've got a lot of nerve saying something like that to me. You of all people."

Helena held one hand up before she could continue her barrage. "I didn't mean that the way it sounded. Well, not exactly. Oh, hell, I never could get things out right. Might have made life a lot easier if I'd ever learned some tact."

"It's apparently not too late."

Helena grinned. "Why start now when the only people it would benefit are you and Luc?"

"Why indeed?" Maryse sighed. "Please just go away, Helena. I've got enough to think about without you mucking things up more."

"Not until I have my say."

"You've had your say for years, and it's been nothing but

aggravation and trouble. You've got five more minutes of my life, Helena, then I *will* pitch myself out that window."

"Fair enough." Helena took a deep breath. "The reason I implied that some of your life has been a waste wasn't because the cure turned out to be a fake, and it certainly wasn't because you married my useless son—that one is totally on Hank."

"Then why . . ."

Helena gave her a sad smile. "It's because in looking for the cure, you shut yourself away from the very society you purported to want to save. How do you even know people are worth saving anymore if you don't get out of that swamp and meet any?"

Maryse started to fling back a retort but clamped her mouth shut, remembering that Sabine had said the same thing. "I meet people," she said finally.

Helena snorted. "Yeah, that Dr. Do-Kiddies being one of them. You've locked yourself away from the world, Maryse, and I know you think you had a good reason to do so, but I'll be the first to tell you that if you don't change, you'll regret it. I do."

Maryse stared at her. "You regret your life? But you had everything . . . well, maybe not in the husband and kid department, but the money, the respect of the town."

Helena waved one hand in dismissal. "Respect? Oh, please, I was *tolerated* by this town, and that was all my own fault. For all intents and purposes, I was the biggest bitch on the face of the Earth. Oh, I might have done a couple of good things with my money, but I never really lived myself. I even chose to marry Harold because I knew I'd never really love him so I wasn't in danger of being hurt."

"I don't understand. Why would marriage have to hurt?"

Helena sighed. "That's my own hang-up. My childhood

was miserable. My father was a tyrant who barely tolerated girls and remained angry with my mother until the day he passed for producing a daughter rather than a son, then having the nerve to die while giving birth."

Maryse stared at Helena in disbelief, unable to comprehend that degree of spite. Unable to imagine a childhood spent with a man who blamed his only child for the gender she'd been born with.

"He died when I was eight," Helena continued, "and all I can remember is being relieved. Then guilty because I was relieved, you know?"

Maryse nodded. "I can see that."

"I stayed fairly locked away from the world with a guardian, a tutor, and a live-in nanny. But when I turned twenty-one and gained control of my inheritance, that's when the circus started. People who'd never spoken a word to me in my life practically lined up at the gate of my house with their hand out. I couldn't even walk into town without someone hitting me up for money—business loans, medical bills, scholarships, it never seemed to end."

Suddenly, Maryse understood. "So you became the biggest bitch in Mudbug because all anyone wanted from you was your money. And you funded the orphanage because you could relate to children that didn't have anyone looking out for them."

Helena nodded. "That was what I told myself—convinced myself was a good reason. But I was wrong, Maryse. Dead wrong."

"How so?"

"There are good people in this town, people who wouldn't have wanted a thing from me. People like your mother, and you, and Mildred." She smiled. "And even your nutty best friend. By shutting myself off, I denied myself the pleasure of friendship, of knowing what it felt like to have someone care for you that wasn't being paid to do it."

She gave Maryse a hard stare. "My life could have been so much more, and it took dying to realize that. Don't make the same mistakes I did, Maryse. This world would be a much better place with you in it."

Maryse looked at Helena, decked out in blue jeans, the "dead people" T-shirt, and neon blue Nikes. A far cry from the unrelieved black she'd always worn. But it was too late to share her newfound style with anyone. Too late to leave a different mark on this Earth. Because for everyone but Maryse and Luc, Helena was already gone, and Maryse had stopped living so long ago that she'd been dead longer than Helena.

Maryse didn't even try to hold in the tears as they rolled out of her eyes. She cried for Helena, the little lost girl and the older lost woman. She cried for herself—the life she'd never bothered to live and had almost lost—and the realization that she still had an opportunity to change it all before it was too late.

She looked up as Helena rose from the bed. "Where are you going?"

"My five minutes are up," Helena said. "And I've probably given you enough to think about." She walked to the door, then looked back. "There is one last thing."

Maryse looked up at her. "What's that?"

"When Johnny broke into your room, I ran out of the hotel desperate to find a way to help. Luc was sitting in a car across the street from the hotel, and if I had to guess, he'd been there for a while and wasn't planning on moving."

"He was watching the hotel," Maryse said. "You sent him to save me. That's how he knew."

Helena nodded. "Luc LeJeune is no Harold or Hank

Henry, Maryse. And I think I overheard him say he needed to pick up some stuff at the office first thing in the morning before he cleared out of town." And with that, she disappeared through the wall.

Maryse rose from the bed and pulled on her shoes, knowing with a certainty she'd never felt before exactly what she needed to do. But first, there was someone else who needed to hear Helena's speech.

Chapter Nineteen

Despite the fact that it was darn near sunrise and nobody had really slept the night before, Maryse figured she'd find Sabine in her shop. Peering through the window of Read 'em and Reap, she saw Sabine sitting at her table in the center of the room, eyes closed and her hands covering a crystal ball. She was wearing her purple robe, one she brought out for only two reasons—stress or trying to contact her parents.

Maryse sighed. All the drama with Maryse and the land and Sabine's own medical worries had probably driven her to the edge. But none of that was going to prevent her from what she needed to do. She took the last couple of steps to the shop entrance and pushed the door open.

Sabine looked up in surprise when the bells over the door jangled, then realizing it was Maryse, her expression changed to worry. She jumped up from her chair and hurried over. "Are you all right?" she asked. "Is everything okay?"

"Actually, I'm not all right." Maryse smiled. "I'm fantastic. I just had an interesting conversation with Helena."

Sabine studied her for a moment. "Are you high? Did the paramedics give you some drugs or something?"

Maryse's smile faltered a bit. Okay, so obviously telling people to take their lives back wasn't her strong suit. How in the world was it that Helena, of all people, did this so much better? Maryse took a deep breath and repeated Helena's story from the beginning. Sabine listened in rapt attention, her eyes growing wider until Maryse wrapped it up with Helena's ultimatum on living life and regrets.

"Wow," Sabine said when Maryse finished. "Helena didn't pull any punches."

"No." Maryse took a deep breath and pushed forward. "And neither do I." She placed her hand on Sabine's arm. "You're not living either, Sabine. Your obsession with your parents has kept you so grounded in the past that you have no future."

Sabine stared at her in surprise, then pulled away her arm. "How can you say that? You know what it's like not to have a parent. How can you blame me for wanting to know something, anything, about mine?"

Shit. This wasn't going so well. "That's not what I meant. Look, Sabine, I'm just excited by my new outlook on life. I want you there with me . . . like you always have been."

Sabine's angry expression softened, but before she could speak, a glow of bright light appeared a couple of feet from the table, and they both stared in disbelief. "What the hell?" Maryse asked as the light swirled round and round, something slowly taking shape in the center. *Please, God, no more ghosts.* She didn't think her heart could take the strain.

As the shape took form, Maryse realized they were looking at a young couple, smiling over at them. The man was tall and thin, the woman petite and slender. Their haircuts and clothes betrayed the era of their existence, and Maryse knew they had been gone from this world for some time. The woman looked directly at Sabine and extended one hand. A flash of silver at the woman's neck caught Maryse's eye and she cried out. "Her necklace. Sabine, look at her necklace."

Sabine looked at the woman, and her hand flew to her throat, clutching the matching locket she wore. The only thing she had of her mothers. "It's them," she whispered.

Maryse nodded, unable to speak.

"They're beautiful," Sabine said, and started to cry. "My parents. I finally know my parents." Sabine took a hesitant step toward the light, but as she moved, the light began to dim and the couple faded away into blackness. With a final blink, they were gone.

"No!" Sabine ran to the spot where the light had been, but there was nothing left to see. She sank onto the floor, tears streaming down her face.

Maryse rushed over to her friend. "Please don't cry," she begged as she sat on the floor and hugged Sabine. "I don't want you to be sad. I don't want anyone I love to be sad, not one more moment of their lives. It's too short."

Sabine choked a bit and laughed. "You ninny. I'm not crying because I'm sad." She pulled back from the hug, and Maryse could see that even through the tears, there was a smile on her face. "I'm happy," Sabine said. "I'm thrilled. I finally got that sliver of closure that I've always prayed for." Sabine grabbed Maryse's shoulders with both hands and shook her. "I saw my parents, Maryse. Do you know what that means?"

Maryse wiped at the tears lurking in the corners of her eyes, wondering that she had a single ounce of fluid in her left to cry after the night she'd had. "It means the world is getting two new members?" Maryse smiled. "I hope it's ready."

Maryse gave Sabine another quick hug, then rose from the floor. "I'd love to stay and make plans for our takeover of humanity, but I have some unfinished business with a fake zoologist."

Sabine smiled. "Let the takeover begin."

Maryse left the shop with a spring in her step. If everything could turn out so good for Sabine, why couldn't it turn out that good for her? But the apparition just outside the shop door brought her up short. Maryse took one look at the guilty expression on Helena Henry's face and knew something was up, and in a flash, she knew exactly what it was.

"You did that," Maryse accused. "You created the image of Sabine's parents."

Helena shrugged and shuffled her feet. "Well, you weren't exactly getting anywhere with that lame speech of yours, and I didn't need you sinking back in to your former existence just because Sabine was stuck in hers." Helena grinned. "Besides, I kinda like the nutbag, and I wanted her to be happy. Is that so bad?"

"I guess not. But making up visions of dead parents to fool a daughter is sort of low, even for trying to make someone happy. You've got to stop manipulating people, Helena. Even if you think it's for their own good."

Helena glared at her. "What do you take me for, a charlatan? I admit, I created the image, but the people were really Sabine's parents, or the likeness at least."

"But how do you know what they looked like?"

Helena shrugged. "I took a look on the other side, and there they were. I think they're always close to her."

Maryse stared. "You can look on the other side? Then why can't you go there?"

Helena gave her a sad smile. "I tried, but they told me it's not my time yet. Apparently, I still have some work to do here."

Maryse smiled and shook her head. "You know, I never thought I'd hear myself say this, but I'm sorta glad you're not going yet, Helena. I would have missed you."

Helena nodded. "Of course you would. Not many have been graced with my stellar personality transformation like you have."

Maryse groaned and pointed a finger at her as they walked down the sidewalk to Maryse's rental car. "That is *not* an invitation to show up unannounced or to harass me over the television channel. Well . . . as soon as I actually have a television, and a house to put it in."

Helena raised her hand as if taking an oath. "I promise I will not intrude without making an appointment. Although, I've already seen you naked, so I don't know what else there is."

"Because I plan on being naked with someone else. That is, if things work out."

Helena grinned. "You know, I always did think Luc had a fantastic butt. I wouldn't mind seeing it just once."

"Helena!" Maryse cried, but the wily ghost walked through the wall of the not-yet-open beauty shop, making following her an impossibility.

Maryse headed to the parking lot and jumped in her rental car. She pulled out onto Main Street and drove through town, then merged onto the gravel road and sped toward the office, her mind whirling like a tornado. What if Luc's interest in her had only been because of his job? What if he had only cared about her enough to not want her dead? Or even worse, what if the sex was so bad that he'd changed his mind?

Good God, the possibilities were endless.

She rounded the corner down from the office and saw Luc's Jeep parked outside. *There's still time to change your mind.* She eased her foot off the accelerator. *You're not even divorced from the first man who made you look like a fool. Do you really want to run that risk again?*

The car rolled to a stop, and she stared at the Jeep once more, biting her lower lip. Was love really worth the risk? But then she remembered Luc's face when he'd lifted her in the alley, his fear that she was hurt, then the utter relief when he realized she was okay. She remembered exactly how warm his arms felt wrapped around her and how the soft touch of his lips grazed her face. And she remembered her body's response to him.

She pressed down the accelerator, and the car leapt forward. Definitely worth it.

Luc looked up in surprise when she walked in the office. "I thought you'd still be in bed," he said.

"Or hiding in a closet?" she joked.

Luc smiled. "No, not you. Although that might have made things easier." He studied her for a moment. "How are you doing?"

Maryse nodded. "I'm fine. I mean, overwhelmed on some things and still disappointed on others, but it will all pass in time. At least that's what I'm telling myself."

"Probably an accurate statement."

Maryse pointed to the box of video cameras Luc was packing. "So I guess you're clearing out, huh?"

"Yeah. I figured you wouldn't need the security equipment anymore, and I sorta appropriated it without permission."

Maryse smiled. "I bet. So how much trouble are you in?"

Luc shrugged. "More than I'd like and less than the boss-man would, I'm sure."

Now or never. Maryse stepped closer to him. "And was it worth it?"

Luc locked his eyes on hers. "Definitely."

Maryse took another step towards him, her body so close she could feel the heat coming off of him. "If you'd like to prove that statement, there's still about ten minutes before the office is supposed to open."

Luc's eyes widened. "Are you sure?"

"I've never been more sure."

Luc smiled and ran his finger across her lips. "You know, that statement lacks punch coming from someone with so much uncertainty in her everyday life."

"Sure, point out my flaws when I'm standing here pouring out my heart."

Luc leaned over and kissed her gently on the lips. "I love you, Maryse Robicheaux. God help me, I'm head over heels for you."

Maryse felt her heart pound in her chest. "Are you sure?"

"I've never been more sure."

"Says the guy who sees ghosts. Like that's not uncertain."

Luc wrapped his arms around Maryse and pulled her close to him. This time his kiss wasn't gentle but sensual, and Maryse felt her legs grow weak. "I love you, too, Luc LeJeune," she said. "God help us both."

Luc laughed. "We're a mixed pair, Maryse. Me with a one-bedroom studio in the city and you living in a hotel. What are we supposed to do about that?"

"Actually, I've been thinking about that . . . about everything that's happened over the last week. I know what I thought was a cure wasn't really, but the thing that made it different is that the mice didn't get sick. I think it's something worth pursuing. If I found a way to alleviate illness during radiation, that wouldn't be a cure, but it'd be a hell of a lot better than the way it is now."

"That's a great idea, Maryse."

"So I was thinking that since your job and the university lab are in New Orleans, maybe keeping your apartment there isn't such a bad idea."

"And what about Mudbug?"

"I've got the insurance money from my cabin and the land lease money coming soon. I was thinking about building again, somewhere on the bayou, just on the outskirts of town. Nothing fancy."

"No more hiding out in boat-access-only living quarters?"

Maryse smiled. "I've missed out on things for too long. I'm not going to make that mistake again. So do you think you can handle living in a small town again . . . part time at least?"

Luc planted small kisses down the side of her neck. "I think I'm going to love it."

"You know," Maryse said as she reached around to squeeze Luc's butt. "I've never made it with an undercover agent before. At least, not that I was aware of."

"Really? So you're telling me there are no other men in your life?"

Maryse grinned. "Well, there was this zoologist, but his exit strategy needed work."

Luc drew her lips to his again, the promise of everything to come in his kiss. "Who says I'm going anywhere?"

Helena Henry stepped out of the beauty shop that evening and crossed Main Street. Maryse and Luc had just pulled up in front of the hotel, and from the rumpled looks of their hair and clothes, Helena had serious doubts they'd been doing any botany back at the office.

She smiled as Mildred and Sabine walked out of the hotel to greet them. Luc took Maryse's hand in his and spoke directly to the two other women. From the ecstatic looks on their faces, Helena had no doubt what news Luc was delivering. He was still talking when Mildred grabbed him in a hug, probably crushing every rib in his body. Even from her place across the street, Helena could see the tears in the hotel owner's eyes.

Helena felt her own eyes mist a bit, both with joy and regret. Pretty soon Maryse would have a whole new mother-in-law to deal with. She could only hope the next one didn't cause Maryse the trouble Helena had.

But all that was behind them now. Maryse was safe, and the land was protected. Luc had put things in motion, and Helena had no doubt that her exhumation was just around the corner. Maybe then she'd get the answers she needed to leave this Earth.

The foursome finished their hugs and walked into the hotel, and Helena had no doubt Mildred would be breaking out a bottle from her champagne stash. Helena looked around at the quaint little town and sighed. It was all so peaceful, so normal.

But for now, someone in Mudbug had still gotten away with murder.

Read ahead for a peek at
Mischief in Mudbug
the next book in the Ghost-in-Law series

COMING FALL 2009!

Sabine LeVeche placed her hands over her crystal ball and looked across the table at Thelma Jenkins. It didn't take psychic ability to know that Thelma's problem was her husband Earl, same as always, which was a good thing since Sabine didn't have an ounce of psychic gift in her body. But today, she would have given anything for the ability to know where Earl had squirreled away his secret stash, *if* the money even existed at all.

"Can you see the money?" Thelma asked.

Sabine held in a sigh. On any other day, she would have pretended to see the money in a suitcase or a box or under a bush, something that would send Thelma happily off on a witch hunt and buy Sabine two weeks of peace and quiet. After all, Thelma didn't need the money, but she couldn't stand the idea of Earl keeping something from her and was convinced he'd been skimming off their gas station profits all fifty years of their marriage.

At least that's how Thelma presented it.

The reality was Alzheimer's was fast taking Earl away from this Earth, and Thelma was desperately looking for something to distract her and fill her time. Finding Earl's mythical treasure fit the bill nicely.

Sabine focused on the crystal ball and tried to remember all the tales she'd told Thelma before and come up with something different. "I see the money . . . no wait, he's taking the money into a jewelry store. He's exchanging it for diamonds . . . a bag of uncut diamonds."

Thelma sucked in a breath, the prospect of hunting for diamonds even more exciting than a box of dirty money. "When did he do that?"

Sabine shook her head. "I can't tell for sure, but he placed the diamonds in a red shoe box and put it in the attic." She squinted at the ball. "The image is fading." She held her hands over the ball another couple of seconds, then looked up at Thelma. "It's gone."

Thelma looked at her, her brow wrinkled in concentration. "The attic, huh? Was it the attic in our house?"

"I couldn't tell for sure, and remember, Thelma, there's no way of knowing if the diamonds are still there. Earl could have moved the diamonds, or even sold them sometime after the vision I saw. But my guess is he hid them where he had easy access, so that would limit it to your house." God forbid Thelma got arrested for breaking into every house in Mudbug and digging through their attics.

"What a load of bullshit!" The voice came from out of nowhere, and Sabine straightened in alarm. She stared at Thelma, but the blue-haired woman just stared back at her.

"Did you hear that?" Sabine asked as she glanced around her shop, hoping that someone was hiding behind one of the many shelves of candles, tarot cards, and other paranormal paraphernalia. But as she peered in between the shelves, she didn't see a thing.

"Hear what?" Thelma asked, glancing around the shop. "There wasn't anyone here when I came in, and no one's come in since."

Sabine nodded. That's what she'd thought, but then where had that voice come from? Unless it was her imagination, and that would definitely be a change from the norm.

"You didn't leave the back door open, did you?" Thelma asked.

"No. In fact, it's broken. The landlord is supposed to fix it tomorrow. Right now, I couldn't open it without a crowbar."

Thelma reached across the table and patted her hand. "You've been under a lot of stress lately, dear, what with people trying to kill Maryse and all. You probably need a vacation."

Sabine nodded. Thelma was probably right.

"Give it a rest." The voice sounded again, and Sabine jumped up from her chair. "That asshole Earl has been teasing Thelma for years over that money."

"Who's there?" Sabine asked, and looked frantically around her shop.

Thelma stared, her eyes wide with shock. "I didn't hear anything," she whispered. "Do you think it's the spirits?"

No, Sabine didn't think it was spirits, but obviously someone was having a bit of fun with her. She could allow herself one imagined voice but not two. She was certain someone was speaking. And then there was the voice. It sounded familiar, but made Sabine's nose crinkle like it was attached to something unpleasant.

"So tell me where the money is," Sabine said loudly, figuring if she played along with the charade, she'd eventually expose the person responsible. "You seem to know more about it than I do."

"She doesn't need the damn money," the voice answered. "She already has more money than Bill Gates and still won't pay for a decent hairdo. Why give her more?"

Sabine froze. She wasn't imagining it. Someone was in her shop. She looked over at Thelma, whose eyes were wide with either fear or excitement. "Is the spirit still talking?" Thelma whispered.

"Oh, yeah," Sabine said, wondering momentarily whether Thelma was going deaf. How could she not hear that? Sabine walked across the room to look between the shelves. Finding them empty, she strode to the front of the store and peered behind the counter. Empty. "They're still talking. They said you don't need the money and you have a bad hairdo."

Thelma gasped and put one hand on her puffy blue hair. "Why that's just downright rude. I didn't think spirits were rude once they crossed over."

"You'd be surprised," Sabine muttered, thinking of what her friend Maryse had about Helena Henry's ghost.

"Oh, for Christ's sake," the voice boomed again. "Tell her the money is in her mattress. She's been sleeping on it for years."

No, it couldn't be. God wouldn't play that unfair. "The money's in your mattress," Sabine said as she rushed over to the table and pulled Thelma out of her chair.

"My mattress?" Thelma repeated as she allowed herself to be hustled to the door. "No wonder Earl never wanted to get rid of that lumpy piece of crap."

Sabine nodded and opened the front door to the shop, pushing a confused but excited Thelma out the door. "I'm sorry, Thelma," Sabine said, "but something's come up that I have to take care of. I'll call you tomorrow."

Thelma shook her head. "You young people are always rushing around to something. Slow down, Sabine. All you've got in this world is time, and when it's done it's done."

Sabine slammed the door shut, locked it, and flipped the "Closed" sign around in the window. *When it's done, it's done.* Like hell. Her heart pounding, she turned slowly around and faced her empty shop.

"I know you're there, Helena," Sabine said, then felt a wave of nausea sweep over her at her own words.

"Well, I'll be damned! You *did* hear me." Helena's voice boomed in the empty shop. "For a minute there, I thought you'd actually gone psychic."

Sabine's gaze swept from side to side, casing every square inch of the tiny shop. "I can hear you, but I can't see you. Where are you exactly?"

"I'm standing next to your table. See?"

Sabine looked at her table but didn't see anything out of the ordinary, that is until her crystal ball began to rise from its stand and hover a good two feet above the table. "I see the ball, but I can't see you."

"Hmm. That's weird, right? I mean, is that supposed to happen?"

"How am I supposed to know? You're the ghost."

"Sure, sure, always trying to make me responsible for everything. Hell, all this paranormal stuff is your bag. I didn't ask to stick around after I died, and no one handed me an instruction manual when I crawled out of my coffin."

Sabine yanked her cell phone from her pocket and punched in a text message. She continued to stare at the ball, still suspended in midair, not even sure what to say, what to do. Aside from drinking, nothing else really came to mind. She was saved from reaching for the bottle by a knock on the shop door.

Sabine hurried to unlock the door and allowed Maryse to enter. "That was fast," Sabine said. *Thank God.*

"Luc and I were having a late breakfast across the street at the café," her friend said, the worry on her face clear as day. "What's wrong? Your text message seemed a bit panicked."

Sabine pointed to the hovering ball. "I sorta have an issue here."

Maryse looked over at the table and frowned. "Helena, what in the world are you trying to do—give people heart attacks? That's not funny."

"Oh, admit it, Maryse, it's a little funny," Helena said. "You shoulda seen the look on Sabine's face."

Maryse shook her head. "I don't need to see that look— I've worn it for over a week now. Would you stop freaking people out and find something to do?" Maryse turned to Sabine. "Please tell me she did not do that in front of a customer."

Sabine shook her head, squinting at the area surrounding the hovering ball, trying to make out a body or form or outline or anything, but she saw absolutely nothing.

"I have plenty to do," Helena argued, "and I was doing some of it. I was helping that fool Thelma find Earl's money. She's been bitching about that money for forty years. Everyone down at the beauty shop is tired of hearing about it."

Maryse sighed. "And how were you planning on helping—hitting Thelma on the head with that ball? It's not like you could whisper it in her ear. No one can hear you but me."

Helena laughed, and Sabine cleared her throat. "Actually, Maryse," Sabine said, "that's the issue. I *can* hear her. I just can't see her."

Maryse stared at Sabine, her jaw slightly open. "You can hear her?"

Sabine nodded. "Loud and clear, unfortunately."

"Oh my God," Maryse said, and sank into a chair. "That can't possibly be good."

"Hey," Helena said, "no use being rude about it. I'm not doing anything to Sabine."

Maryse glared at the ghost. "Yeah, you weren't doing anything to me either, but not long after you appeared people started trying to kill me."

Sabine stared at Maryse. "Oh my God! You don't think . . . I mean . . ."

Maryse cast a worried look from the hovering ball to Sabine. "There's no way of knowing for sure, and God knows, this is one of those time I wish I was a decent liar. But it's like you told me before, if it involves Helena, it can't possibly be good."

A Taste of Magic

Tracy Madison

"Fun, quirky and delicious!'
—Annette Blair, National Bestselling Author
of *Never Been Witched*

MIXING IT UP

Today is Elizabeth Stevens's birthday, and not only is it the one-year anniversary of her husband leaving her, it's also the day her bakery is required to make a cake—for her ex's next wedding. If there's a bitter taste in her mouth, no one can blame her.

But today, Liz is about to receive a gift. Her Grandma Verda isn't just wacky; she's a little witchy. An ancient gypsy magic has been passed through the family bloodline for generations, and it's Liz's turn to be empowered. Henceforth, everything she bakes will have a dash of delight and a pinch of wishes-can-come-true. From her hunky policeman neighbor, to her gorgeous personal trainer, to her bum of an ex-husband, everyone Liz knows is going to taste her power. Revenge is sweet…and it's only the first dish to be served.

ISBN 13: 978-0-505-52810-0

☐ **YES!**

Sign me up for the Love Spell Book Club and send my FREE BOOKS! If I choose to stay in the club, I will pay only $8.50* each month, a savings of $6.48!

NAME: _____

ADDRESS: _____

TELEPHONE: _____

EMAIL: _____

☐ I want to pay by credit card.

☐ **VISA**   ☐ **MasterCard**   ☐ **DISCOVER**

ACCOUNT #: _____

EXPIRATION DATE: _____

SIGNATURE: _____

Mail this page along with $2.00 shipping and handling to:
Love Spell Book Club
PO Box 6640
Wayne, PA 19087
Or fax (must include credit card information) to:
610-995-9274
You can also sign up online at **www.dorchesterpub.com**.
*Plus $2.00 for shipping. Offer open to residents of the U.S. and Canada only.
Canadian residents please call 1-800-481-9191 for pricing information.
If under 18, a parent or guardian must sign. Terms, prices and conditions subject to change. Subscription subject to acceptance. Dorchester Publishing reserves the right to reject any order or cancel any subscription.